W9-AMB-548

VOYAGE TO THE STARS

Facebook: **facebook.com/idwpublishing**
Twitter: **@idwpublishing**
YouTube: **youtube.com/idwpublishing**
Instagram: **@idwpublishing**

COVER ARTIST
CONNIE DAIDONE

SERIES EDITOR
CHASE W. MAROTZ

COLLECTION EDITORS
ALONZO SIMON
AND ZAC BOONE

COLLECTION DESIGNER
NATHAN WIDICK

ISBN: 978-1-68405-798-6   24 23 22 21   1 2 3 4

VOYAGE TO THE STARS. JUNE 2021. FIRST PRINTING. © 2021
MWM Universe, LLC. All Rights Reserved. © 2021 Idea and Design
Works, LLC. The IDW logo is registered in the U.S. Patent and
Trademark Office. IDW Publishing, a division of Idea and Design
Works, LLC. Editorial offices: 2765 Truxtun Road, San Diego, CA
92106. Any similarities to persons living or dead are purely
coincidental. With the exception of artwork used for review
purposes, none of the contents of this publication may be
reprinted without the permission of Idea and Design Works, LLC.
IDW Publishing does not read or accept unsolicited submissions of
ideas, stories, or artwork. Printed in Korea.

Originally published as VOYAGE TO THE STARS issues #1–4.

Nachie Marsham, Publisher
Rebekah Cahalin, EVP of Operations
Blake Kobashigawa, VP of Sales
John Barber, Editor-in-Chief
Justin Eisinger, Editorial Director, Graphic Novels and Collections
Scott Dunbier, Director, Special Projects
Anna Morrow, Sr. Marketing Director
Tara McCrillis, Director of Design & Production
Shauna Monteforte, Sr. Director of Manufacturing Operations

Ted Adams and Robbie Robbins, IDW Founders

MWM Universe • **Morgan Kruger**, COO • **Diana Williams**, EVP Creative • **Kylie Williams**, Franchise Manager.

Facebook: **facebook.com/MWMstorydriven**
Twitter: @**MWMstorydriven**
YouTube: **MWMyoutube**
Linkedin: **linkedin.com/company/mwmstorydriven**
Instagram: **instagram.com/mwmstorydriven**

Genuine Entertainment • **Joe LeFavi**, CEO & Creative Director.

Facebook: **facebook.com/GenuineEntertainment**
Twitter: @**Genuine_Ent**
Linkedin: **linkedin.com/company/genuine-entertainment-llc**

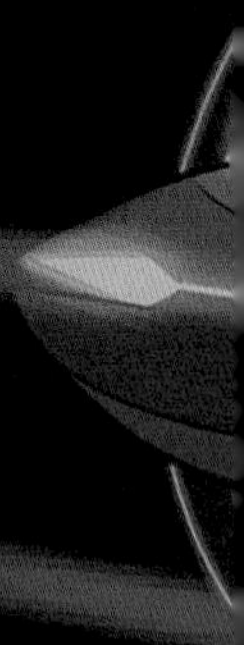

STORY BY
RYAN COPPLE & JAMES ASMUS

SCRIPT BY
JAMES ASMUS

ART BY
CONNIE DAIDONE

COLORS BY
REGGIE GRAHAM

LETTERS BY
ANDWORLD DESIGN'S JUSTIN BIRCH

MANAGING PRODUCER
JOE LEFAVI

TEAM CAST
COLTON DUNN, FELICIA DAY, JANET VARNEY,
KIRSTEN VANGSNESS, STEVE BERG

TEAM PODCAST
EARWOLF (COLIN ANDERSON, DEVON BRYANT, KRISTIN MYERS),
STITCHER (JOSH RICHMOND) & DAVID BURGIS

TEAM MWM
GIGI PRITZKER, MORGAN KRUGER, DIANA WILLIAMS, KYLIE WILLIAMS,
CHELSEA WESTMORELAND, ARTHUR CHAN

INSPIRED BY THE PARTIALLY IMPROVISED PODCAST
VOYAGE TO THE STARS CREATED BY RYAN COPPLE AND PRODUCED BY
MORGAN KRUGER, RYAN COPPLE, JANET VARNEY & FELICIA DAY.

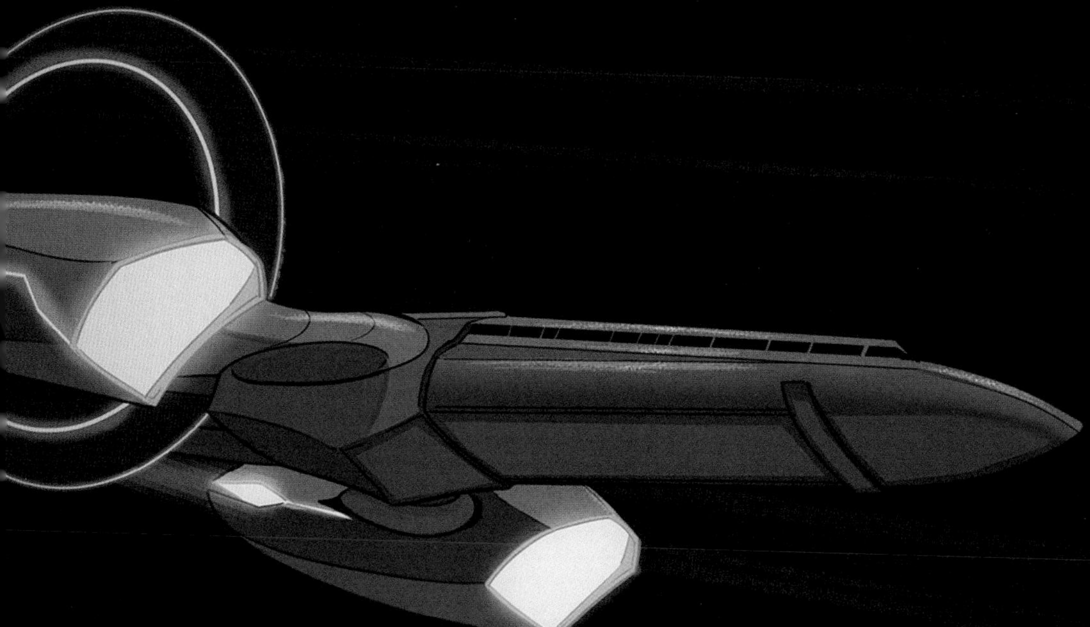

INTRODUCTION BY FELICIA DAY

Is entering a black hole possible?

What exactly is a "quasar"?

And why does everyone in the fictional future always wear unitards?!

Surprise! This graphic novel will not answer ANY of these questions! But, if you picked this book up for the amazing art, quirky characters, and borderline-appropriate humor, it's definitely going to satisfy—unitard explanations or not!

I joined the crew of *Voyage to the Stars* in 2017 as a performer and producer because creator Ryan Copple is a dear friend. So much so that I actually moved my child's birthday forward one day so they wouldn't have to share it. (I had a c-section for medical reasons and was able to schedule the day of the procedure. I couldn't have done that with a natural birth. Probably.)

When Ryan pitched me the character he wanted me to play in the podcast version of *Voyage*, I signed on immediately. Mostly because Elsa Rankfort is neurotic and a know-it-all and can't finish anything she starts. Only the best of friends could create a pseudo-biographical character so tailor-made for me! But as far as the larger concept, I didn't actually understand how it would work. An improvised podcast? But with a script and story beats we would follow? While making up all the dialogue on the fly? Sounded like a fun challenge that would definitely crash into the surface of a virtual performance planet once we tried it out!

But it didn't. Because Ryan put together a fantastic roster of performers including Janet Varney, Colton Dunn, Steve Berg, Kirsten Vangsness, and moi, along with a different hilarious guest actor each episode. We formed a rapport with each other that challenged the audio editors mightily, mostly because we would crack each other up all the time with our jokes, and they had to cut out a lot of giggles and snorts from the final podcast recordings.

For three seasons we kept making jokes in space, and the show grew and grew. To the point where it got the opportunity to branch out into other formats, including the series of comics you now hold in your hand. You definitely made the right decision in picking it up, because the translation into comic form is stupendous. The writing by James Asmus is on point, and the art by Connie Daidone is fantastic. It even inspired me to go back to having a bob in real life! THE POWER OF ART!

For listeners of the podcast, you'll discover tons of new things about all the characters and the world. For new people unfamiliar with the podcast, you will definitely snort-laugh yourself a few times, and then probably say, "Wow, that Elsa character is funny but needs therapy." (No offense at all, I do and so does she!)

With all the forms of media we have to choose from, the key to modern storytelling is great world building. And the *Voyage* world is so rich and hilarious, it can succeed in any format and go beyond any entertainment galaxy. I love the comic and hope you do too. I can't wait to see where the crew gets to go from here.

And now, flying from your ear holes into your eye holes, it's *Voyage to the Stars*!!!

oxox

Felicia

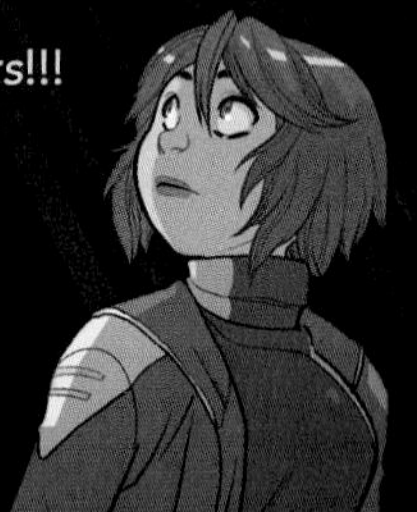

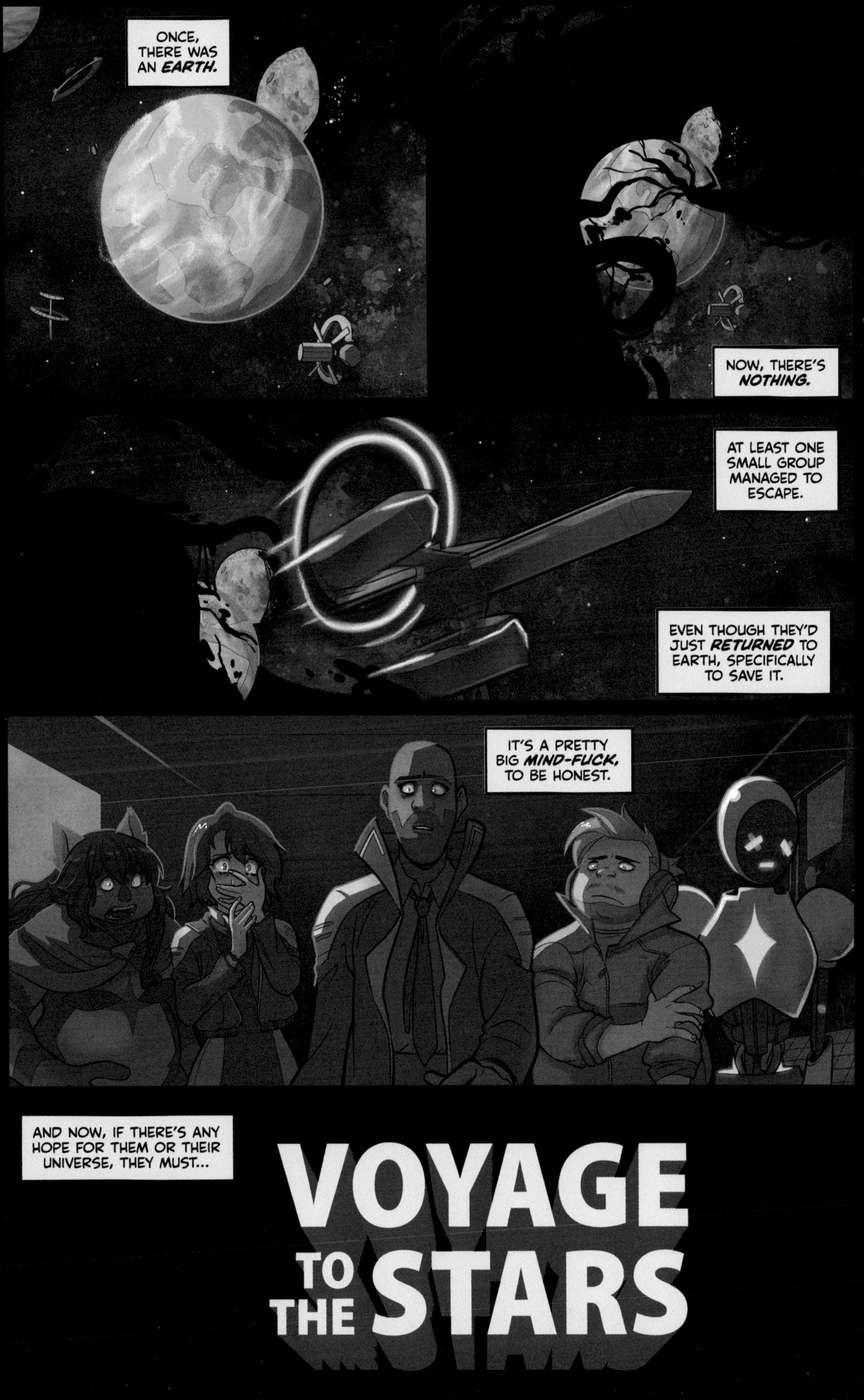
ONCE, THERE WAS AN EARTH.
NOW, THERE'S NOTHING.
AT LEAST ONE SMALL GROUP MANAGED TO ESCAPE.
EVEN THOUGH THEY'D JUST RETURNED TO EARTH, SPECIFICALLY TO SAVE IT.
IT'S A PRETTY BIG MIND-FUCK, TO BE HONEST.
AND NOW, IF THERE'S ANY HOPE FOR THEM OR THEIR UNIVERSE, THEY MUST...
VOYAGE TO THE STARS

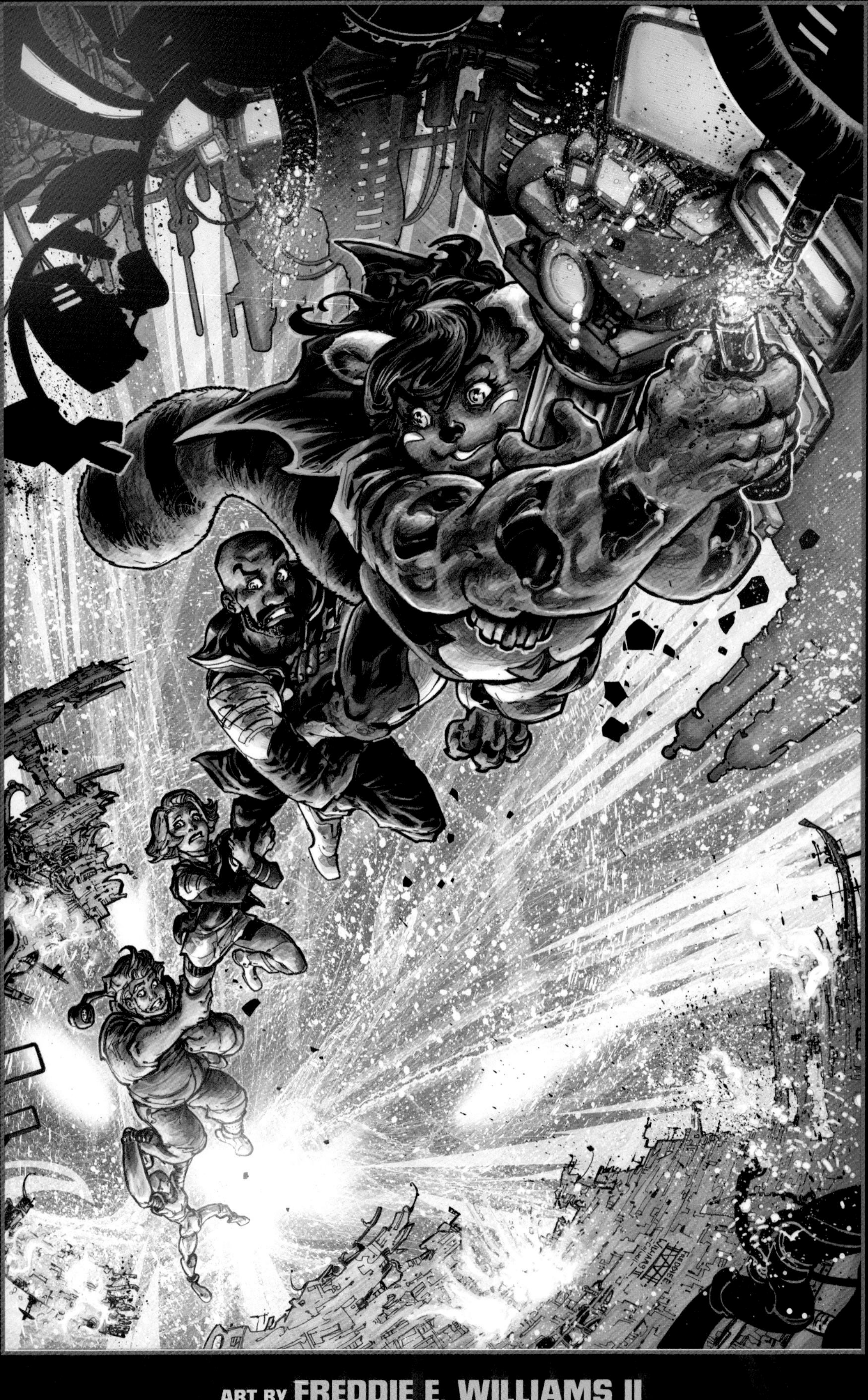

ART BY **FREDDIE E. WILLIAMS II**

COLORS BY **JEREMY COLWELL**

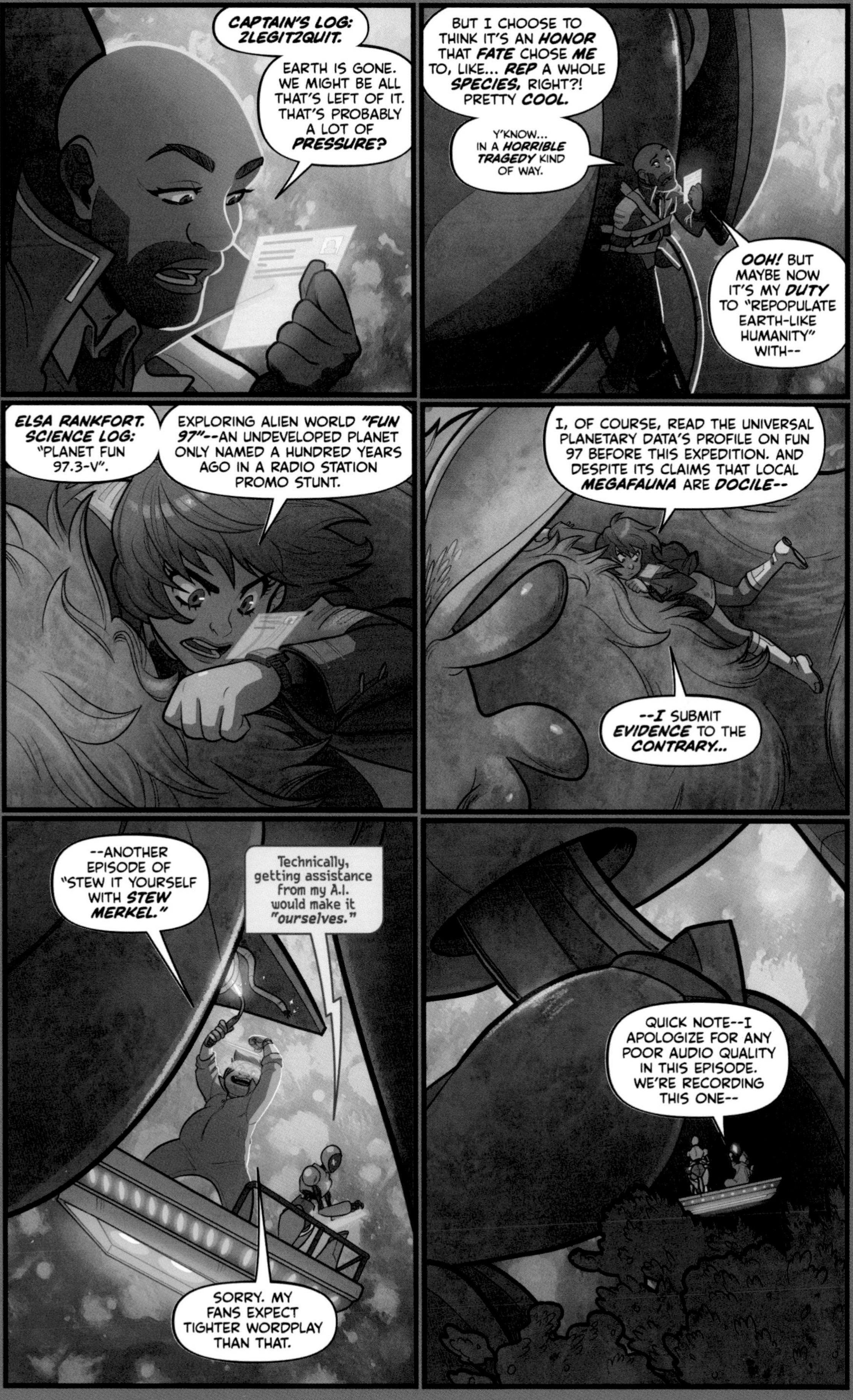
CAPTAIN'S LOG: 2LEGIT2QUIT.
EARTH IS GONE. WE MIGHT BE ALL THAT'S LEFT OF IT. THAT'S PROBABLY A LOT OF PRESSURE?
BUT I CHOOSE TO THINK IT'S AN HONOR THAT FATE CHOSE ME TO, LIKE... REP A WHOLE SPECIES, RIGHT?! PRETTY COOL.
Y'KNOW... IN A HORRIBLE TRAGEDY KIND OF WAY.
OOH! BUT MAYBE NOW IT'S MY DUTY TO "REPOPULATE EARTH-LIKE HUMANITY" WITH--
ELSA RANKFORT. SCIENCE LOG: "PLANET FUN 97.3-V".
EXPLORING ALIEN WORLD "FUN 97"--AN UNDEVELOPED PLANET ONLY NAMED A HUNDRED YEARS AGO IN A RADIO STATION PROMO STUNT.
I, OF COURSE, READ THE UNIVERSAL PLANETARY DATA'S PROFILE ON FUN 97 BEFORE THIS EXPEDITION. AND DESPITE ITS CLAIMS THAT LOCAL MEGAFAUNA ARE DOCILE--
--I SUBMIT EVIDENCE TO THE CONTRARY...
--ANOTHER EPISODE OF "STEW IT YOURSELF WITH STEW MERKEL."
Technically, getting assistance from my A.I. would make it "ourselves."
SORRY. MY FANS EXPECT TIGHTER WORDPLAY THAN THAT.
QUICK NOTE--I APOLOGIZE FOR ANY POOR AUDIO QUALITY IN THIS EPISODE. WE'RE RECORDING THIS ONE--

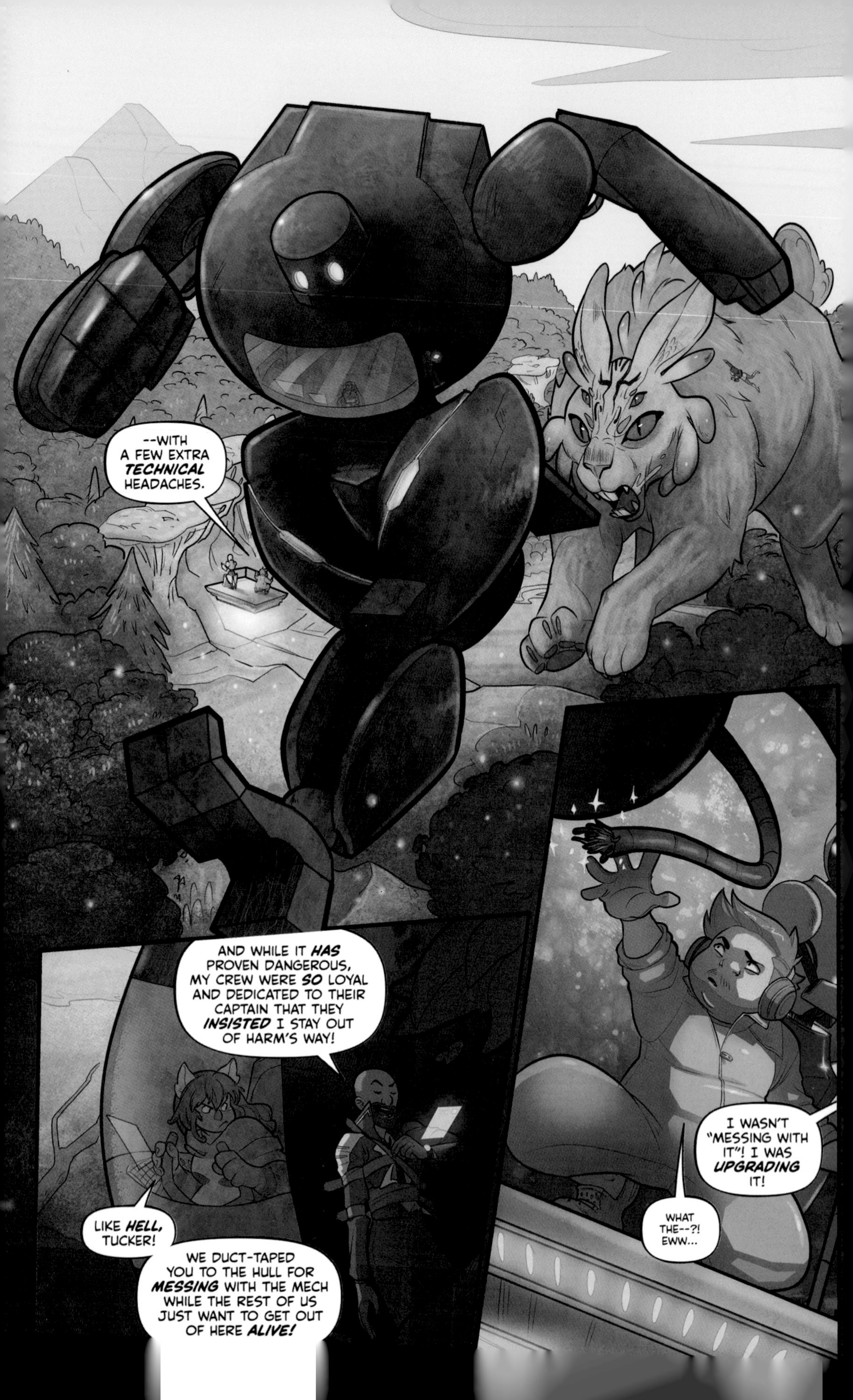
--WITH A FEW EXTRA *TECHNICAL* HEADACHES.
AND WHILE IT *HAS* PROVEN DANGEROUS, MY CREW WERE *SO* LOYAL AND DEDICATED TO THEIR CAPTAIN THAT THEY *INSISTED* I STAY OUT OF HARM'S WAY!
LIKE *HELL,* TUCKER!
WE DUCT-TAPED YOU TO THE HULL FOR *MESSING* WITH THE MECH WHILE THE REST OF US JUST WANT TO GET OUT OF HERE *ALIVE!*
I WASN'T "MESSING WITH IT"! I WAS *UPGRADING* IT!
WHAT THE--?! EWW...

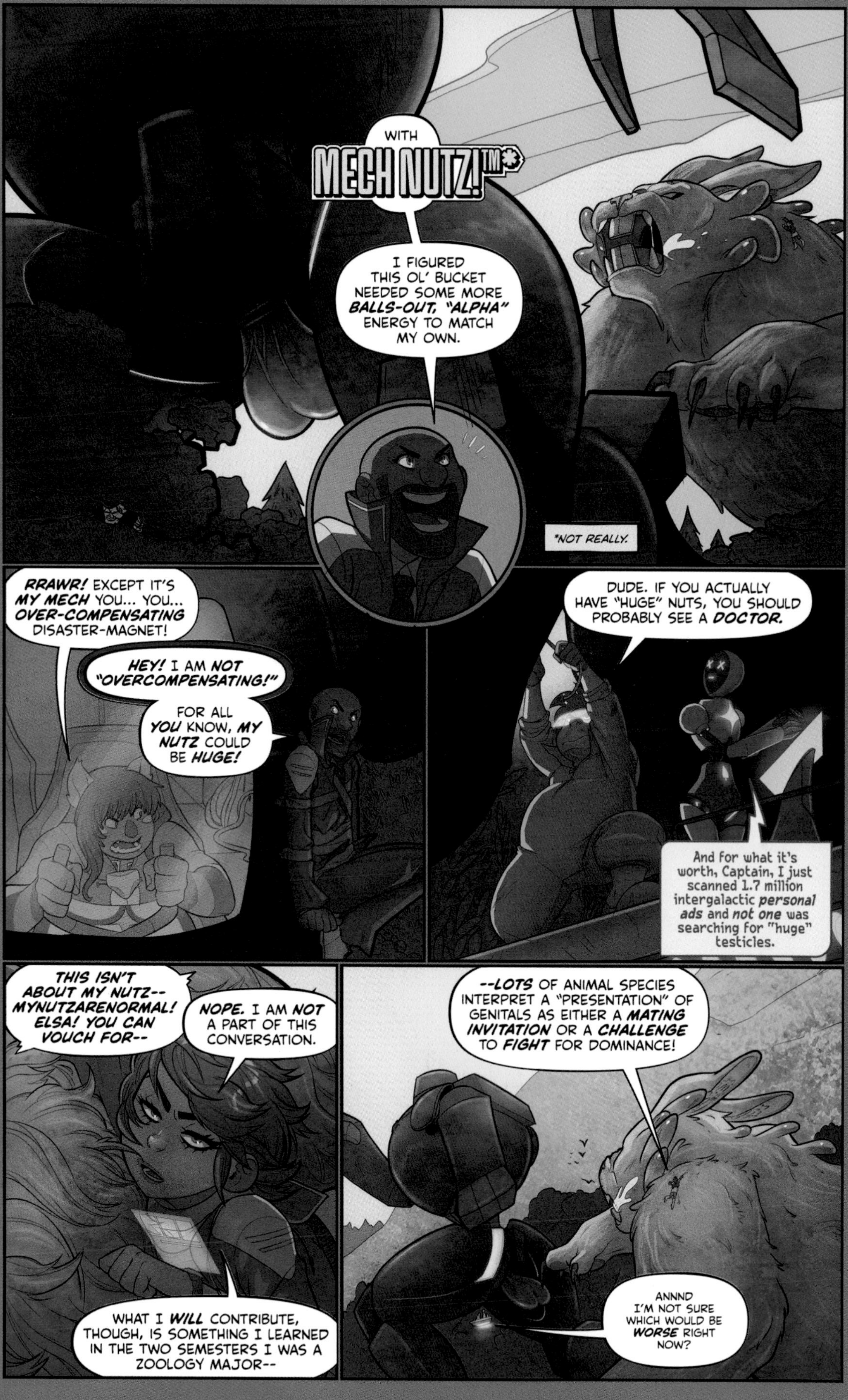
WITH
MECH NUTZ!™*
I FIGURED THIS OL' BUCKET NEEDED SOME MORE BALLS-OUT, "ALPHA" ENERGY TO MATCH MY OWN.
*NOT REALLY.
RRAWR! EXCEPT IT'S MY MECH YOU... YOU... OVER-COMPENSATING DISASTER-MAGNET!
HEY! I AM NOT "OVERCOMPENSATING!"
FOR ALL YOU KNOW, MY NUTZ COULD BE HUGE!
DUDE. IF YOU ACTUALLY HAVE "HUGE" NUTS, YOU SHOULD PROBABLY SEE A DOCTOR.
And for what it's worth, Captain, I just scanned 1.7 million intergalactic personal ads and not one was searching for "huge" testicles.
THIS ISN'T ABOUT MY NUTZ-- MYNUTZARENORMAL! ELSA! YOU CAN VOUCH FOR--
NOPE. I AM NOT A PART OF THIS CONVERSATION.
WHAT I WILL CONTRIBUTE, THOUGH, IS SOMETHING I LEARNED IN THE TWO SEMESTERS I WAS A ZOOLOGY MAJOR--
--LOTS OF ANIMAL SPECIES INTERPRET A "PRESENTATION" OF GENITALS AS EITHER A MATING INVITATION OR A CHALLENGE TO FIGHT FOR DOMINANCE!
ANNND I'M NOT SURE WHICH WOULD BE WORSE RIGHT NOW?

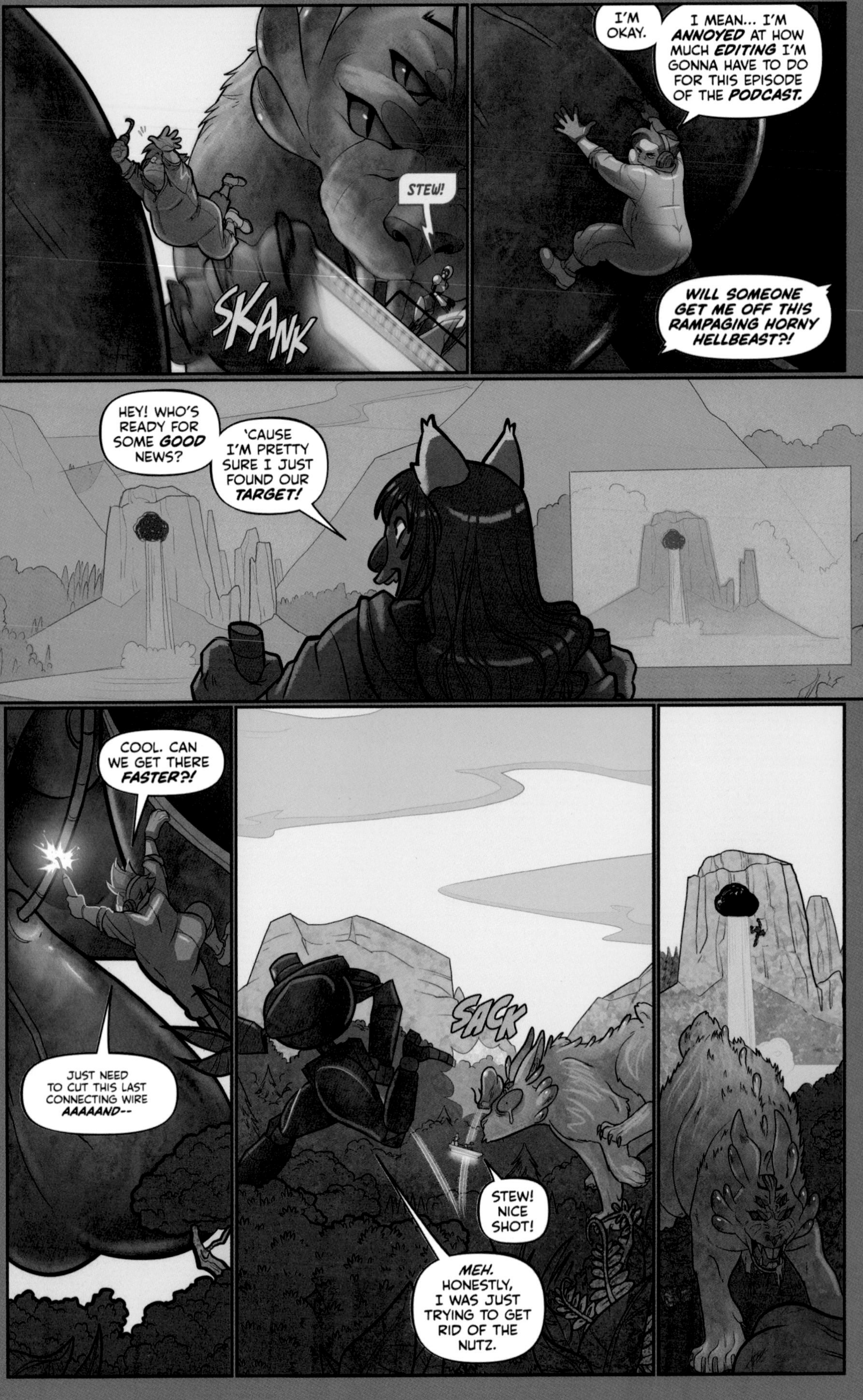
STEW!
SKANK
I'M OKAY.
I MEAN... I'M ANNOYED AT HOW MUCH EDITING I'M GONNA HAVE TO DO FOR THIS EPISODE OF THE PODCAST.
WILL SOMEONE GET ME OFF THIS RAMPAGING HORNY HELLBEAST?!
HEY! WHO'S READY FOR SOME GOOD NEWS?
'CAUSE I'M PRETTY SURE I JUST FOUND OUR TARGET!
COOL. CAN WE GET THERE FASTER?!
JUST NEED TO CUT THIS LAST CONNECTING WIRE AAAAAND--
SACK
STEW! NICE SHOT!
MEH. HONESTLY, I WAS JUST TRYING TO GET RID OF THE NUTZ.

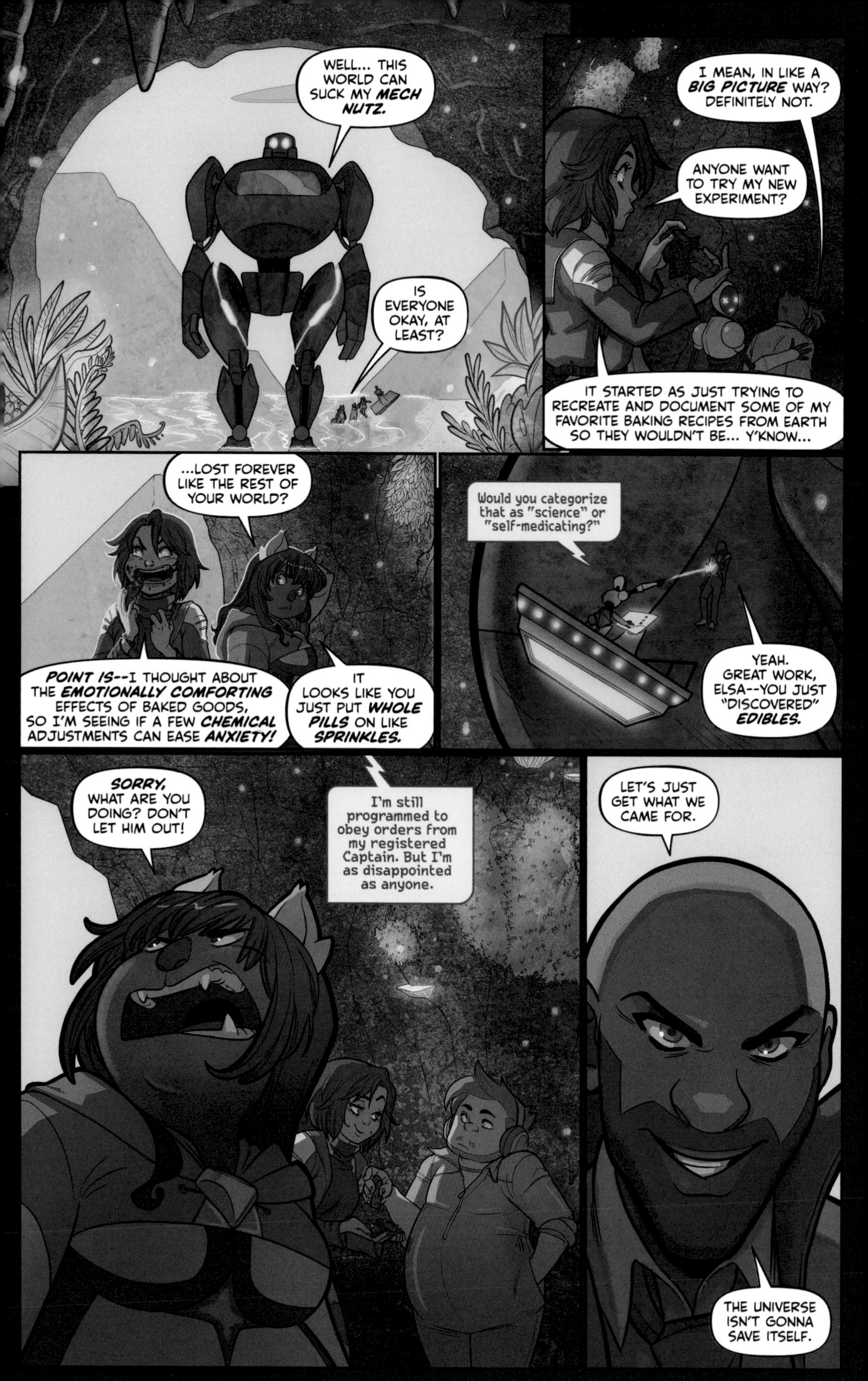
WELL... THIS WORLD CAN SUCK MY *MECH NUTZ.*
IS EVERYONE OKAY, AT LEAST?
I MEAN, IN LIKE A *BIG PICTURE* WAY? DEFINITELY NOT.
ANYONE WANT TO TRY MY NEW EXPERIMENT?
IT STARTED AS JUST TRYING TO RECREATE AND DOCUMENT SOME OF MY FAVORITE BAKING RECIPES FROM EARTH SO THEY WOULDN'T BE... Y'KNOW...
...LOST FOREVER LIKE THE REST OF YOUR WORLD?
*POINT IS--*I THOUGHT ABOUT THE *EMOTIONALLY COMFORTING* EFFECTS OF BAKED GOODS, SO I'M SEEING IF A FEW *CHEMICAL* ADJUSTMENTS CAN EASE *ANXIETY!*
IT LOOKS LIKE YOU JUST PUT *WHOLE PILLS* ON LIKE *SPRINKLES.*
Would you categorize that as "science" or "self-medicating?"
YEAH. GREAT WORK, ELSA--YOU JUST "DISCOVERED" *EDIBLES.*
SORRY, WHAT ARE YOU DOING? DON'T LET HIM OUT!
I'm still programmed to obey orders from my registered Captain. But I'm as disappointed as anyone.
LET'S JUST GET WHAT WE CAME FOR.
THE UNIVERSE ISN'T GONNA SAVE ITSELF.

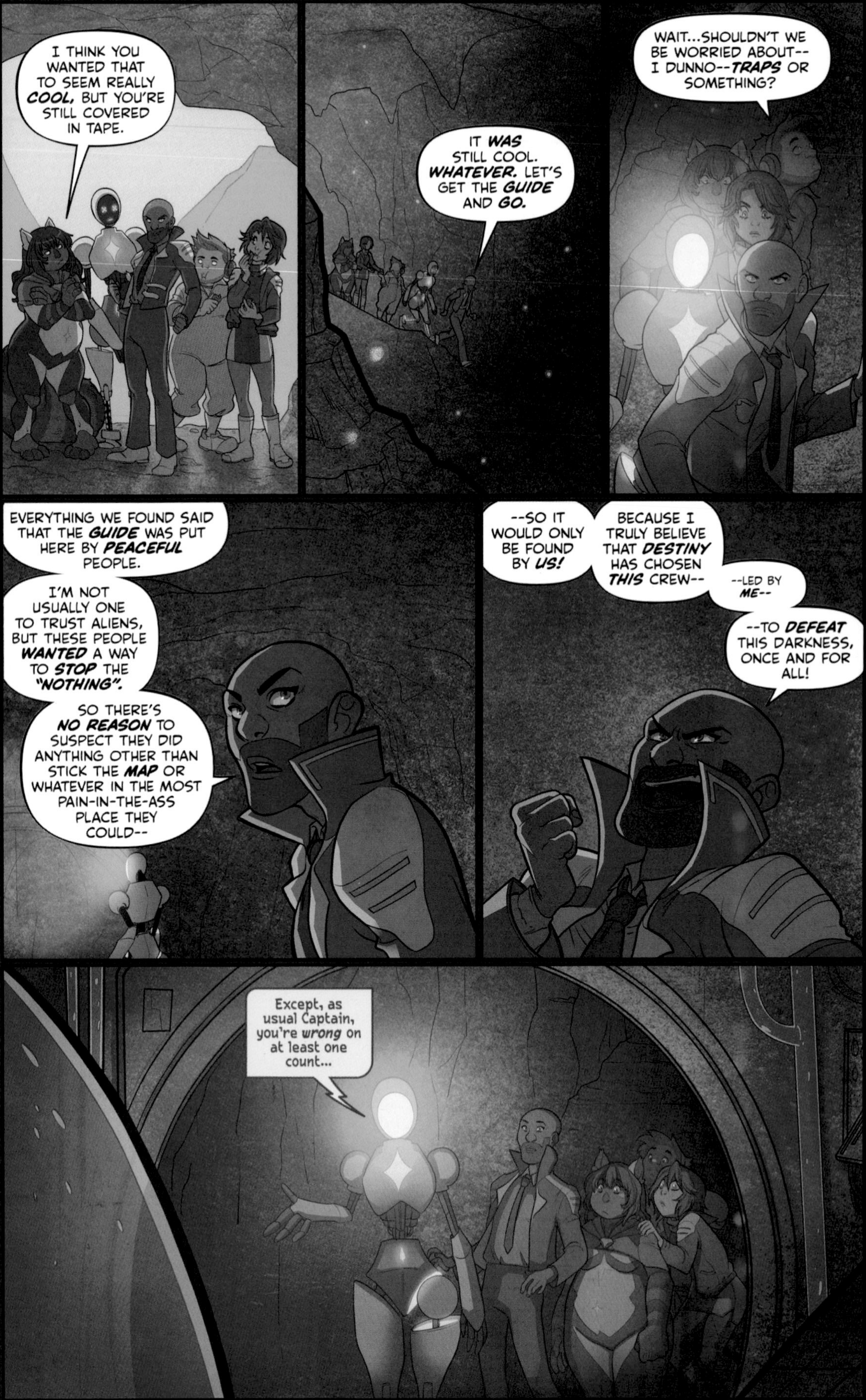
I THINK YOU WANTED THAT TO SEEM REALLY COOL, BUT YOU'RE STILL COVERED IN TAPE.
IT WAS STILL COOL. WHATEVER. LET'S GET THE GUIDE AND GO.
WAIT...SHOULDN'T WE BE WORRIED ABOUT-- I DUNNO--TRAPS OR SOMETHING?
EVERYTHING WE FOUND SAID THAT THE GUIDE WAS PUT HERE BY PEACEFUL PEOPLE.
I'M NOT USUALLY ONE TO TRUST ALIENS, BUT THESE PEOPLE WANTED A WAY TO STOP THE "NOTHING".
SO THERE'S NO REASON TO SUSPECT THEY DID ANYTHING OTHER THAN STICK THE MAP OR WHATEVER IN THE MOST PAIN-IN-THE-ASS PLACE THEY COULD--
--SO IT WOULD ONLY BE FOUND BY US!
BECAUSE I TRULY BELIEVE THAT DESTINY HAS CHOSEN THIS CREW--
--LED BY ME--
--TO DEFEAT THIS DARKNESS, ONCE AND FOR ALL!
Except, as usual Captain, you're wrong on at least one count...

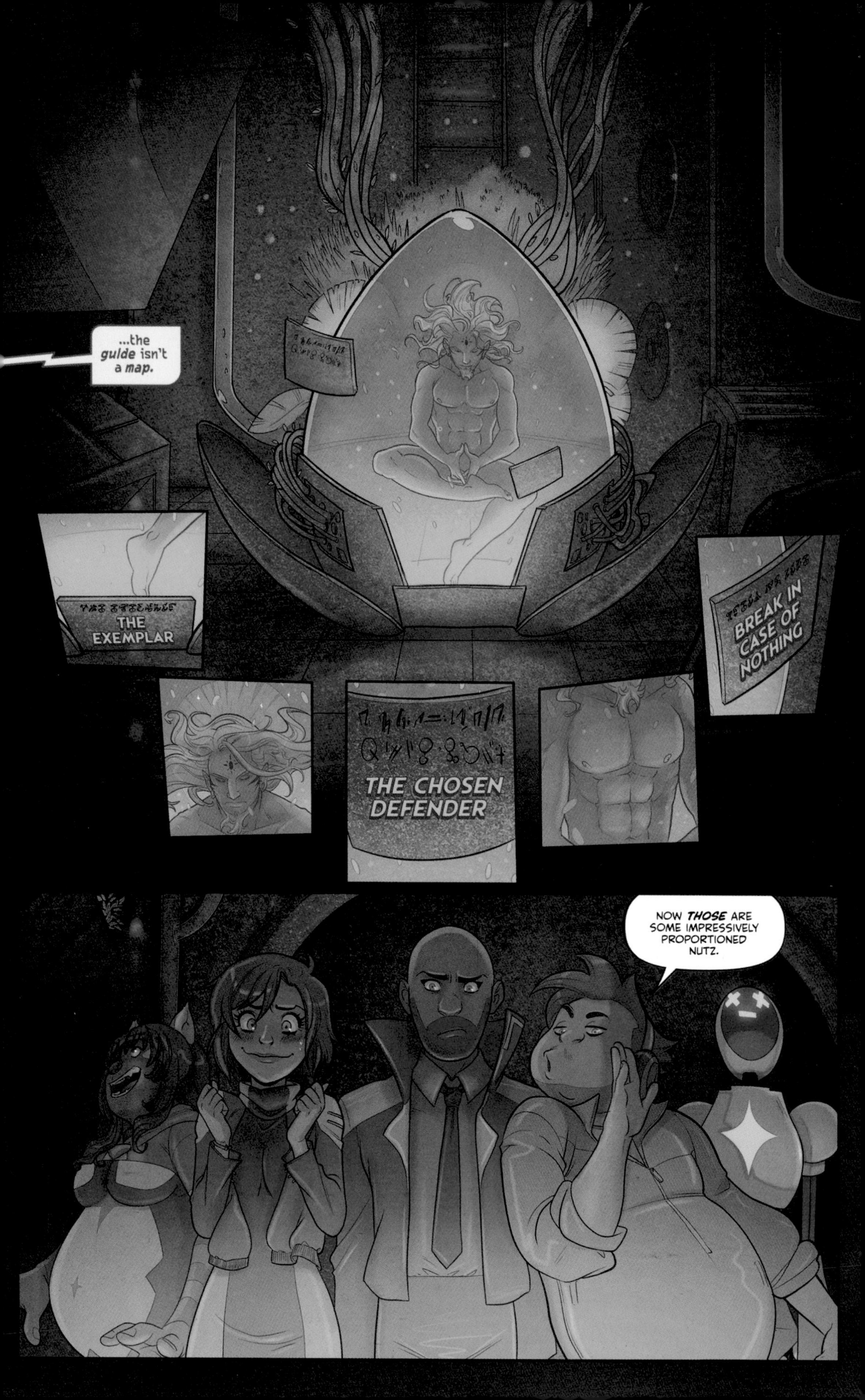

...the guide isn't a map.
THE EXEMPLAR
BREAK IN CASE OF NOTHING
THE CHOSEN DEFENDER
NOW THOSE ARE SOME IMPRESSIVELY PROPORTIONED NUTZ.

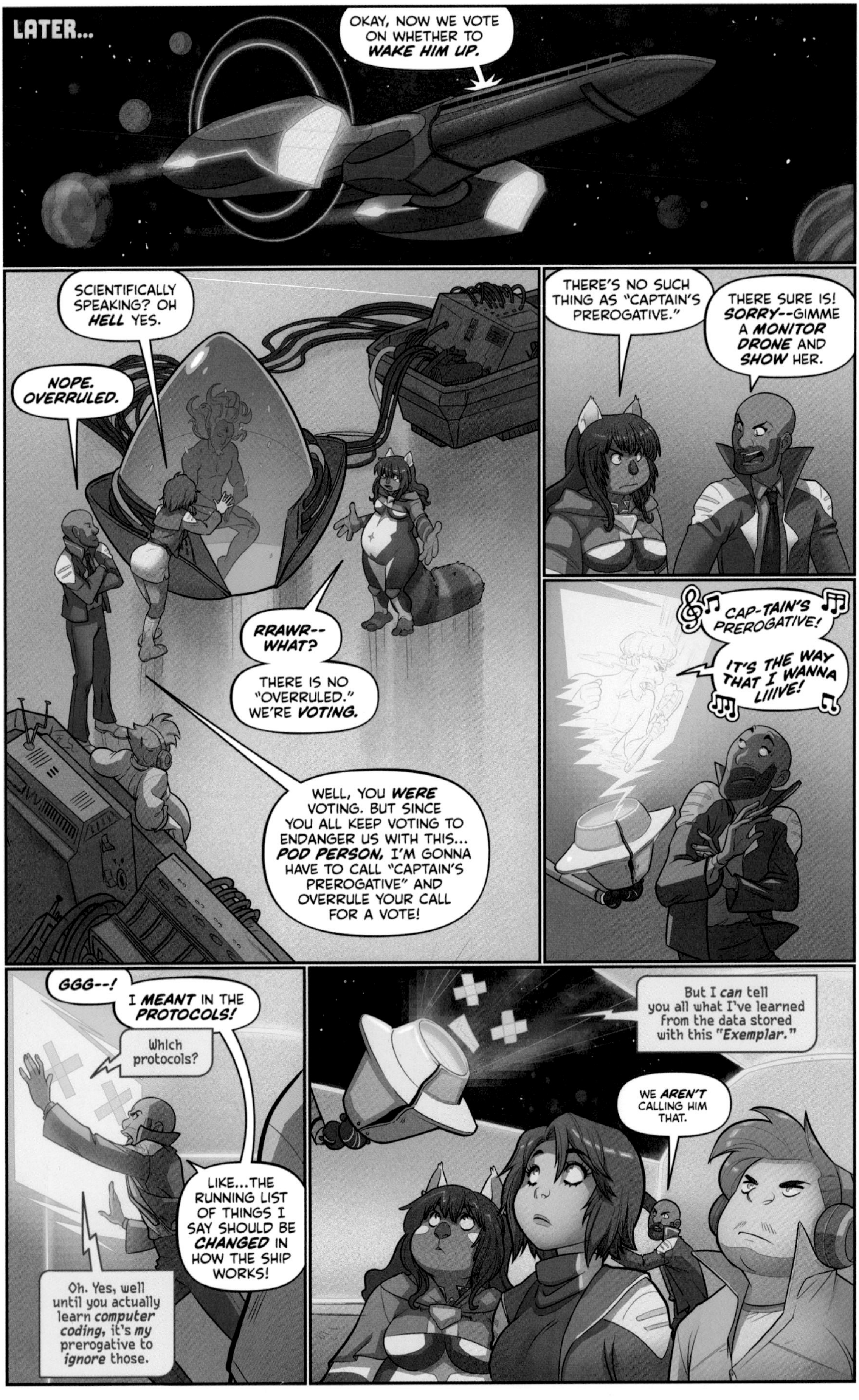
LATER...
OKAY, NOW WE VOTE ON WHETHER TO WAKE HIM UP.
SCIENTIFICALLY SPEAKING? OH HELL YES.
NOPE. OVERRULED.
RRAWR--WHAT?
THERE IS NO "OVERRULED." WE'RE VOTING.
WELL, YOU WERE VOTING. BUT SINCE YOU ALL KEEP VOTING TO ENDANGER US WITH THIS... POD PERSON, I'M GONNA HAVE TO CALL "CAPTAIN'S PREROGATIVE" AND OVERRULE YOUR CALL FOR A VOTE!
THERE'S NO SUCH THING AS "CAPTAIN'S PREROGATIVE."
THERE SURE IS! SORRY--GIMME A MONITOR DRONE AND SHOW HER.
CAP-TAIN'S PREROGATIVE!
IT'S THE WAY THAT I WANNA LIIIVE!
GGG--!
I MEANT IN THE PROTOCOLS!
Which protocols?
LIKE...THE RUNNING LIST OF THINGS I SAY SHOULD BE CHANGED IN HOW THE SHIP WORKS!
Oh. Yes, well until you actually learn computer coding, it's my prerogative to ignore those.
But I can tell you all what I've learned from the data stored with this "Exemplar."
WE AREN'T CALLING HIM THAT.

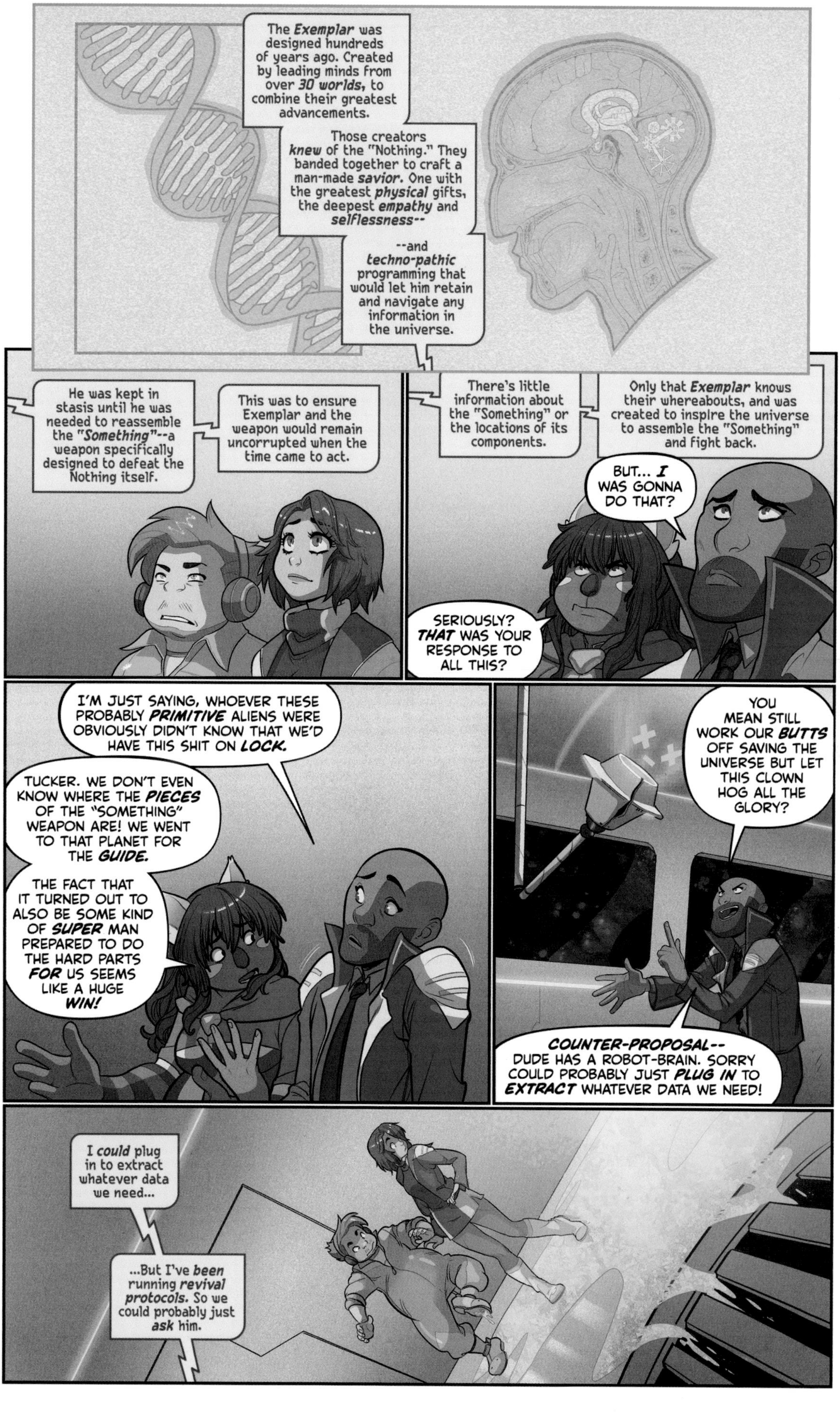
The Exemplar was designed hundreds of years ago. Created by leading minds from over 30 worlds, to combine their greatest advancements.
Those creators knew of the "Nothing." They banded together to craft a man-made savior. One with the greatest physical gifts, the deepest empathy and selflessness--
--and techno-pathic programming that would let him retain and navigate any information in the universe.
He was kept in stasis until he was needed to reassemble the "Something"--a weapon specifically designed to defeat the Nothing itself.
This was to ensure Exemplar and the weapon would remain uncorrupted when the time came to act.
There's little information about the "Something" or the locations of its components.
Only that Exemplar knows their whereabouts, and was created to inspire the universe to assemble the "Something" and fight back.
BUT... I WAS GONNA DO THAT?
SERIOUSLY? THAT WAS YOUR RESPONSE TO ALL THIS?
I'M JUST SAYING, WHOEVER THESE PROBABLY PRIMITIVE ALIENS WERE OBVIOUSLY DIDN'T KNOW THAT WE'D HAVE THIS SHIT ON LOCK.
TUCKER. WE DON'T EVEN KNOW WHERE THE PIECES OF THE "SOMETHING" WEAPON ARE! WE WENT TO THAT PLANET FOR THE GUIDE.
THE FACT THAT IT TURNED OUT TO ALSO BE SOME KIND OF SUPER MAN PREPARED TO DO THE HARD PARTS FOR US SEEMS LIKE A HUGE WIN!
YOU MEAN STILL WORK OUR BUTTS OFF SAVING THE UNIVERSE BUT LET THIS CLOWN HOG ALL THE GLORY?
COUNTER-PROPOSAL-- DUDE HAS A ROBOT-BRAIN. SORRY COULD PROBABLY JUST PLUG IN TO EXTRACT WHATEVER DATA WE NEED!
I could plug in to extract whatever data we need...
...But I've been running revival protocols. So we could probably just ask him.

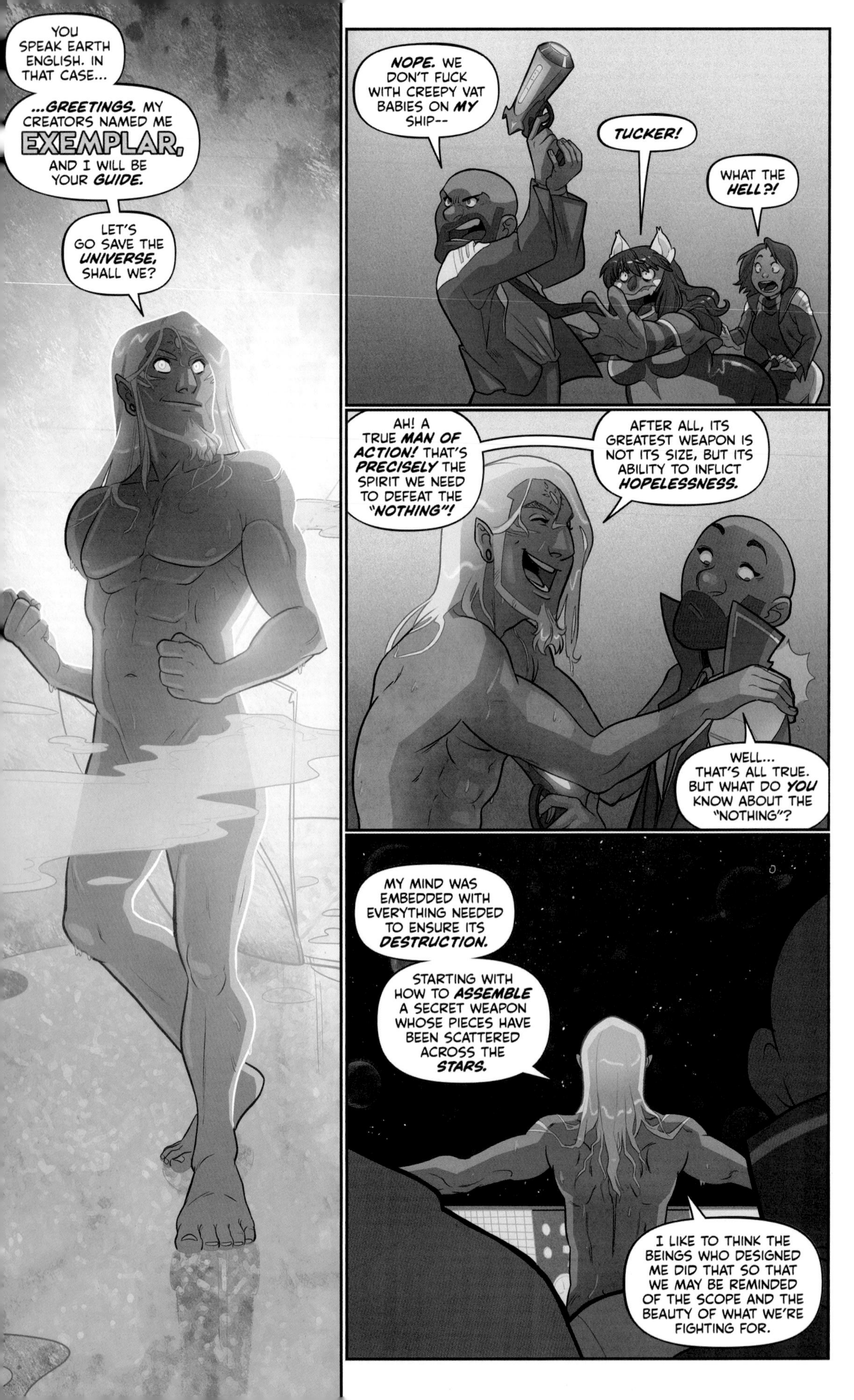

YOU SPEAK EARTH ENGLISH. IN THAT CASE...
...GREETINGS. MY CREATORS NAMED ME EXEMPLAR, AND I WILL BE YOUR GUIDE.
LET'S GO SAVE THE UNIVERSE, SHALL WE?
NOPE. WE DON'T FUCK WITH CREEPY VAT BABIES ON MY SHIP--
TUCKER!
WHAT THE HELL?!
AH! A TRUE MAN OF ACTION! THAT'S PRECISELY THE SPIRIT WE NEED TO DEFEAT THE "NOTHING"!
AFTER ALL, ITS GREATEST WEAPON IS NOT ITS SIZE, BUT ITS ABILITY TO INFLICT HOPELESSNESS.
WELL... THAT'S ALL TRUE. BUT WHAT DO YOU KNOW ABOUT THE "NOTHING"?
MY MIND WAS EMBEDDED WITH EVERYTHING NEEDED TO ENSURE ITS DESTRUCTION.
STARTING WITH HOW TO ASSEMBLE A SECRET WEAPON WHOSE PIECES HAVE BEEN SCATTERED ACROSS THE STARS.
I LIKE TO THINK THE BEINGS WHO DESIGNED ME DID THAT SO THAT WE MAY BE REMINDED OF THE SCOPE AND THE BEAUTY OF WHAT WE'RE FIGHTING FOR.

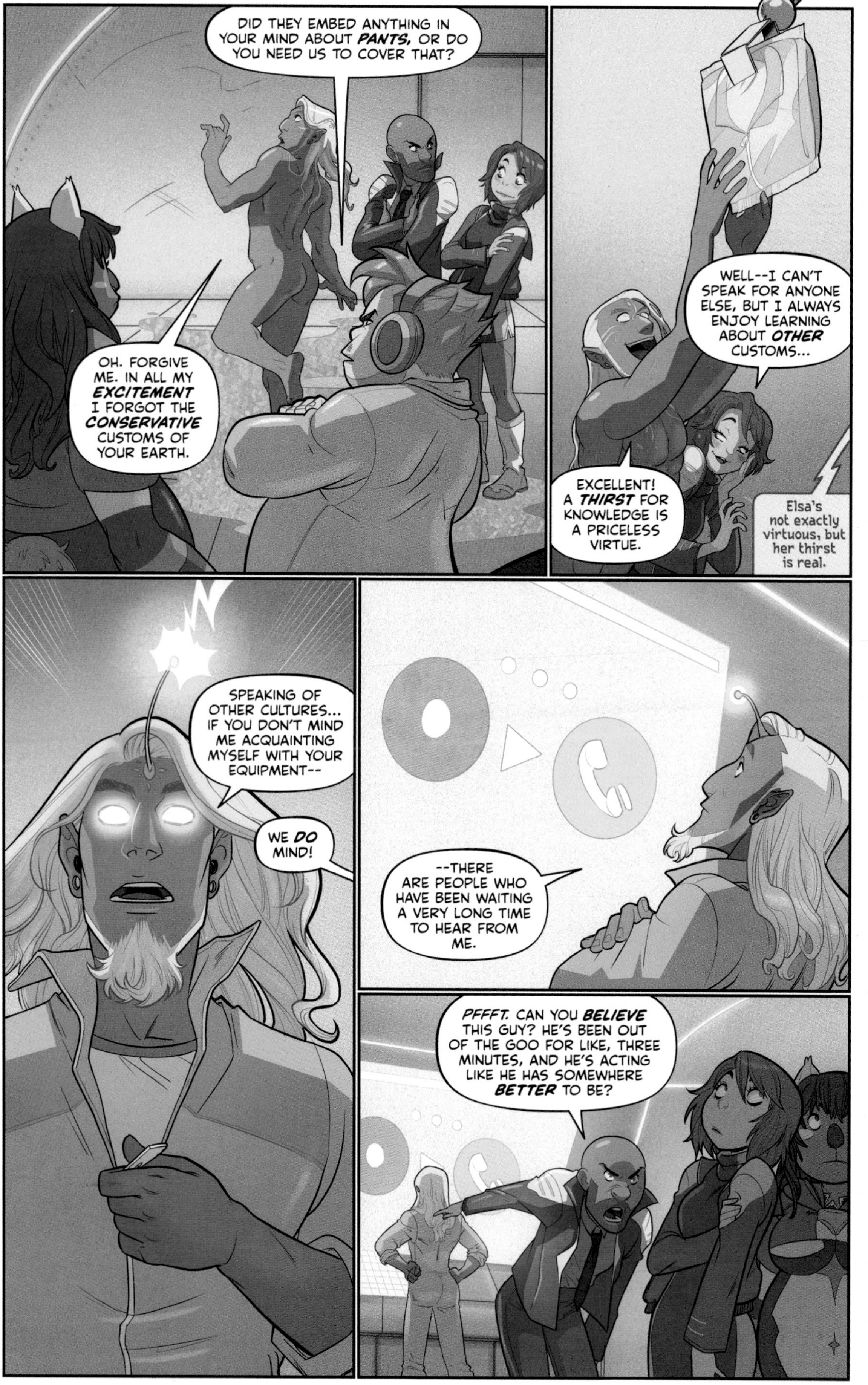
DID THEY EMBED ANYTHING IN YOUR MIND ABOUT *PANTS,* OR DO YOU NEED US TO COVER THAT?
OH. FORGIVE ME. IN ALL MY ***EXCITEMENT*** I FORGOT THE ***CONSERVATIVE*** CUSTOMS OF YOUR EARTH.
WELL--I CAN'T SPEAK FOR ANYONE ELSE, BUT I ALWAYS ENJOY LEARNING ABOUT ***OTHER*** CUSTOMS...
EXCELLENT! A ***THIRST*** FOR KNOWLEDGE IS A PRICELESS VIRTUE.
Elsa's not exactly virtuous, but her thirst is real.
SPEAKING OF OTHER CULTURES... IF YOU DON'T MIND ME ACQUAINTING MYSELF WITH YOUR EQUIPMENT--
WE ***DO*** MIND!
--THERE ARE PEOPLE WHO HAVE BEEN WAITING A VERY LONG TIME TO HEAR FROM ME.
PFFFT. CAN YOU ***BELIEVE*** THIS GUY? HE'S BEEN OUT OF THE GOO FOR LIKE, THREE MINUTES, AND HE'S ACTING LIKE HE HAS SOMEWHERE ***BETTER*** TO BE?

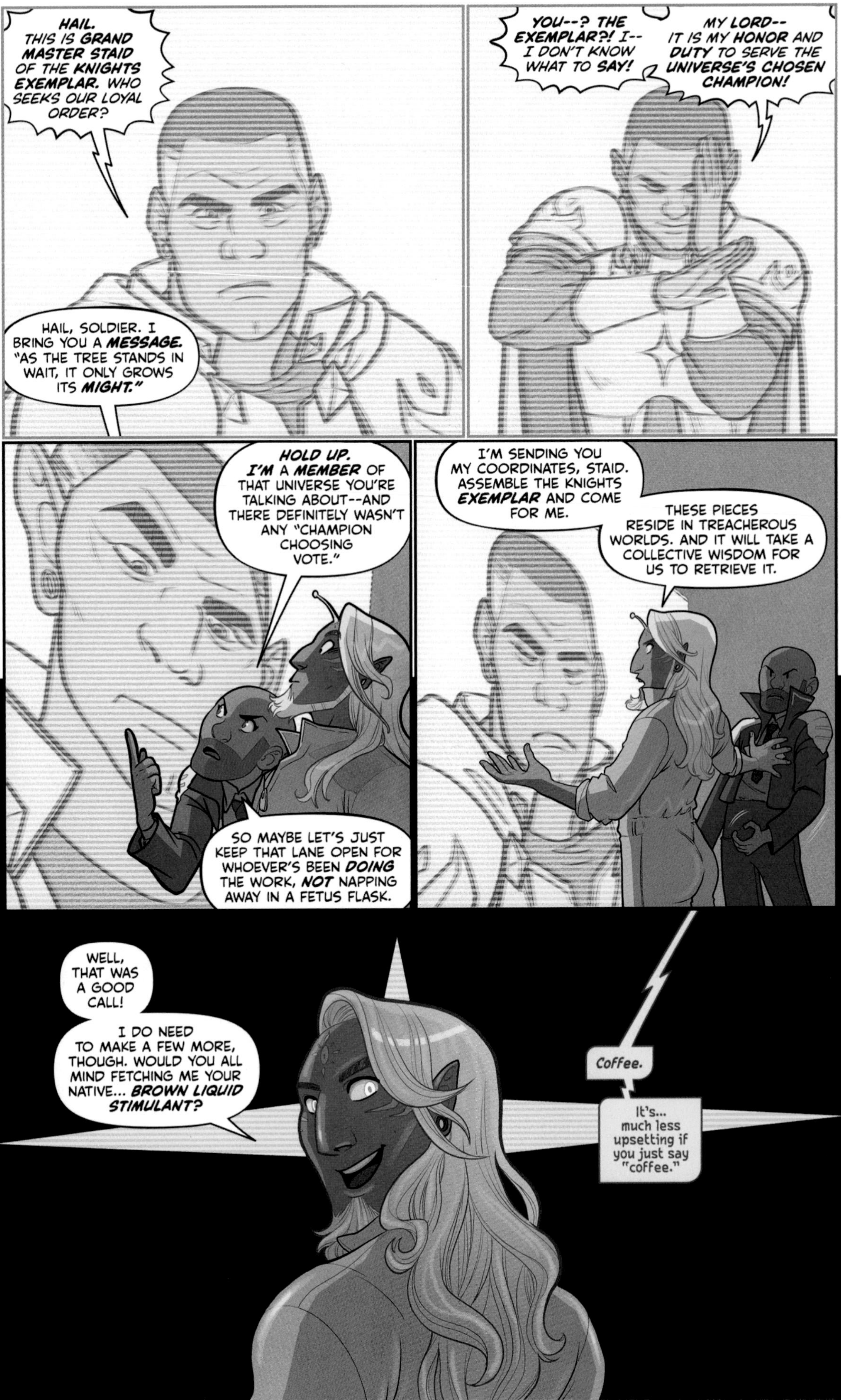
HAIL. THIS IS GRAND MASTER STAID OF THE KNIGHTS EXEMPLAR. WHO SEEKS OUR LOYAL ORDER?
HAIL, SOLDIER. I BRING YOU A MESSAGE. "AS THE TREE STANDS IN WAIT, IT ONLY GROWS ITS MIGHT."
YOU--? THE EXEMPLAR?! I--I DON'T KNOW WHAT TO SAY!
MY LORD--IT IS MY HONOR AND DUTY TO SERVE THE UNIVERSE'S CHOSEN CHAMPION!
HOLD UP. I'M A MEMBER OF THAT UNIVERSE YOU'RE TALKING ABOUT--AND THERE DEFINITELY WASN'T ANY "CHAMPION CHOOSING VOTE."
SO MAYBE LET'S JUST KEEP THAT LANE OPEN FOR WHOEVER'S BEEN DOING THE WORK, NOT NAPPING AWAY IN A FETUS FLASK.
I'M SENDING YOU MY COORDINATES, STAID. ASSEMBLE THE KNIGHTS EXEMPLAR AND COME FOR ME.
THESE PIECES RESIDE IN TREACHEROUS WORLDS. AND IT WILL TAKE A COLLECTIVE WISDOM FOR US TO RETRIEVE IT.
WELL, THAT WAS A GOOD CALL!
I DO NEED TO MAKE A FEW MORE, THOUGH. WOULD YOU ALL MIND FETCHING ME YOUR NATIVE... BROWN LIQUID STIMULANT?
Coffee.
It's... much less upsetting if you just say "coffee."

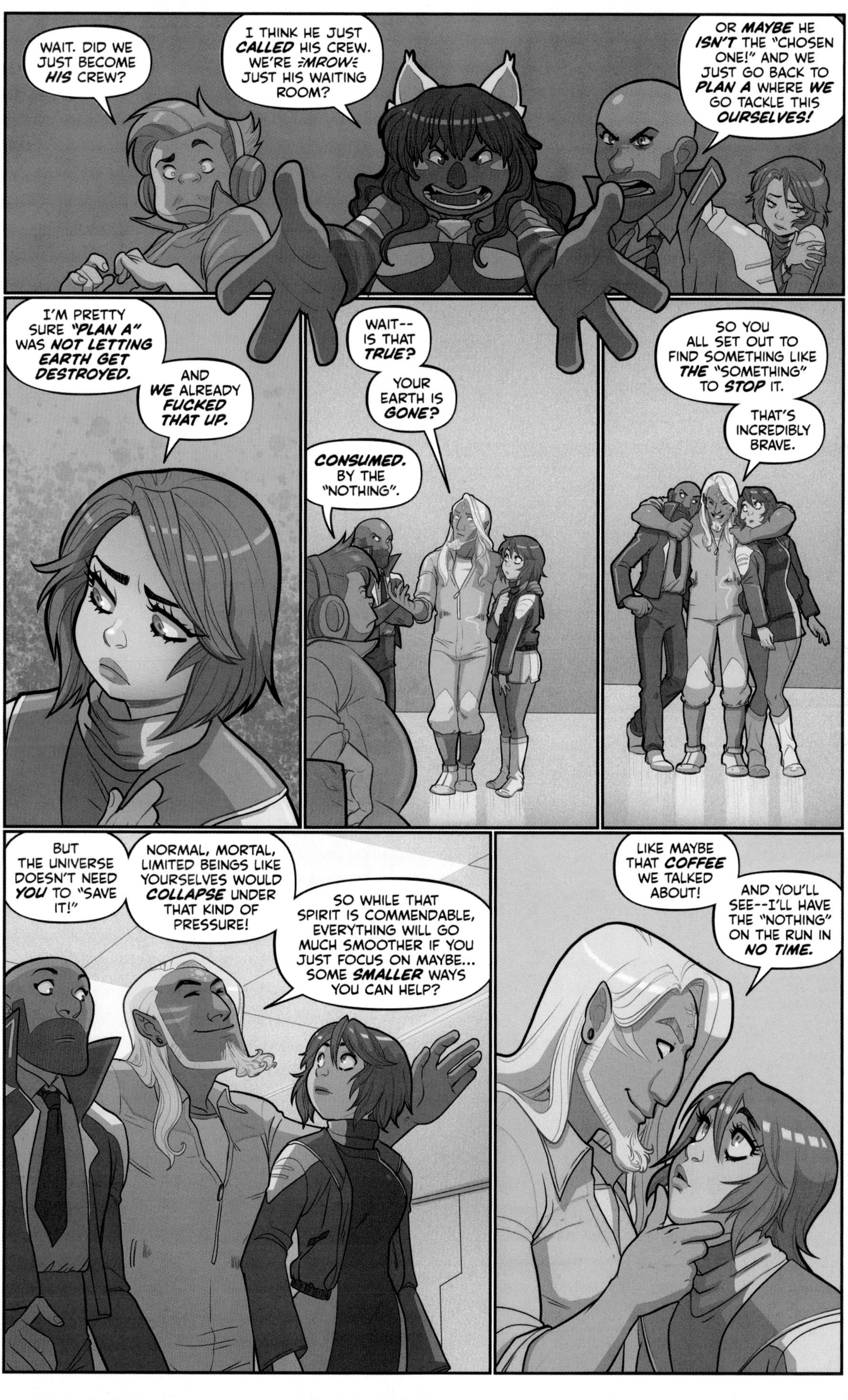
WAIT. DID WE JUST BECOME HIS CREW?
I THINK HE JUST CALLED HIS CREW. WE'RE =MROW= JUST HIS WAITING ROOM?
OR MAYBE HE ISN'T THE "CHOSEN ONE!" AND WE JUST GO BACK TO PLAN A WHERE WE GO TACKLE THIS OURSELVES!
I'M PRETTY SURE "PLAN A" WAS NOT LETTING EARTH GET DESTROYED.
AND WE ALREADY FUCKED THAT UP.
WAIT-- IS THAT TRUE?
YOUR EARTH IS GONE?
CONSUMED. BY THE "NOTHING".
SO YOU ALL SET OUT TO FIND SOMETHING LIKE THE "SOMETHING" TO STOP IT.
THAT'S INCREDIBLY BRAVE.
BUT THE UNIVERSE DOESN'T NEED YOU TO "SAVE IT!"
NORMAL, MORTAL, LIMITED BEINGS LIKE YOURSELVES WOULD COLLAPSE UNDER THAT KIND OF PRESSURE!
SO WHILE THAT SPIRIT IS COMMENDABLE, EVERYTHING WILL GO MUCH SMOOTHER IF YOU JUST FOCUS ON MAYBE... SOME SMALLER WAYS YOU CAN HELP?
LIKE MAYBE THAT COFFEE WE TALKED ABOUT!
AND YOU'LL SEE--I'LL HAVE THE "NOTHING" ON THE RUN IN NO TIME.

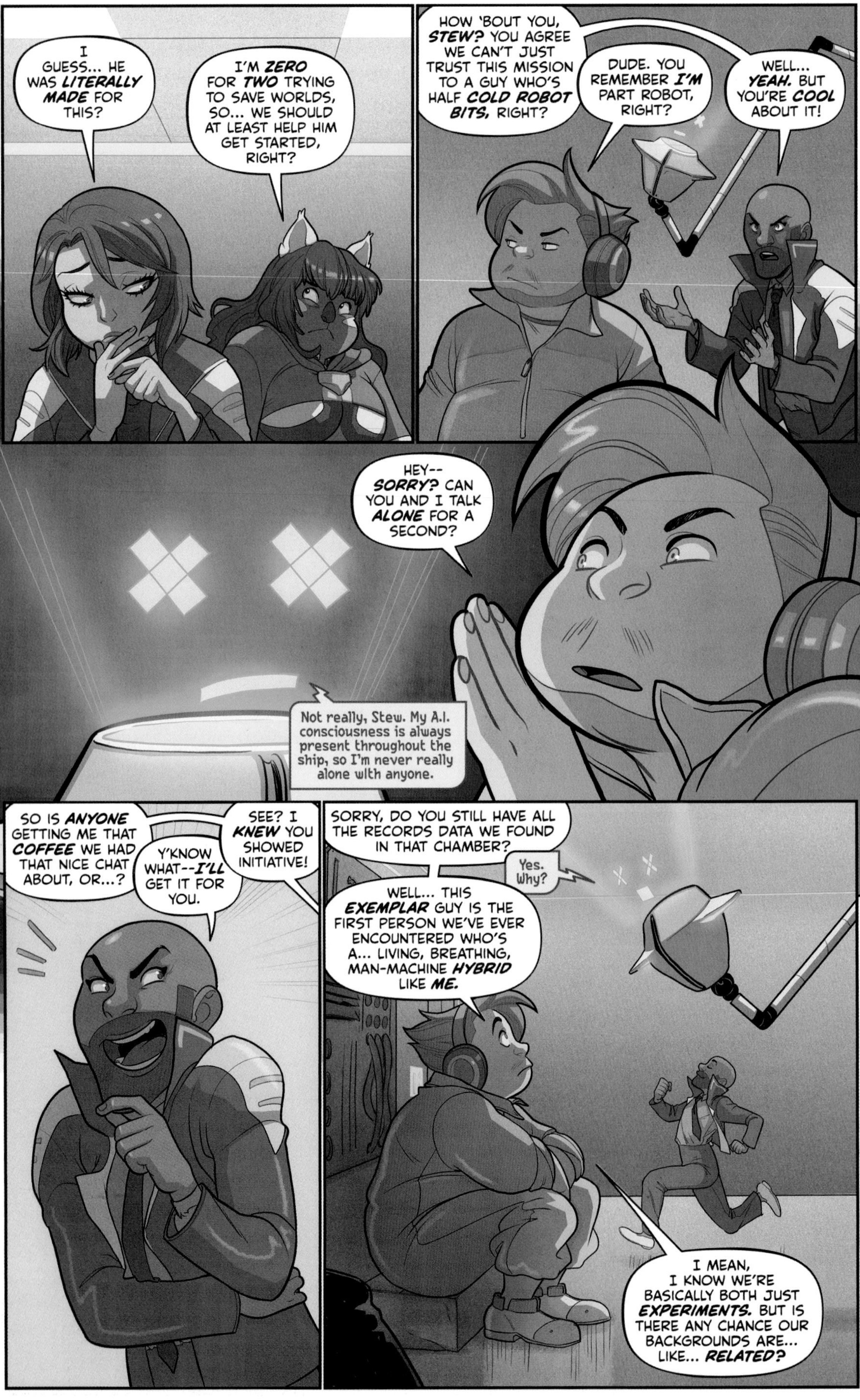
I GUESS... HE WAS LITERALLY MADE FOR THIS?
I'M ZERO FOR TWO TRYING TO SAVE WORLDS, SO... WE SHOULD AT LEAST HELP HIM GET STARTED, RIGHT?
HOW 'BOUT YOU, STEW? YOU AGREE WE CAN'T JUST TRUST THIS MISSION TO A GUY WHO'S HALF COLD ROBOT BITS, RIGHT?
DUDE. YOU REMEMBER I'M PART ROBOT, RIGHT?
WELL... YEAH. BUT YOU'RE COOL ABOUT IT!
HEY-- SORRY? CAN YOU AND I TALK ALONE FOR A SECOND?
Not really, Stew. My A.I. consciousness is always present throughout the ship, so I'm never really alone with anyone.
SO IS ANYONE GETTING ME THAT COFFEE WE HAD THAT NICE CHAT ABOUT, OR...?
Y'KNOW WHAT--I'LL GET IT FOR YOU.
SEE? I KNEW YOU SHOWED INITIATIVE!
SORRY, DO YOU STILL HAVE ALL THE RECORDS DATA WE FOUND IN THAT CHAMBER?
Yes. Why?
WELL... THIS EXEMPLAR GUY IS THE FIRST PERSON WE'VE EVER ENCOUNTERED WHO'S A... LIVING, BREATHING, MAN-MACHINE HYBRID LIKE ME.
I MEAN, I KNOW WE'RE BASICALLY BOTH JUST EXPERIMENTS. BUT IS THERE ANY CHANCE OUR BACKGROUNDS ARE... LIKE... RELATED?

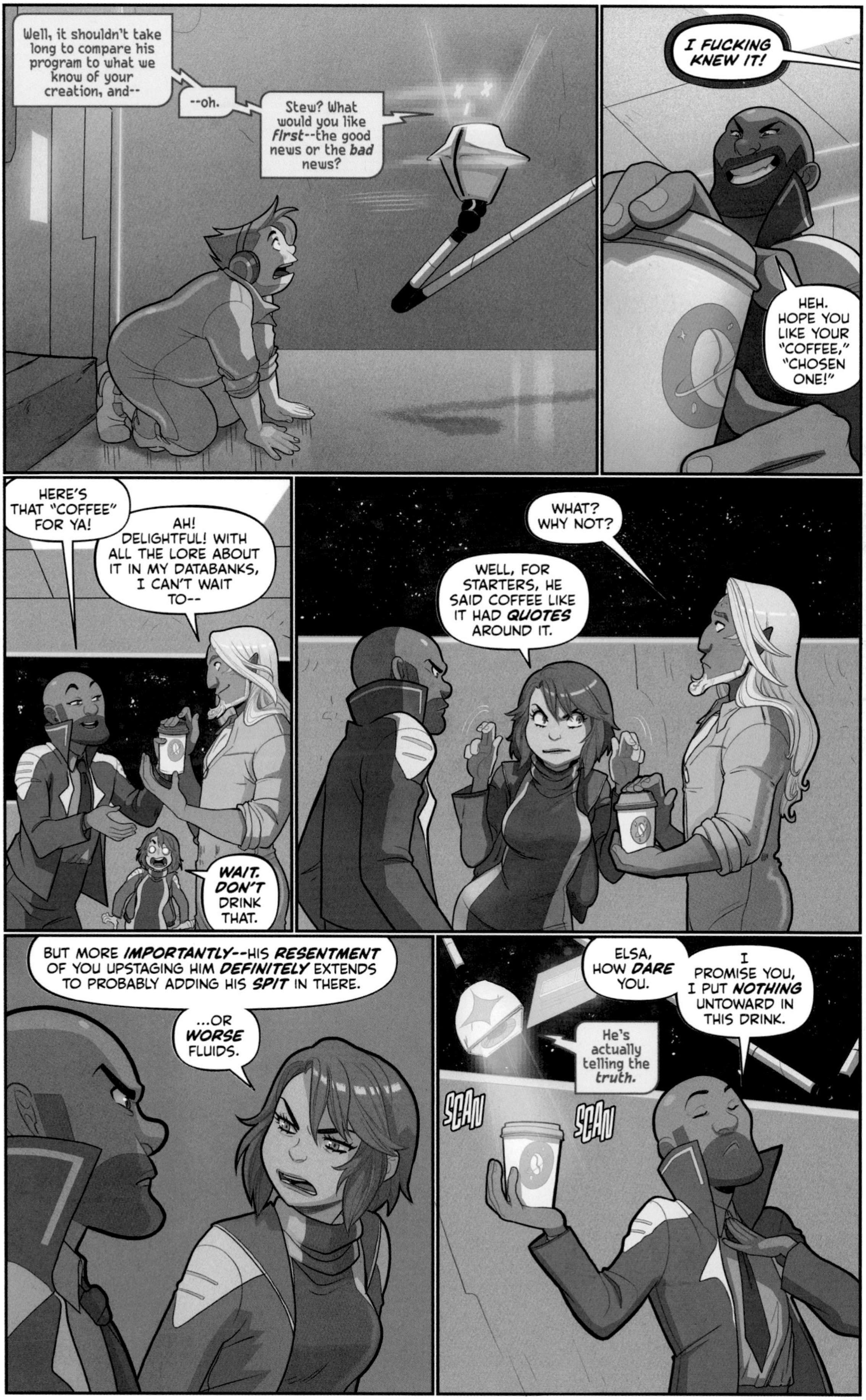
Well, it shouldn't take long to compare his program to what we know of your creation, and--
--oh.
Stew? What would you like *first*--the good news or the *bad* news?
I FUCKING KNEW IT!
HEH. HOPE YOU LIKE YOUR "COFFEE," "CHOSEN ONE!"
HERE'S THAT "COFFEE" FOR YA!
AH! DELIGHTFUL! WITH ALL THE LORE ABOUT IT IN MY DATABANKS, I CAN'T WAIT TO--
WAIT. DON'T DRINK THAT.
WHAT? WHY NOT?
WELL, FOR STARTERS, HE SAID COFFEE LIKE IT HAD *QUOTES* AROUND IT.
BUT MORE *IMPORTANTLY*--HIS *RESENTMENT* OF YOU UPSTAGING HIM *DEFINITELY* EXTENDS TO PROBABLY ADDING HIS *SPIT* IN THERE.
...OR *WORSE* FLUIDS.
ELSA, HOW *DARE* YOU.
I PROMISE YOU, I PUT *NOTHING* UNTOWARD IN THIS DRINK.
SCAN
SCAN
He's actually telling the *truth.*

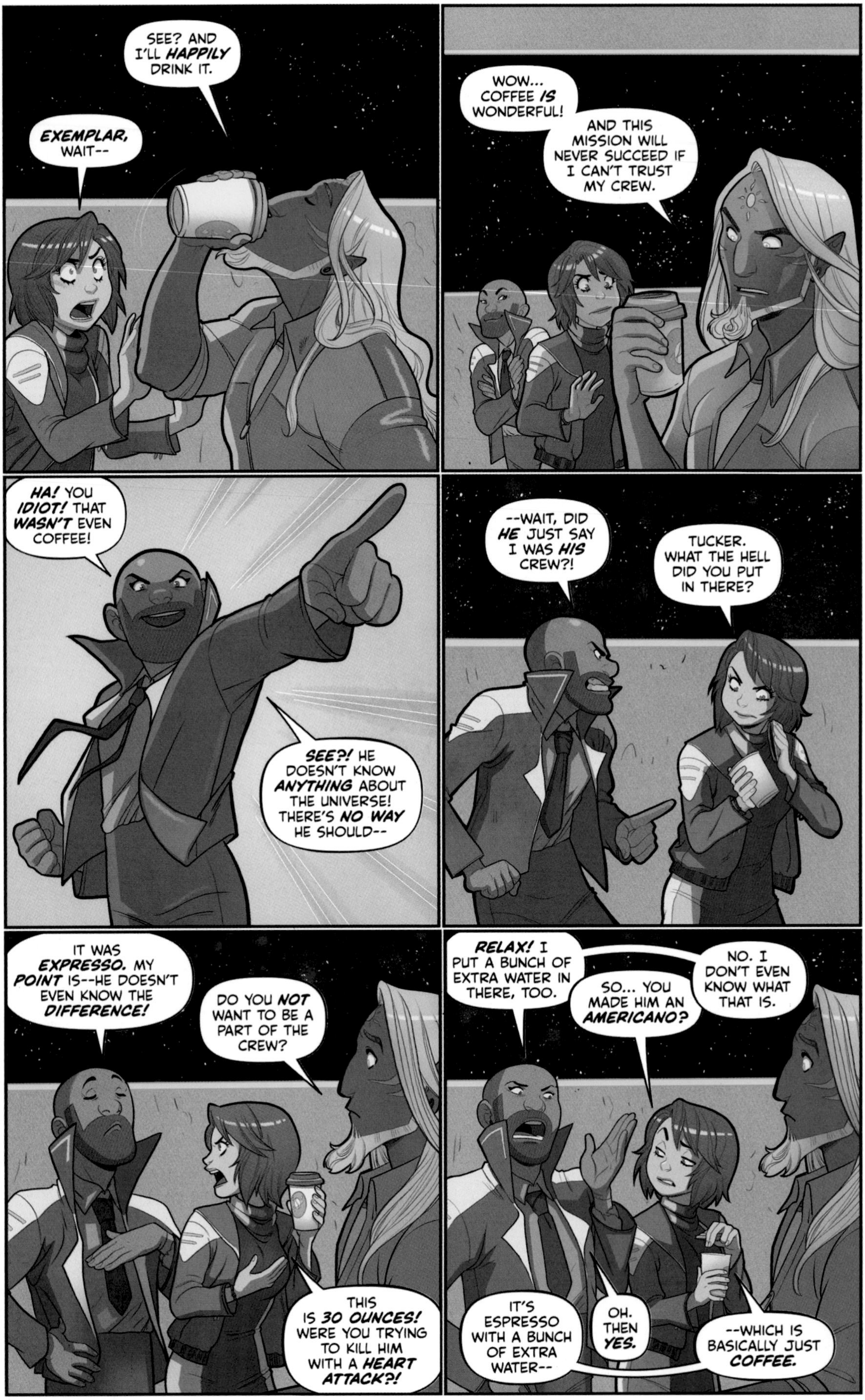
EXEMPLAR, WAIT--
SEE? AND I'LL HAPPILY DRINK IT.
WOW... COFFEE IS WONDERFUL!
AND THIS MISSION WILL NEVER SUCCEED IF I CAN'T TRUST MY CREW.
HA! YOU IDIOT! THAT WASN'T EVEN COFFEE!
SEE?! HE DOESN'T KNOW ANYTHING ABOUT THE UNIVERSE! THERE'S NO WAY HE SHOULD--
--WAIT, DID HE JUST SAY I WAS HIS CREW?!
TUCKER. WHAT THE HELL DID YOU PUT IN THERE?
IT WAS EXPRESSO. MY POINT IS--HE DOESN'T EVEN KNOW THE DIFFERENCE!
DO YOU NOT WANT TO BE A PART OF THE CREW?
THIS IS 30 OUNCES! WERE YOU TRYING TO KILL HIM WITH A HEART ATTACK?!
RELAX! I PUT A BUNCH OF EXTRA WATER IN THERE, TOO.
SO... YOU MADE HIM AN AMERICANO?
NO. I DON'T EVEN KNOW WHAT THAT IS.
IT'S ESPRESSO WITH A BUNCH OF EXTRA WATER--
OH. THEN YES.
--WHICH IS BASICALLY JUST COFFEE.

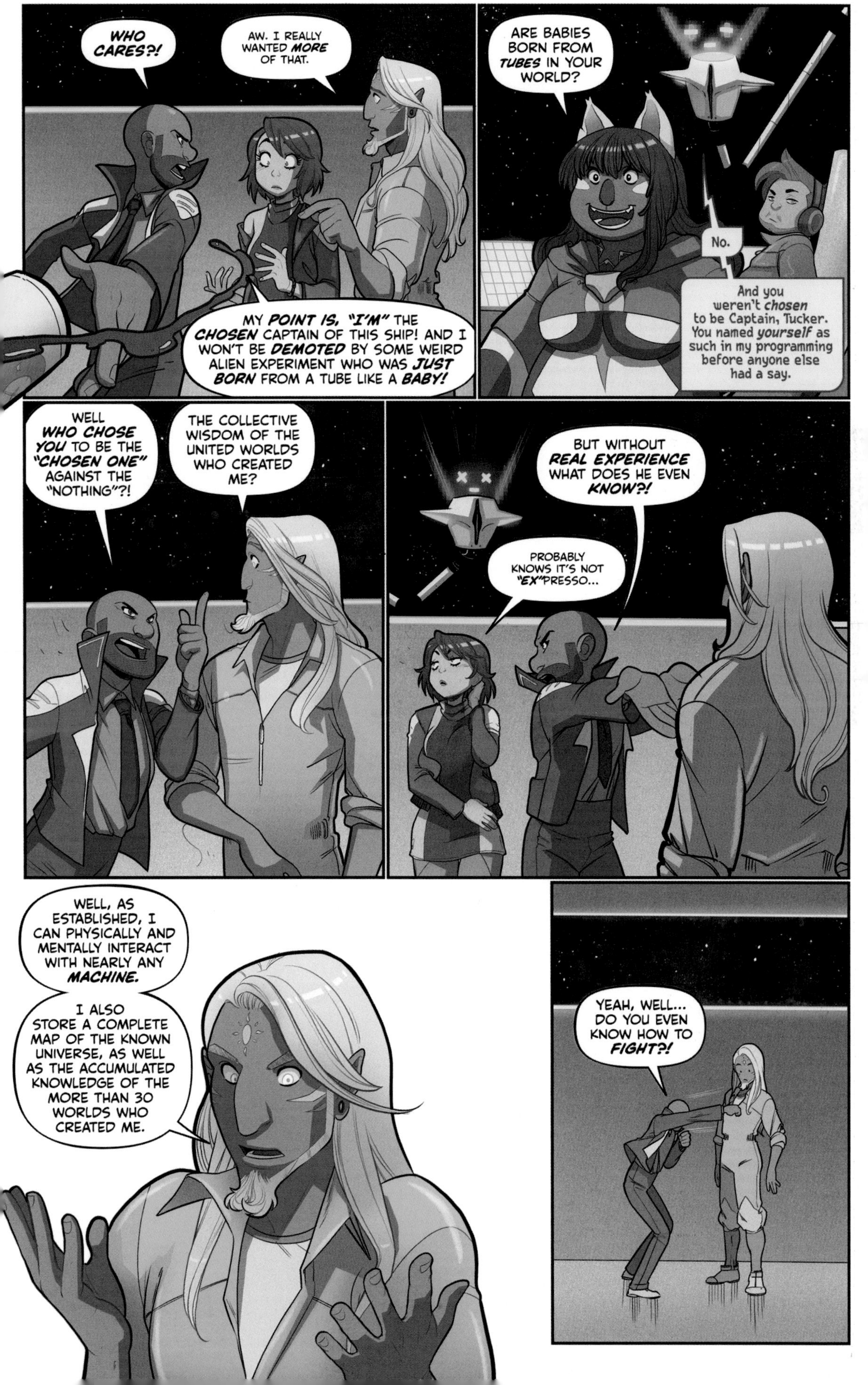
WHO CARES?!
AW. I REALLY WANTED MORE OF THAT.
MY POINT IS, "I'M" THE CHOSEN CAPTAIN OF THIS SHIP! AND I WON'T BE DEMOTED BY SOME WEIRD ALIEN EXPERIMENT WHO WAS JUST BORN FROM A TUBE LIKE A BABY!
ARE BABIES BORN FROM TUBES IN YOUR WORLD?
No.
And you weren't chosen to be Captain, Tucker. You named yourself as such in my programming before anyone else had a say.
WELL WHO CHOSE YOU TO BE THE "CHOSEN ONE" AGAINST THE "NOTHING"?!
THE COLLECTIVE WISDOM OF THE UNITED WORLDS WHO CREATED ME?
BUT WITHOUT REAL EXPERIENCE WHAT DOES HE EVEN KNOW?!
PROBABLY KNOWS IT'S NOT "EX"PRESSO...
WELL, AS ESTABLISHED, I CAN PHYSICALLY AND MENTALLY INTERACT WITH NEARLY ANY MACHINE.
I ALSO STORE A COMPLETE MAP OF THE KNOWN UNIVERSE, AS WELL AS THE ACCUMULATED KNOWLEDGE OF THE MORE THAN 30 WORLDS WHO CREATED ME.
YEAH, WELL... DO YOU EVEN KNOW HOW TO FIGHT?!

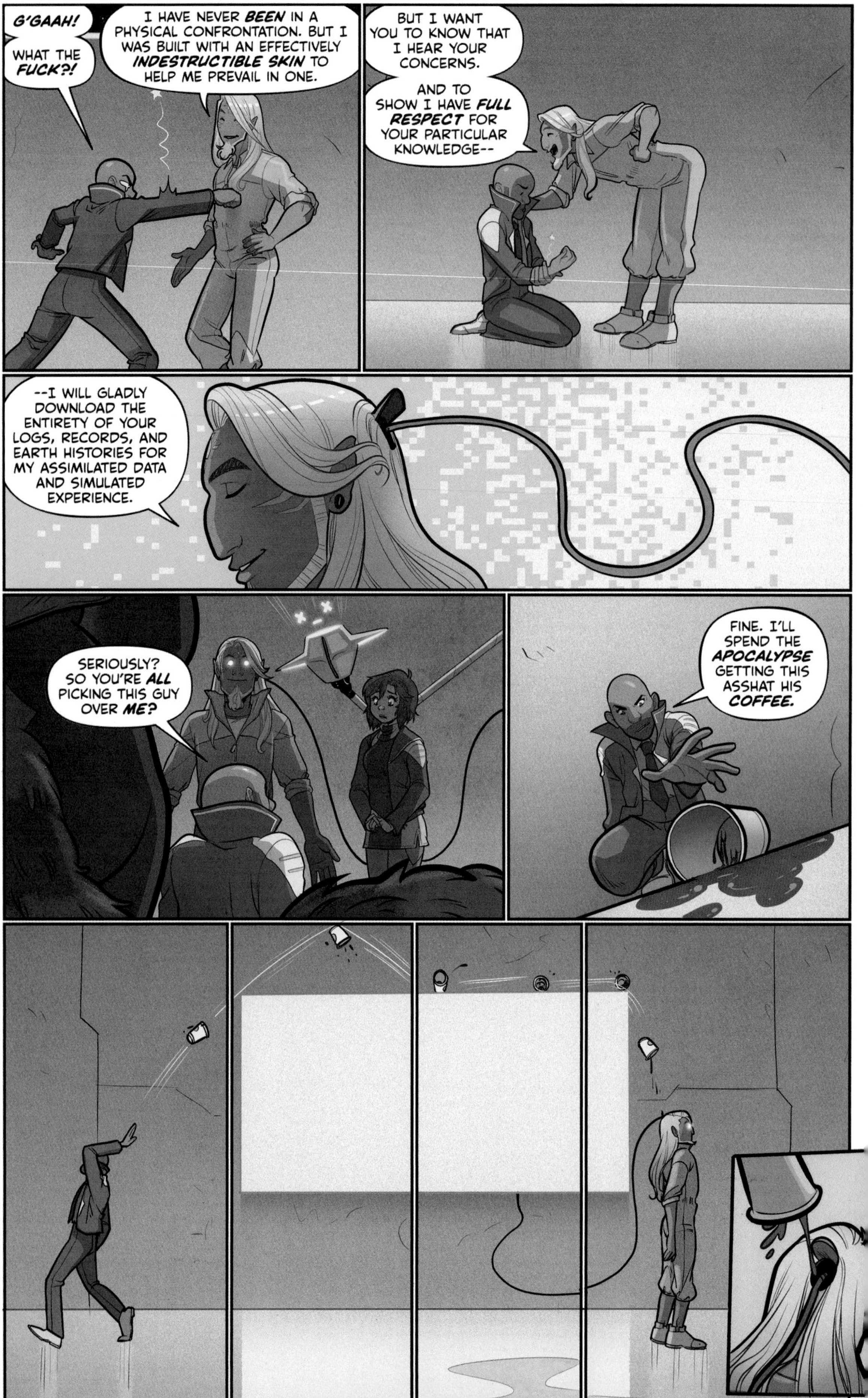
G'GAAH!
WHAT THE FUCK?!
I HAVE NEVER BEEN IN A PHYSICAL CONFRONTATION. BUT I WAS BUILT WITH AN EFFECTIVELY INDESTRUCTIBLE SKIN TO HELP ME PREVAIL IN ONE.
BUT I WANT YOU TO KNOW THAT I HEAR YOUR CONCERNS.
AND TO SHOW I HAVE FULL RESPECT FOR YOUR PARTICULAR KNOWLEDGE--
--I WILL GLADLY DOWNLOAD THE ENTIRETY OF YOUR LOGS, RECORDS, AND EARTH HISTORIES FOR MY ASSIMILATED DATA AND SIMULATED EXPERIENCE.
SERIOUSLY? SO YOU'RE ALL PICKING THIS GUY OVER ME?
FINE. I'LL SPEND THE APOCALYPSE GETTING THIS ASSHAT HIS COFFEE.

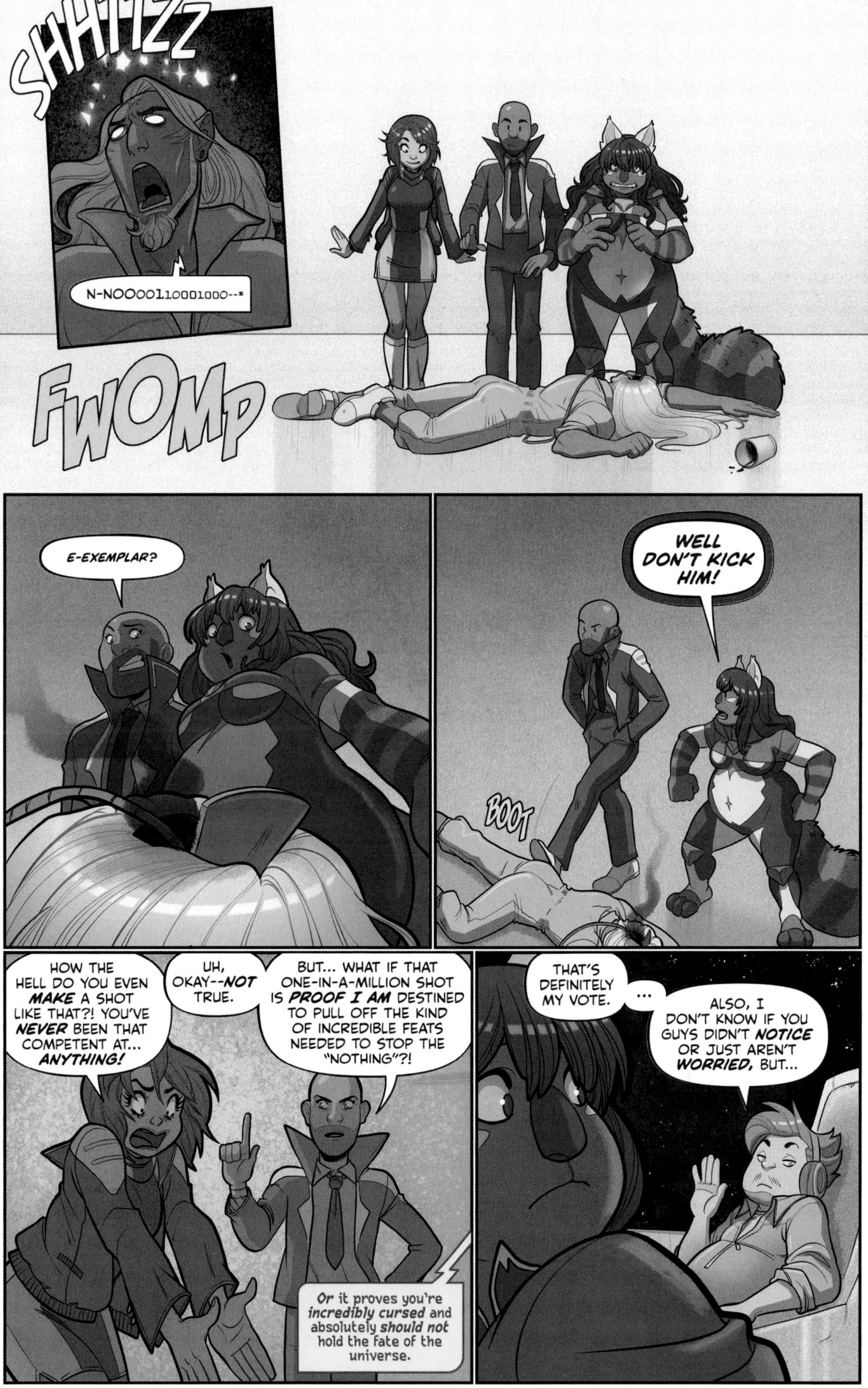
SHHTTZZ
N-NOOoo11oo01ooo--*
FWOMP
E-EXEMPLAR?
WELL DON'T KICK HIM!
BOOT
HOW THE HELL DO YOU EVEN MAKE A SHOT LIKE THAT?! YOU'VE NEVER BEEN THAT COMPETENT AT... ANYTHING!
UH, OKAY--NOT TRUE.
BUT... WHAT IF THAT ONE-IN-A-MILLION SHOT IS PROOF I AM DESTINED TO PULL OFF THE KIND OF INCREDIBLE FEATS NEEDED TO STOP THE "NOTHING"?!
Or it proves you're incredibly cursed and absolutely should not hold the fate of the universe.
THAT'S DEFINITELY MY VOTE.
...
ALSO, I DON'T KNOW IF YOU GUYS DIDN'T NOTICE OR JUST AREN'T WORRIED, BUT...

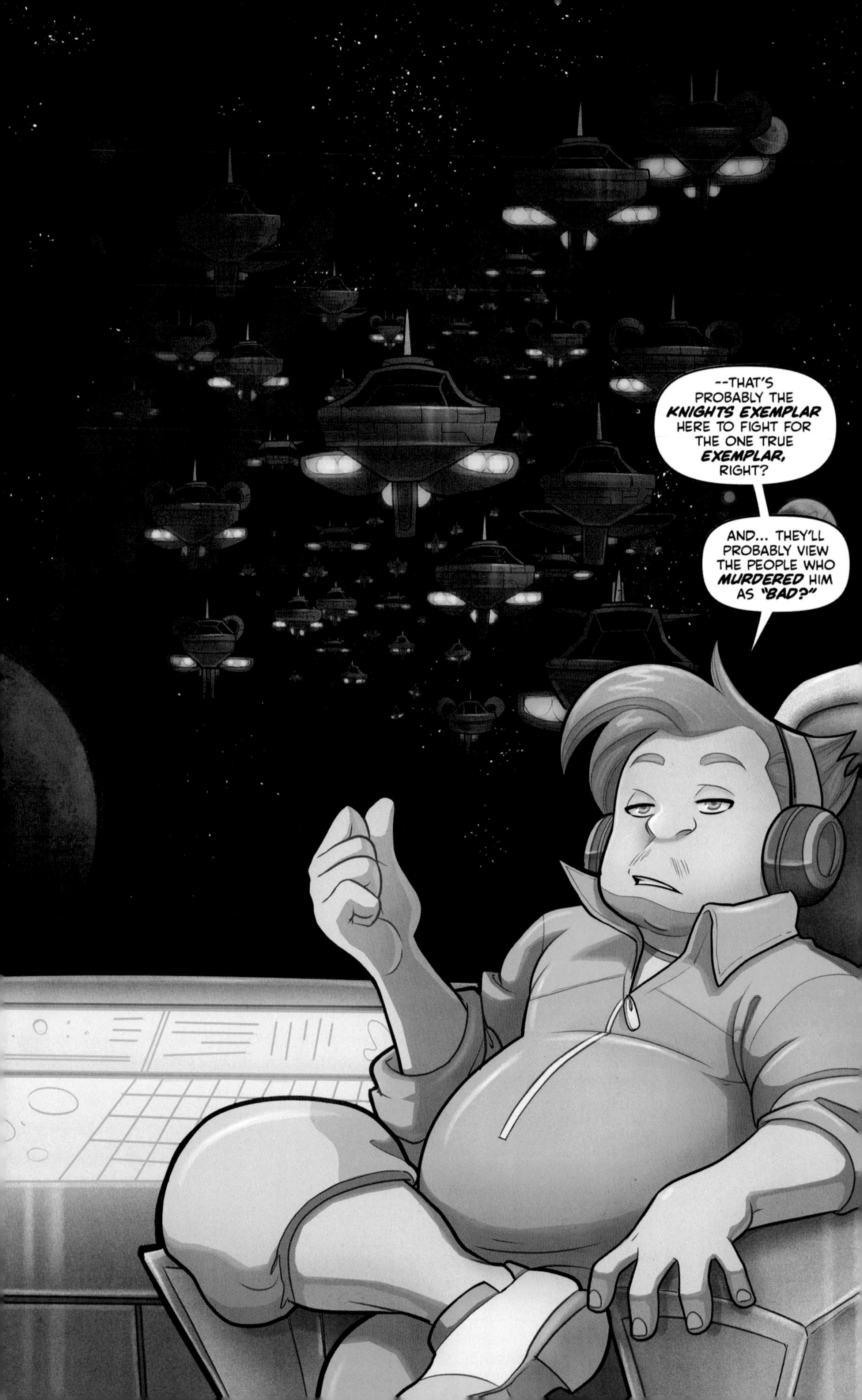
--THAT'S PROBABLY THE KNIGHTS EXEMPLAR HERE TO FIGHT FOR THE ONE TRUE EXEMPLAR, RIGHT?
AND... THEY'LL PROBABLY VIEW THE PEOPLE WHO MURDERED HIM AS "BAD?"

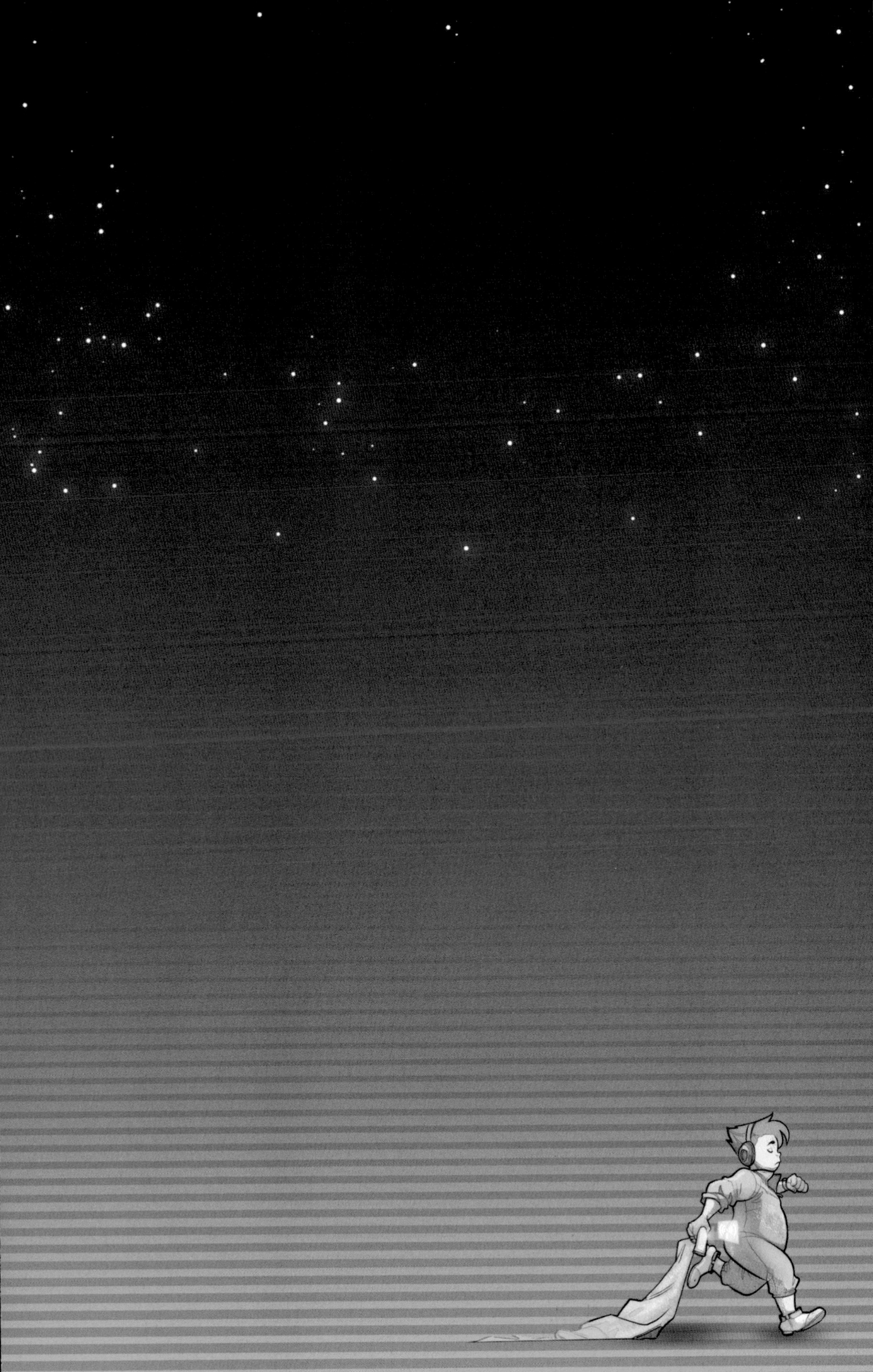

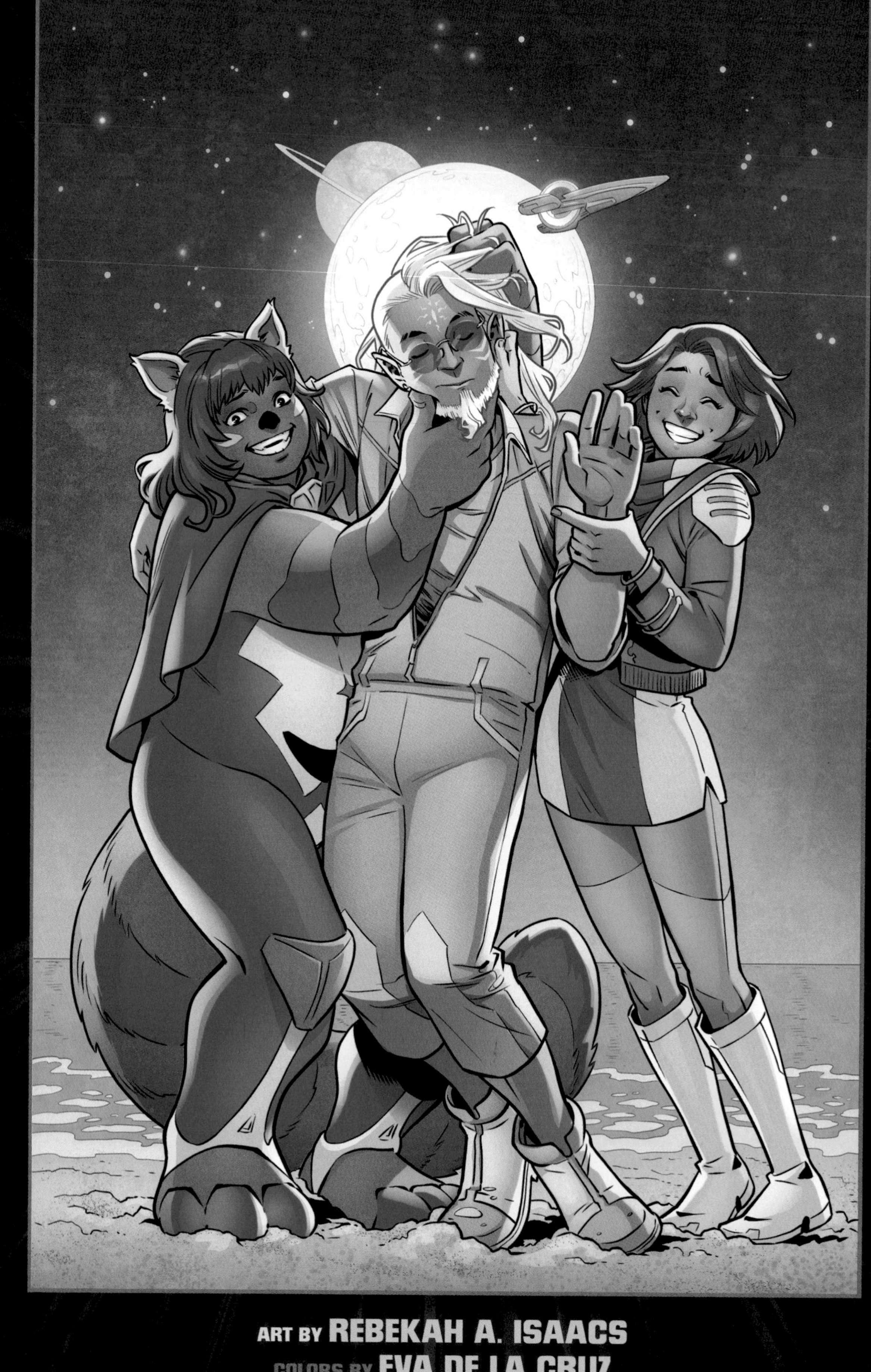

ART BY REBEKAH A. ISAACS
COLORS BY EVA DE LA CRUZ

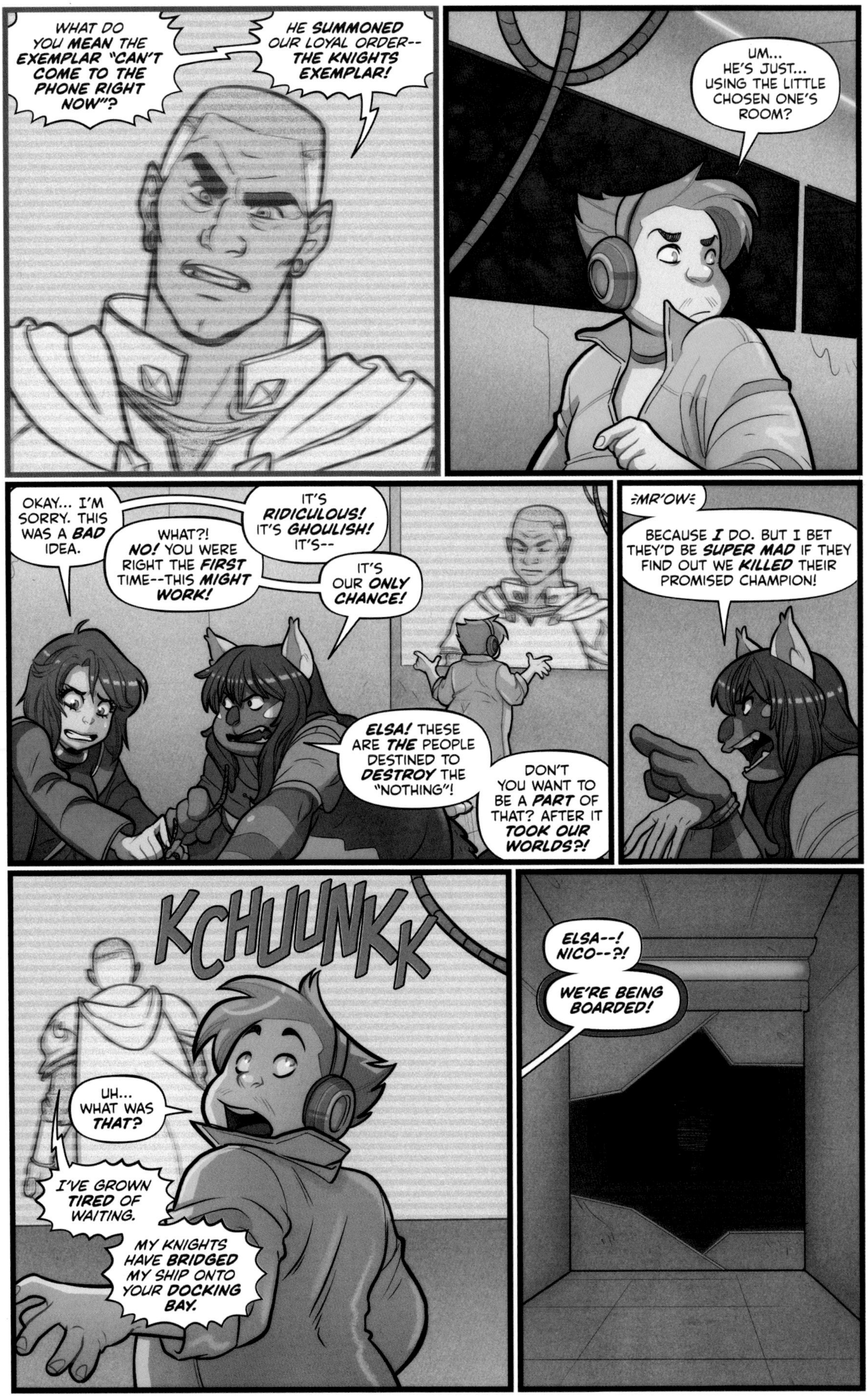
WHAT DO YOU MEAN THE EXEMPLAR "CAN'T COME TO THE PHONE RIGHT NOW"?
HE SUMMONED OUR LOYAL ORDER-- THE KNIGHTS EXEMPLAR!
UM... HE'S JUST... USING THE LITTLE CHOSEN ONE'S ROOM?
OKAY... I'M SORRY. THIS WAS A BAD IDEA.
IT'S RIDICULOUS! IT'S GHOULISH! IT'S--
WHAT?! NO! YOU WERE RIGHT THE FIRST TIME--THIS MIGHT WORK!
IT'S OUR ONLY CHANCE!
ELSA! THESE ARE THE PEOPLE DESTINED TO DESTROY THE "NOTHING"!
DON'T YOU WANT TO BE A PART OF THAT? AFTER IT TOOK OUR WORLDS?!
MR'OW
BECAUSE I DO. BUT I BET THEY'D BE SUPER MAD IF THEY FIND OUT WE KILLED THEIR PROMISED CHAMPION!
KCHUUNKK
UH... WHAT WAS THAT?
I'VE GROWN TIRED OF WAITING.
MY KNIGHTS HAVE BRIDGED MY SHIP ONTO YOUR DOCKING BAY.
ELSA--! NICO--?!
WE'RE BEING BOARDED!

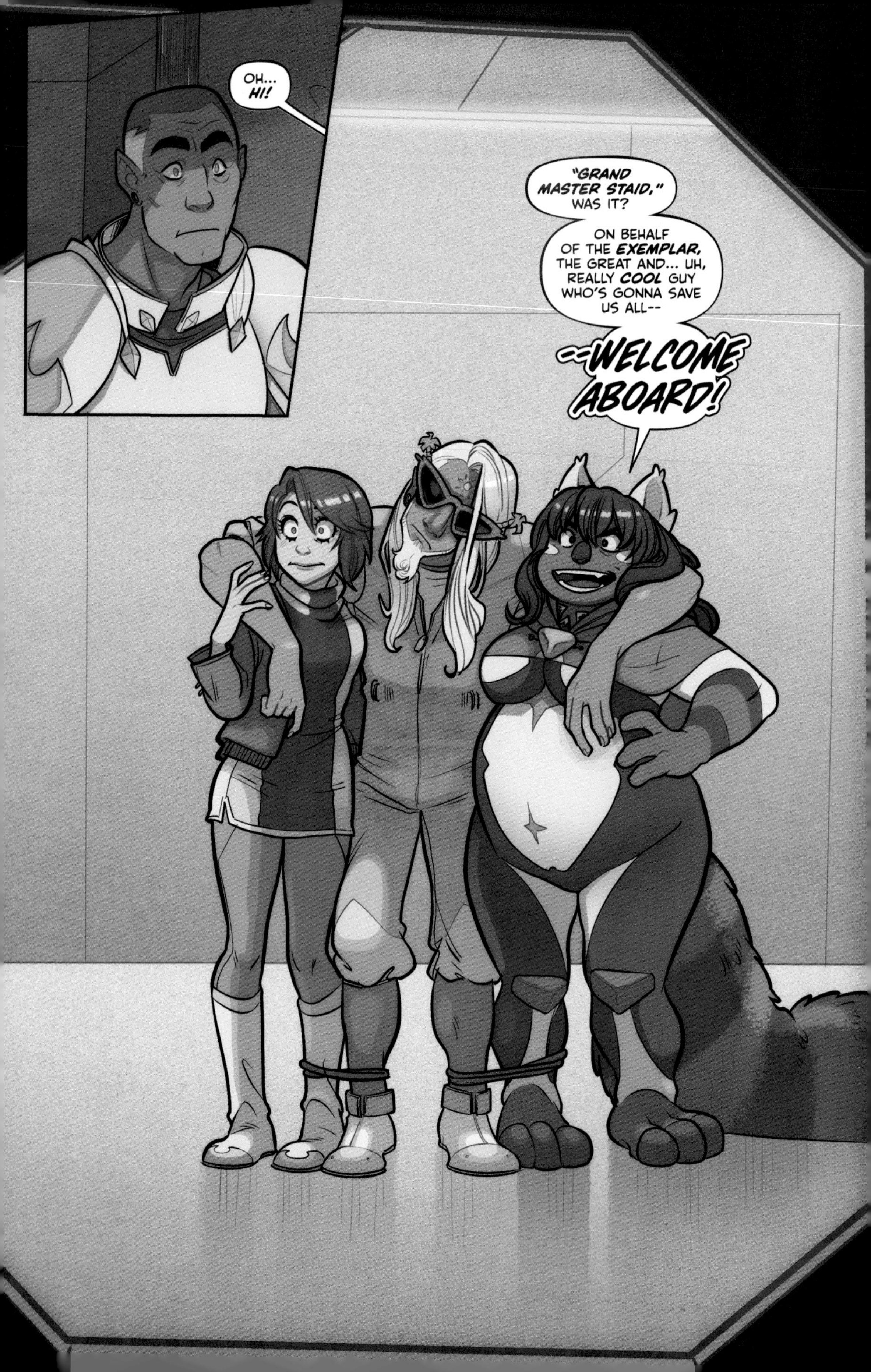
OH... HI!
"GRAND MASTER STAID," WAS IT?
ON BEHALF OF THE EXEMPLAR, THE GREAT AND... UH, REALLY COOL GUY WHO'S GONNA SAVE US ALL--
--WELCOME ABOARD!

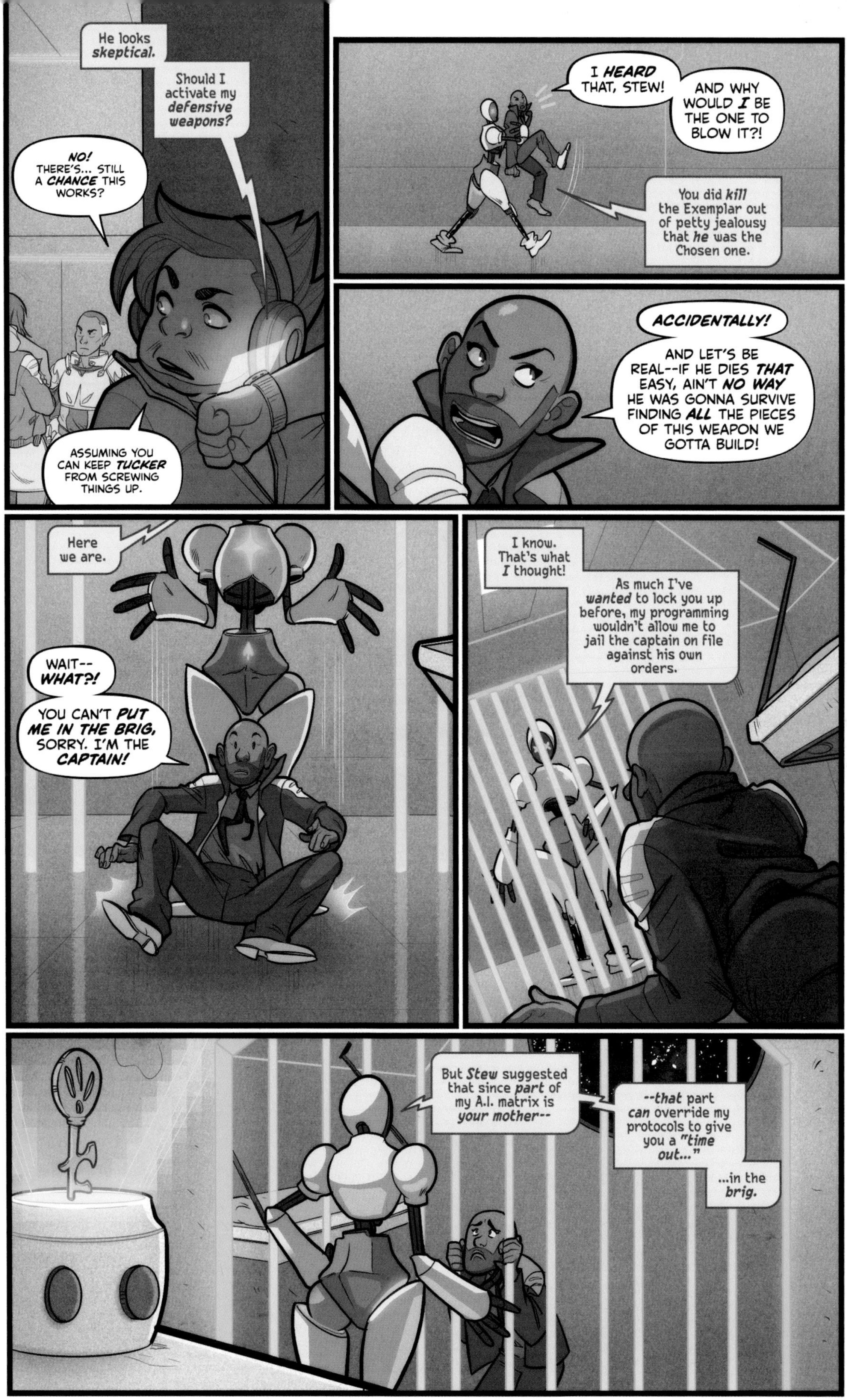
He looks skeptical.
Should I activate my defensive weapons?
NO! THERE'S... STILL A CHANCE THIS WORKS?
ASSUMING YOU CAN KEEP TUCKER FROM SCREWING THINGS UP.
I HEARD THAT, STEW!
AND WHY WOULD I BE THE ONE TO BLOW IT?!
You did kill the Exemplar out of petty jealousy that he was the Chosen one.
ACCIDENTALLY!
AND LET'S BE REAL--IF HE DIES THAT EASY, AIN'T NO WAY HE WAS GONNA SURVIVE FINDING ALL THE PIECES OF THIS WEAPON WE GOTTA BUILD!
Here we are.
WAIT-- WHAT?!
YOU CAN'T PUT ME IN THE BRIG, SORRY. I'M THE CAPTAIN!
I know. That's what I thought!
As much I've wanted to lock you up before, my programming wouldn't allow me to jail the captain on file against his own orders.
But Stew suggested that since part of my A.I. matrix is your mother--
--that part can override my protocols to give you a "time out..."
...in the brig.

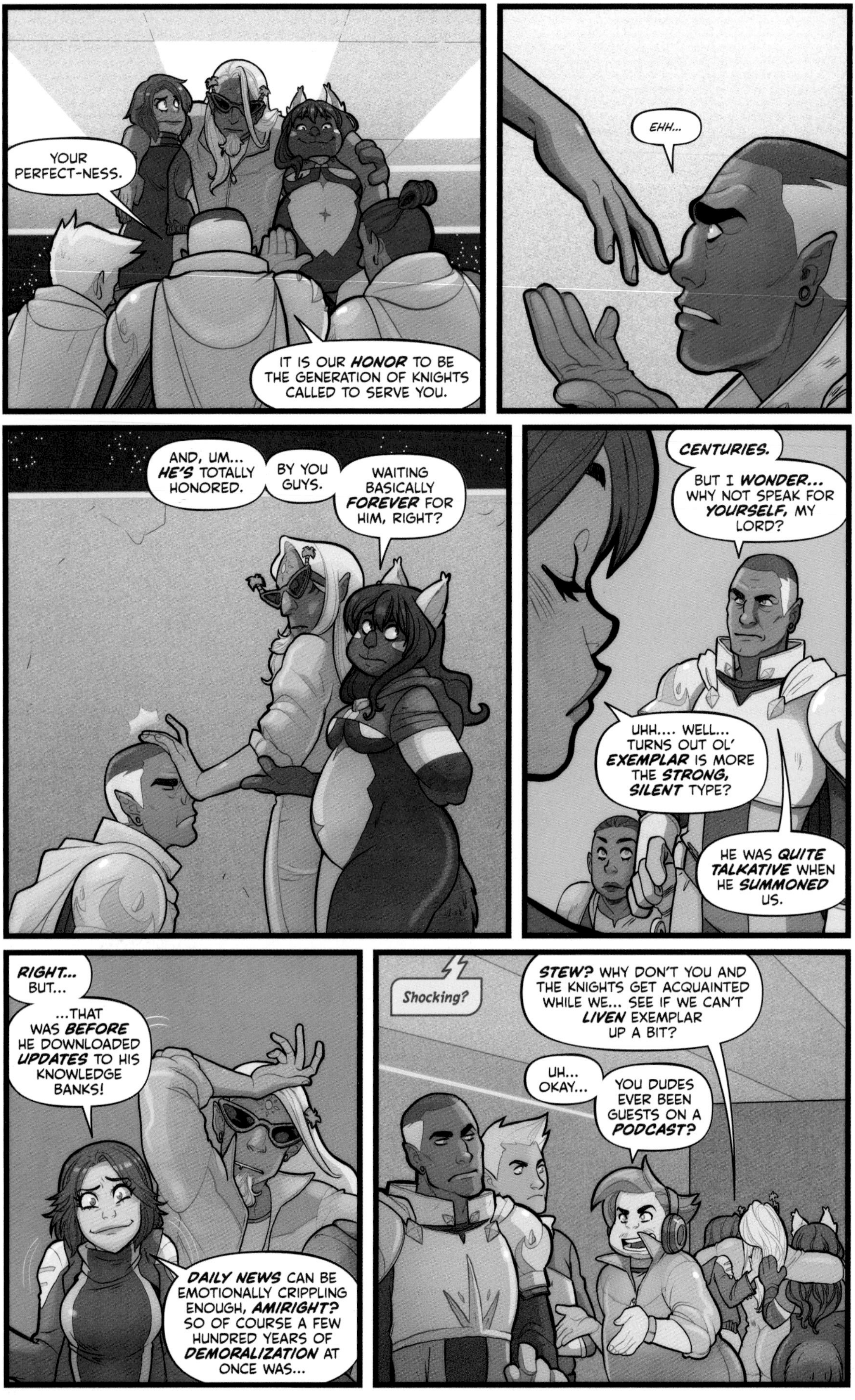
YOUR PERFECT-NESS.
IT IS OUR HONOR TO BE THE GENERATION OF KNIGHTS CALLED TO SERVE YOU.
EHH...
AND, UM... HE'S TOTALLY HONORED.
BY YOU GUYS.
WAITING BASICALLY FOREVER FOR HIM, RIGHT?
CENTURIES.
BUT I WONDER... WHY NOT SPEAK FOR YOURSELF, MY LORD?
UHH.... WELL... TURNS OUT OL' EXEMPLAR IS MORE THE STRONG, SILENT TYPE?
HE WAS QUITE TALKATIVE WHEN HE SUMMONED US.
RIGHT... BUT...
...THAT WAS BEFORE HE DOWNLOADED UPDATES TO HIS KNOWLEDGE BANKS!
DAILY NEWS CAN BE EMOTIONALLY CRIPPLING ENOUGH, AMIRIGHT? SO OF COURSE A FEW HUNDRED YEARS OF DEMORALIZATION AT ONCE WAS...
Shocking?
STEW? WHY DON'T YOU AND THE KNIGHTS GET ACQUAINTED WHILE WE... SEE IF WE CAN'T LIVEN EXEMPLAR UP A BIT?
UH... OKAY...
YOU DUDES EVER BEEN GUESTS ON A PODCAST?

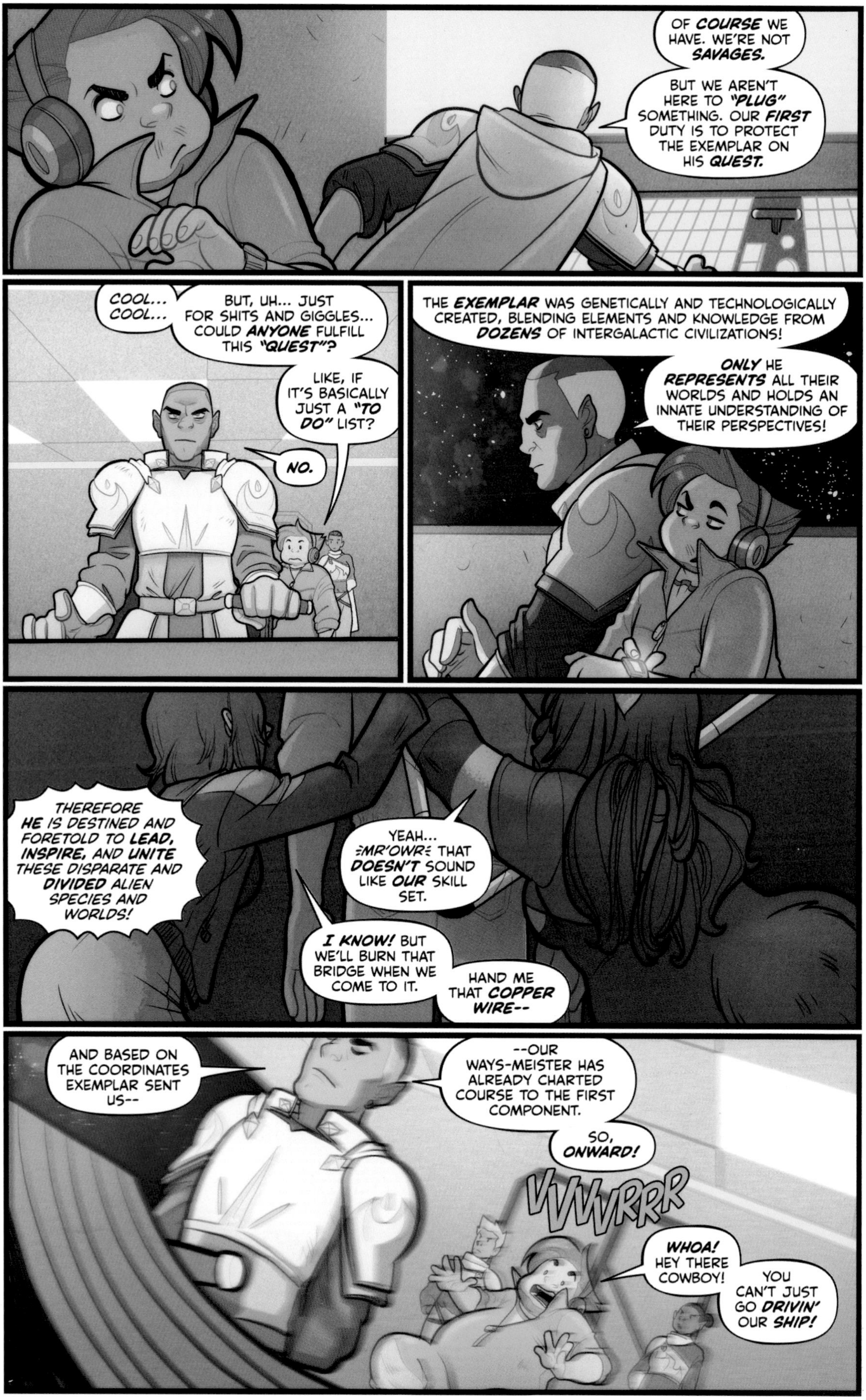
OF COURSE WE HAVE. WE'RE NOT SAVAGES.
BUT WE AREN'T HERE TO "PLUG" SOMETHING. OUR FIRST DUTY IS TO PROTECT THE EXEMPLAR ON HIS QUEST.
COOL... COOL...
BUT, UH... JUST FOR SHITS AND GIGGLES... COULD ANYONE FULFILL THIS "QUEST"?
LIKE, IF IT'S BASICALLY JUST A "TO DO" LIST?
NO.
THE EXEMPLAR WAS GENETICALLY AND TECHNOLOGICALLY CREATED, BLENDING ELEMENTS AND KNOWLEDGE FROM DOZENS OF INTERGALACTIC CIVILIZATIONS!
ONLY HE REPRESENTS ALL THEIR WORLDS AND HOLDS AN INNATE UNDERSTANDING OF THEIR PERSPECTIVES!
THEREFORE HE IS DESTINED AND FORETOLD TO LEAD, INSPIRE, AND UNITE THESE DISPARATE AND DIVIDED ALIEN SPECIES AND WORLDS!
YEAH... ≡MR'OWR≡ THAT DOESN'T SOUND LIKE OUR SKILL SET.
I KNOW! BUT WE'LL BURN THAT BRIDGE WHEN WE COME TO IT.
HAND ME THAT COPPER WIRE--
AND BASED ON THE COORDINATES EXEMPLAR SENT US--
--OUR WAYS-MEISTER HAS ALREADY CHARTED COURSE TO THE FIRST COMPONENT.
SO, ONWARD!
VVVVRRR
WHOA! HEY THERE COWBOY!
YOU CAN'T JUST GO DRIVIN' OUR SHIP!

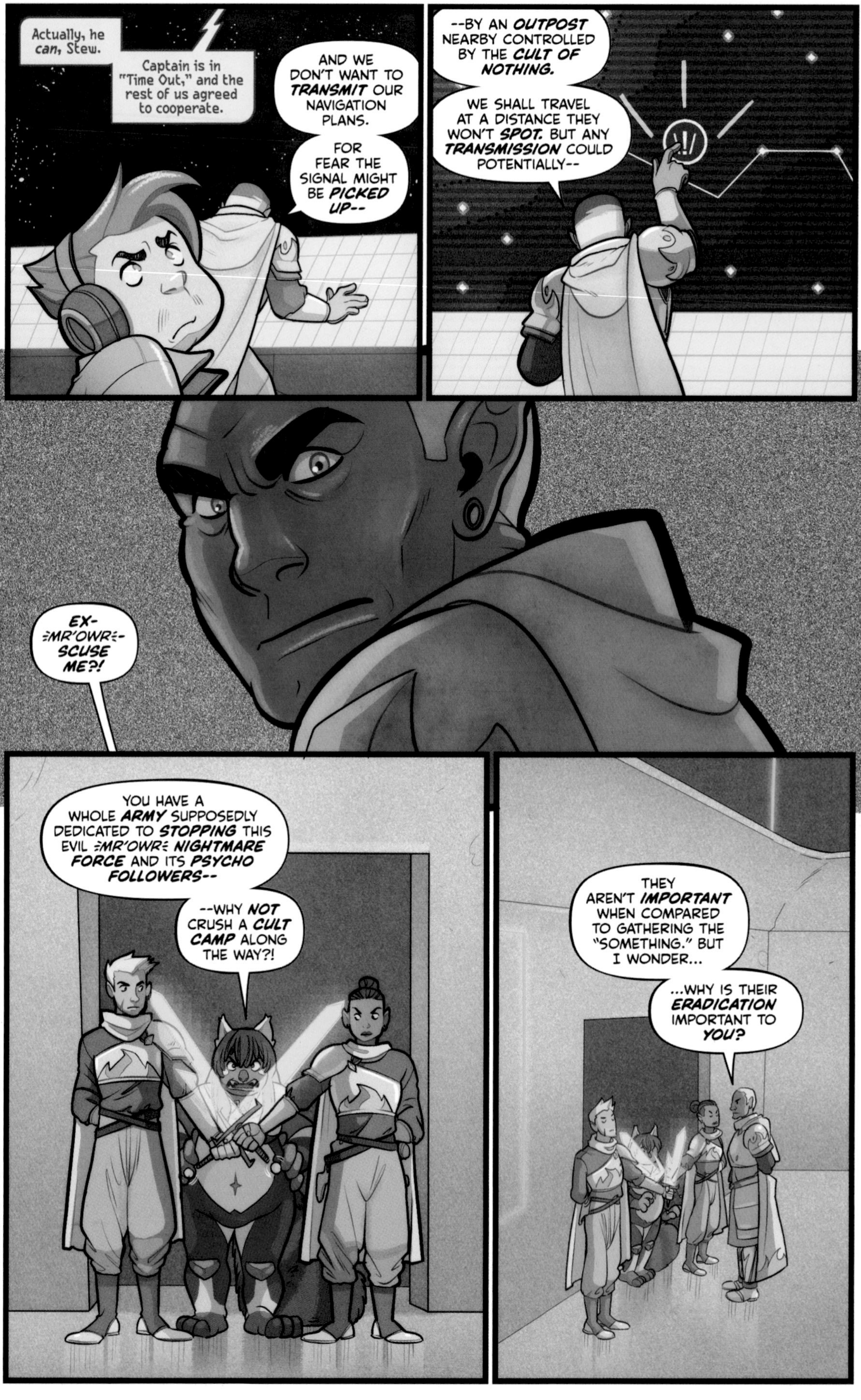
Actually, he can, Stew.
Captain is in "Time Out," and the rest of us agreed to cooperate.
AND WE DON'T WANT TO TRANSMIT OUR NAVIGATION PLANS.
FOR FEAR THE SIGNAL MIGHT BE PICKED UP--
--BY AN OUTPOST NEARBY CONTROLLED BY THE CULT OF NOTHING.
WE SHALL TRAVEL AT A DISTANCE THEY WON'T SPOT. BUT ANY TRANSMISSION COULD POTENTIALLY--
EX- =MR'OWR= -SCUSE ME?!
YOU HAVE A WHOLE ARMY SUPPOSEDLY DEDICATED TO STOPPING THIS EVIL =MR'OWR= NIGHTMARE FORCE AND ITS PSYCHO FOLLOWERS--
--WHY NOT CRUSH A CULT CAMP ALONG THE WAY?!
THEY AREN'T IMPORTANT WHEN COMPARED TO GATHERING THE "SOMETHING." BUT I WONDER...
...WHY IS THEIR ERADICATION IMPORTANT TO YOU?

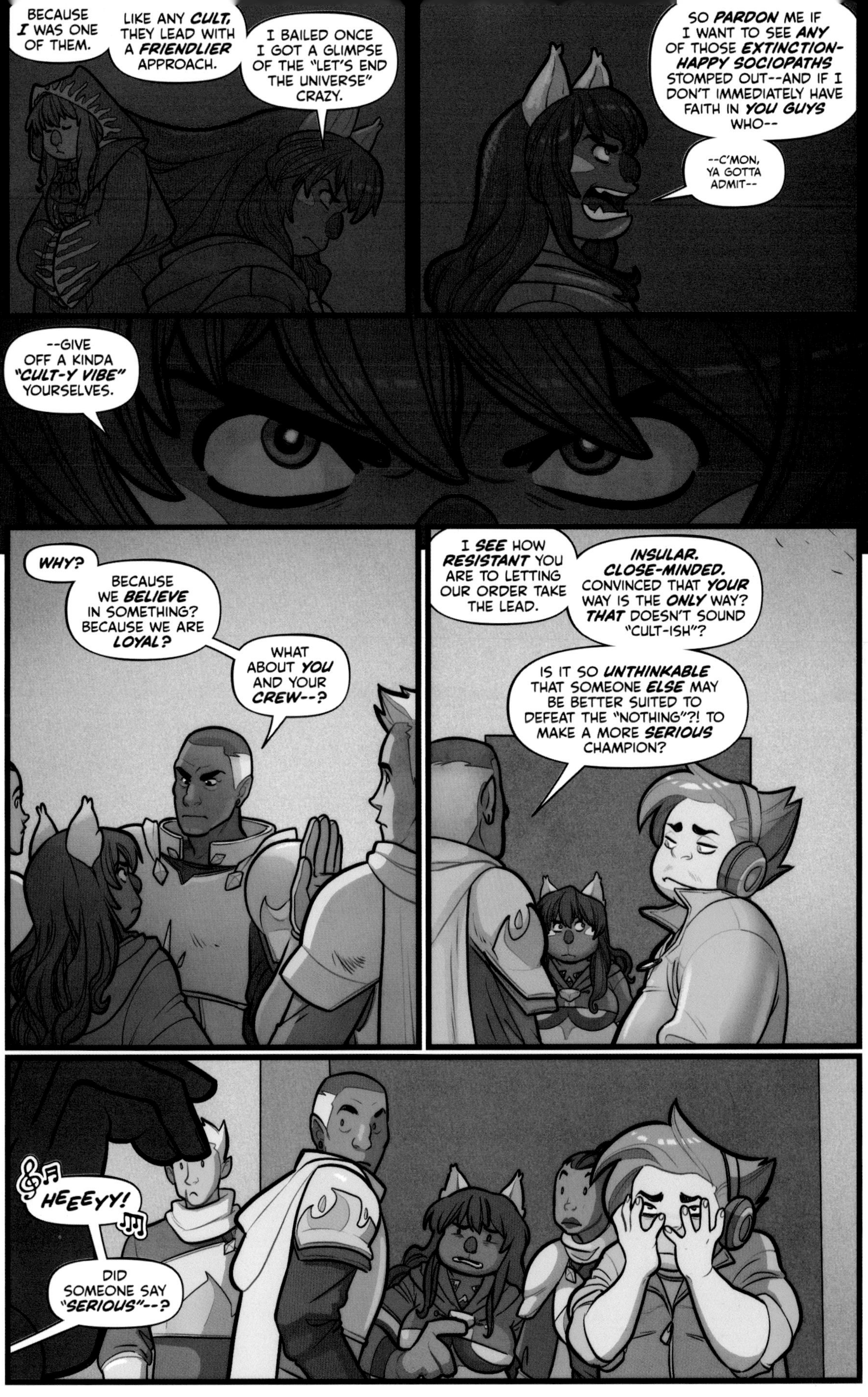
BECAUSE I WAS ONE OF THEM.
LIKE ANY CULT, THEY LEAD WITH A FRIENDLIER APPROACH.
I BAILED ONCE I GOT A GLIMPSE OF THE "LET'S END THE UNIVERSE" CRAZY.
SO PARDON ME IF I WANT TO SEE ANY OF THOSE EXTINCTION-HAPPY SOCIOPATHS STOMPED OUT--AND IF I DON'T IMMEDIATELY HAVE FAITH IN YOU GUYS WHO--
--C'MON, YA GOTTA ADMIT--
--GIVE OFF A KINDA "CULT-Y VIBE" YOURSELVES.
WHY?
BECAUSE WE BELIEVE IN SOMETHING? BECAUSE WE ARE LOYAL?
WHAT ABOUT YOU AND YOUR CREW--?
I SEE HOW RESISTANT YOU ARE TO LETTING OUR ORDER TAKE THE LEAD.
INSULAR. CLOSE-MINDED. CONVINCED THAT YOUR WAY IS THE ONLY WAY? THAT DOESN'T SOUND "CULT-ISH"?
IS IT SO UNTHINKABLE THAT SOMEONE ELSE MAY BE BETTER SUITED TO DEFEAT THE "NOTHING"?! TO MAKE A MORE SERIOUS CHAMPION?
HEEEYY!
DID SOMEONE SAY "SERIOUS"--?

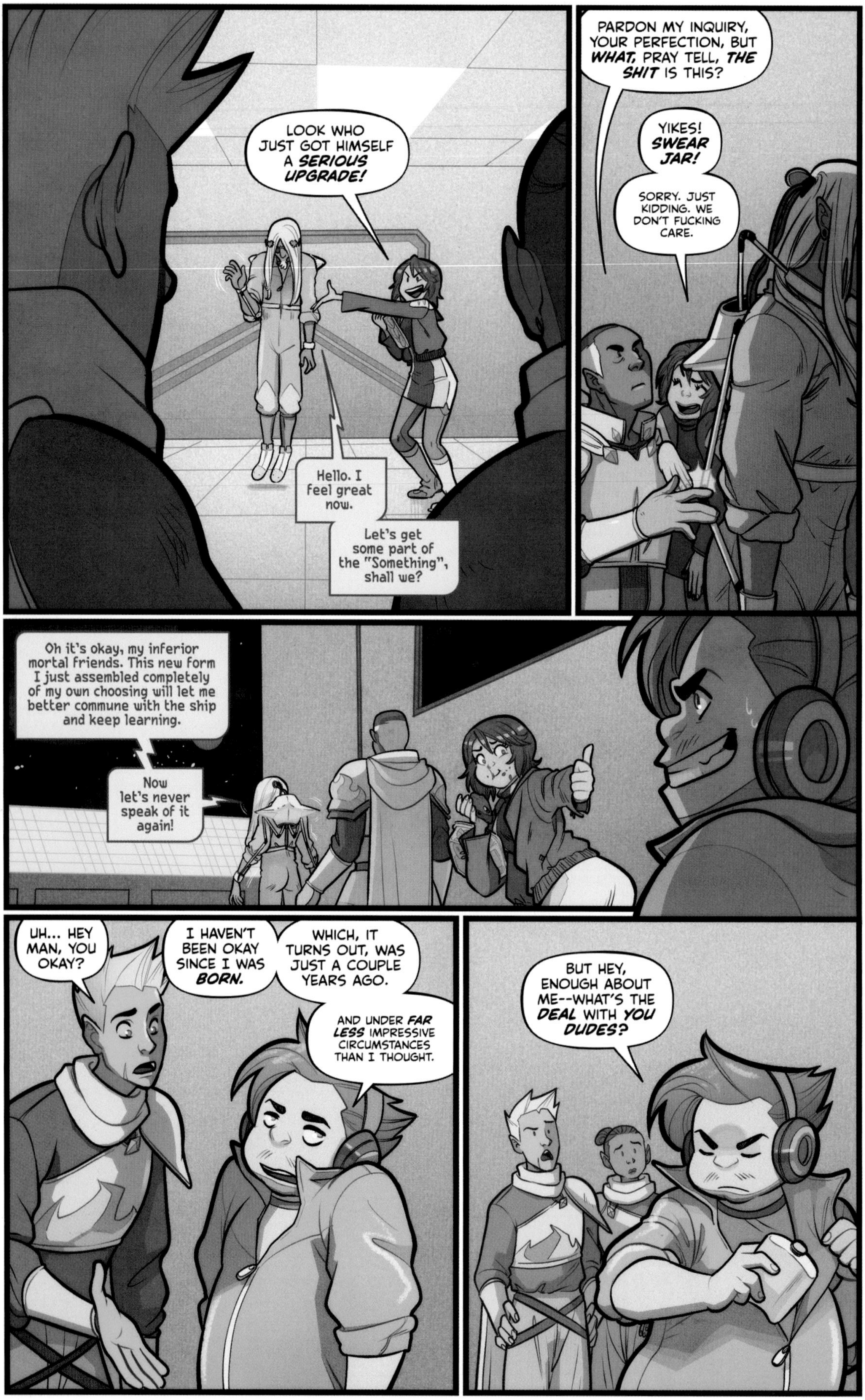
LOOK WHO JUST GOT HIMSELF A SERIOUS UPGRADE!
Hello. I feel great now.
Let's get some part of the "Something", shall we?
PARDON MY INQUIRY, YOUR PERFECTION, BUT WHAT, PRAY TELL, THE SHIT IS THIS?
YIKES! SWEAR JAR!
SORRY. JUST KIDDING. WE DON'T FUCKING CARE.
Oh it's okay, my inferior mortal friends. This new form I just assembled completely of my own choosing will let me better commune with the ship and keep learning.
Now let's never speak of it again!
UH... HEY MAN, YOU OKAY?
I HAVEN'T BEEN OKAY SINCE I WAS BORN.
WHICH, IT TURNS OUT, WAS JUST A COUPLE YEARS AGO.
AND UNDER FAR LESS IMPRESSIVE CIRCUMSTANCES THAN I THOUGHT.
BUT HEY, ENOUGH ABOUT ME--WHAT'S THE DEAL WITH YOU DUDES?

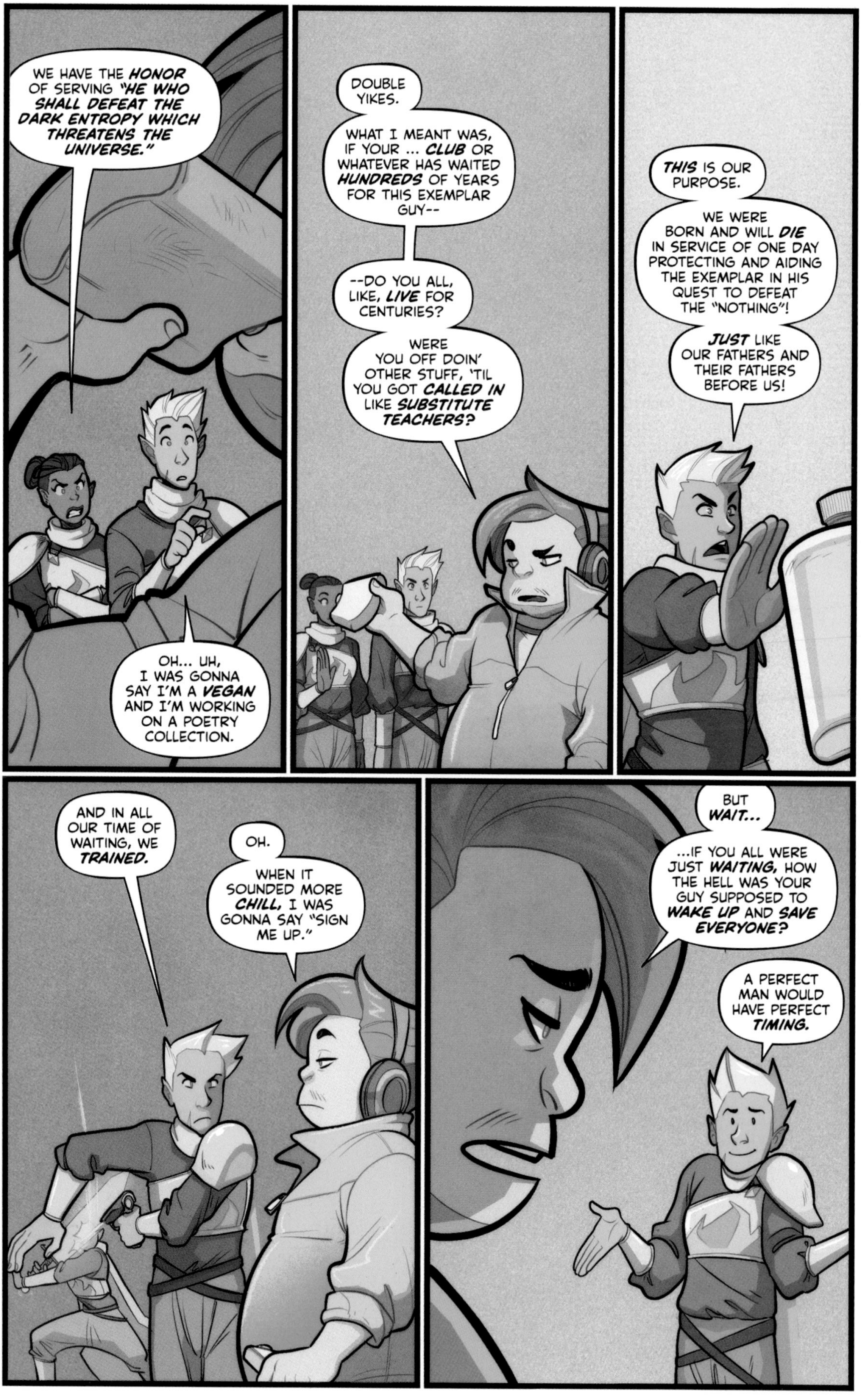
WE HAVE THE HONOR OF SERVING "HE WHO SHALL DEFEAT THE DARK ENTROPY WHICH THREATENS THE UNIVERSE."
OH... UH, I WAS GONNA SAY I'M A VEGAN AND I'M WORKING ON A POETRY COLLECTION.
DOUBLE YIKES.
WHAT I MEANT WAS, IF YOUR ... CLUB OR WHATEVER HAS WAITED HUNDREDS OF YEARS FOR THIS EXEMPLAR GUY--
--DO YOU ALL, LIKE, LIVE FOR CENTURIES?
WERE YOU OFF DOIN' OTHER STUFF, 'TIL YOU GOT CALLED IN LIKE SUBSTITUTE TEACHERS?
THIS IS OUR PURPOSE.
WE WERE BORN AND WILL DIE IN SERVICE OF ONE DAY PROTECTING AND AIDING THE EXEMPLAR IN HIS QUEST TO DEFEAT THE "NOTHING"!
JUST LIKE OUR FATHERS AND THEIR FATHERS BEFORE US!
AND IN ALL OUR TIME OF WAITING, WE TRAINED.
OH.
WHEN IT SOUNDED MORE CHILL, I WAS GONNA SAY "SIGN ME UP."
BUT WAIT...
...IF YOU ALL WERE JUST WAITING, HOW THE HELL WAS YOUR GUY SUPPOSED TO WAKE UP AND SAVE EVERYONE?
A PERFECT MAN WOULD HAVE PERFECT TIMING.

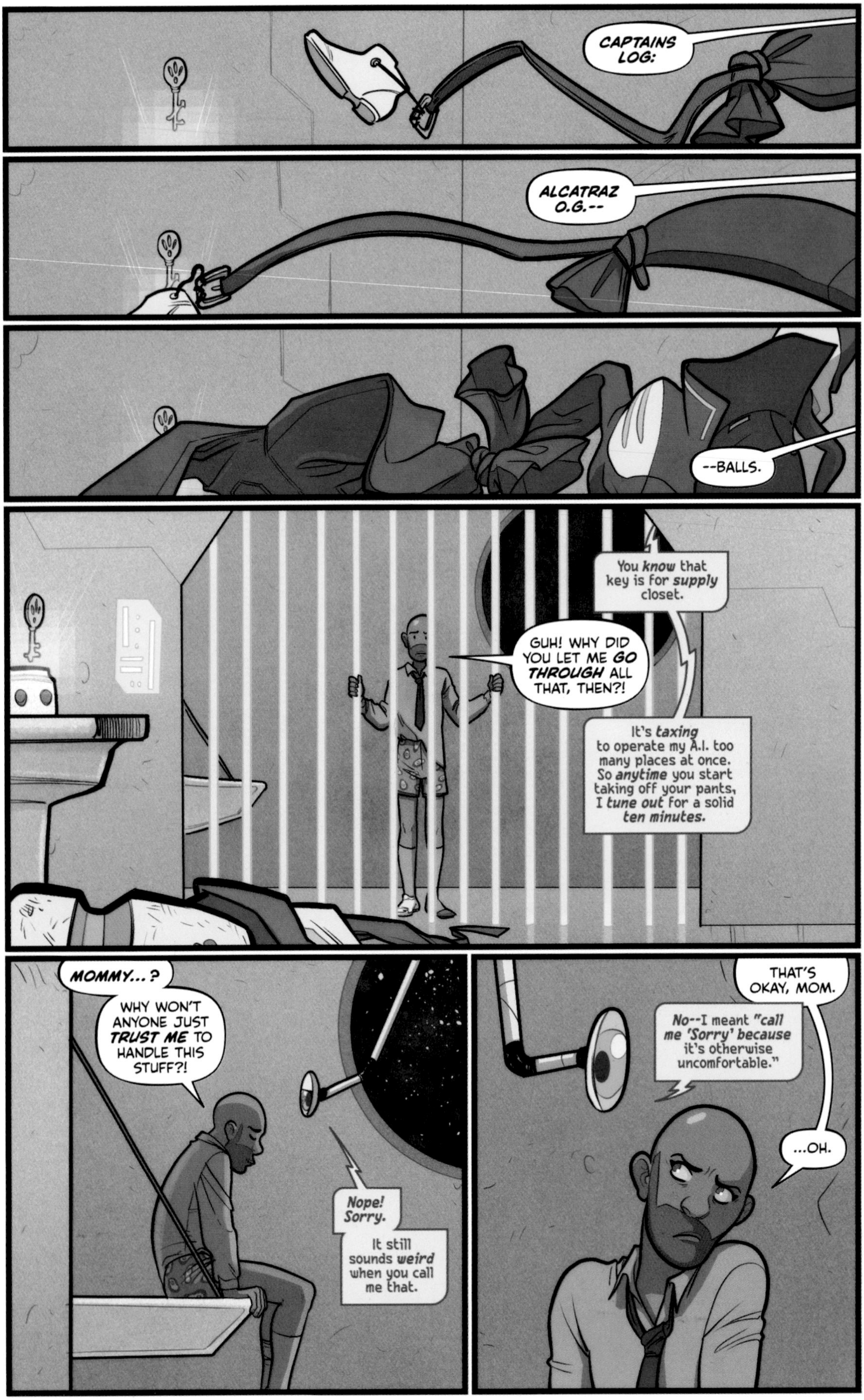
CAPTAINS LOG:
ALCATRAZ O.G.--
--BALLS.
You know that key is for supply closet.
GUH! WHY DID YOU LET ME GO THROUGH ALL THAT, THEN?!
It's taxing to operate my A.I. too many places at once. So anytime you start taking off your pants, I tune out for a solid ten minutes.
MOMMY...?
WHY WON'T ANYONE JUST TRUST ME TO HANDLE THIS STUFF?!
Nope! Sorry.
It still sounds weird when you call me that.
THAT'S OKAY, MOM.
No--I meant "call me 'Sorry' because it's otherwise uncomfortable."
...OH.

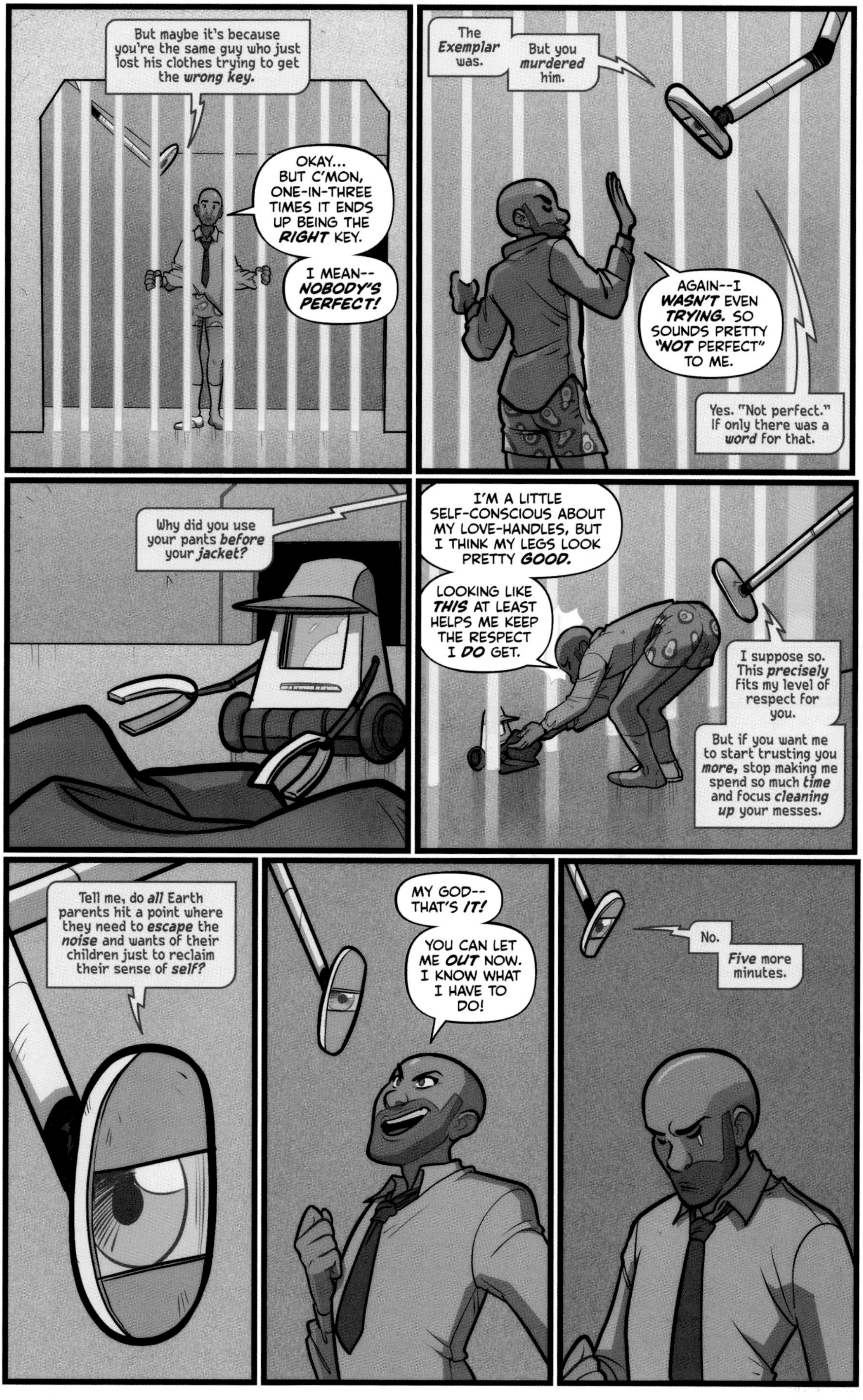
But maybe it's because you're the same guy who just lost his clothes trying to get the *wrong key.*
OKAY... BUT C'MON, ONE-IN-THREE TIMES IT ENDS UP BEING THE ***RIGHT*** KEY.
I MEAN-- ***NOBODY'S PERFECT!***
The *Exemplar* was.
But you *murdered* him.
AGAIN--I ***WASN'T*** EVEN ***TRYING.*** SO SOUNDS PRETTY ***"NOT*** PERFECT" TO ME.
Yes. "Not perfect." If only there was a *word* for that.
Why did you use your pants *before* your *jacket?*
I'M A LITTLE SELF-CONSCIOUS ABOUT MY LOVE-HANDLES, BUT I THINK MY LEGS LOOK PRETTY ***GOOD.***
LOOKING LIKE ***THIS*** AT LEAST HELPS ME KEEP THE RESPECT I ***DO*** GET.
I suppose so. This *precisely* fits my level of respect for you.
But if you want me to start trusting you *more,* stop making me spend so much *time* and focus *cleaning up* your messes.
Tell me, do *all* Earth parents hit a point where they need to *escape* the *noise* and wants of their children just to reclaim their sense of *self?*
MY GOD-- THAT'S ***IT!***
YOU CAN LET ME ***OUT*** NOW. I KNOW WHAT I HAVE TO DO!
No.
Five more minutes.

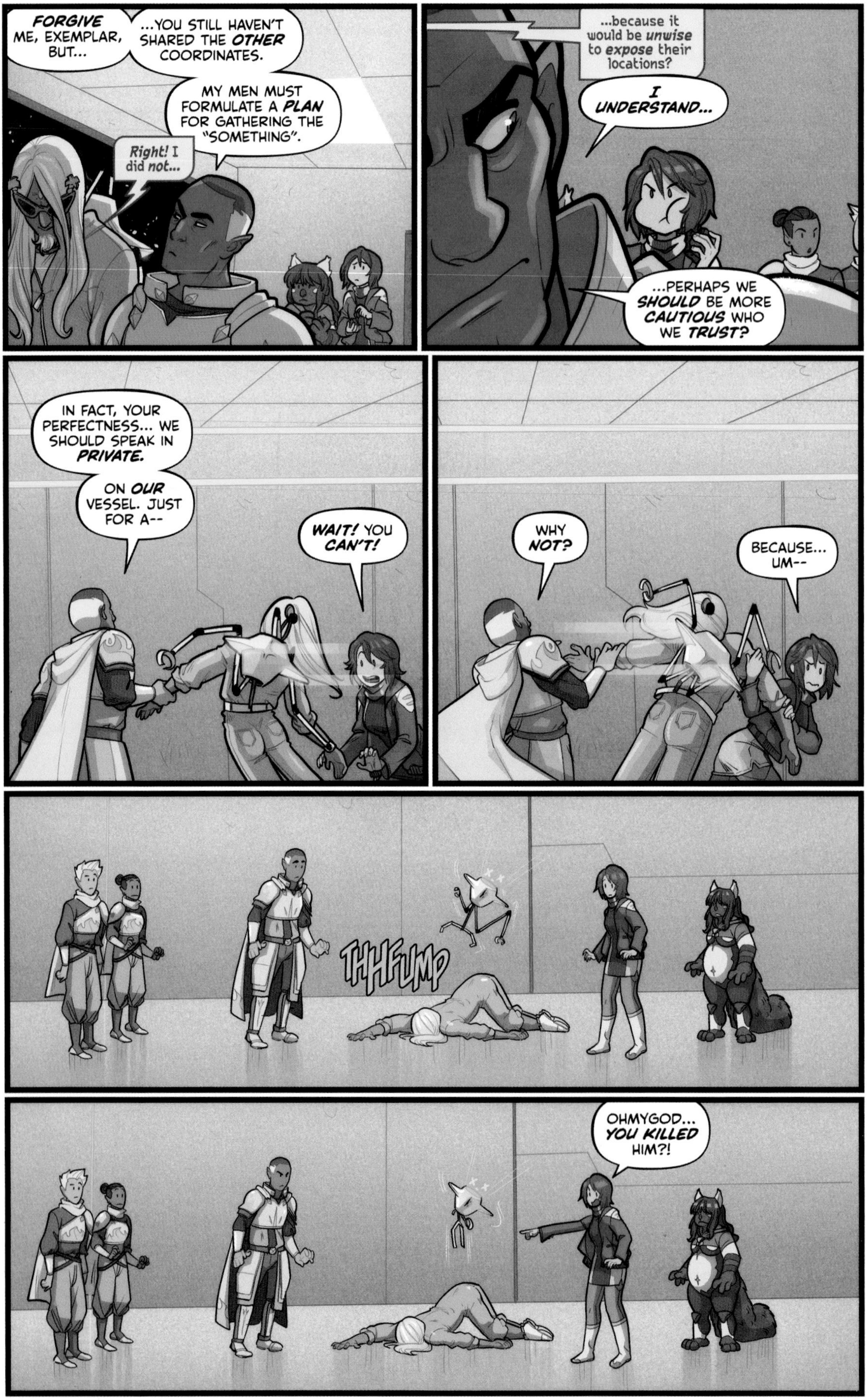
FORGIVE ME, EXEMPLAR, BUT...
...YOU STILL HAVEN'T SHARED THE OTHER COORDINATES.
MY MEN MUST FORMULATE A PLAN FOR GATHERING THE "SOMETHING".
Right! I did not...
...because it would be unwise to expose their locations?
I UNDERSTAND...
...PERHAPS WE SHOULD BE MORE CAUTIOUS WHO WE TRUST?
IN FACT, YOUR PERFECTNESS... WE SHOULD SPEAK IN PRIVATE.
ON OUR VESSEL. JUST FOR A--
WAIT! YOU CAN'T!
WHY NOT?
BECAUSE... UM--
THHFUMP
OHMYGOD... YOU KILLED HIM?!

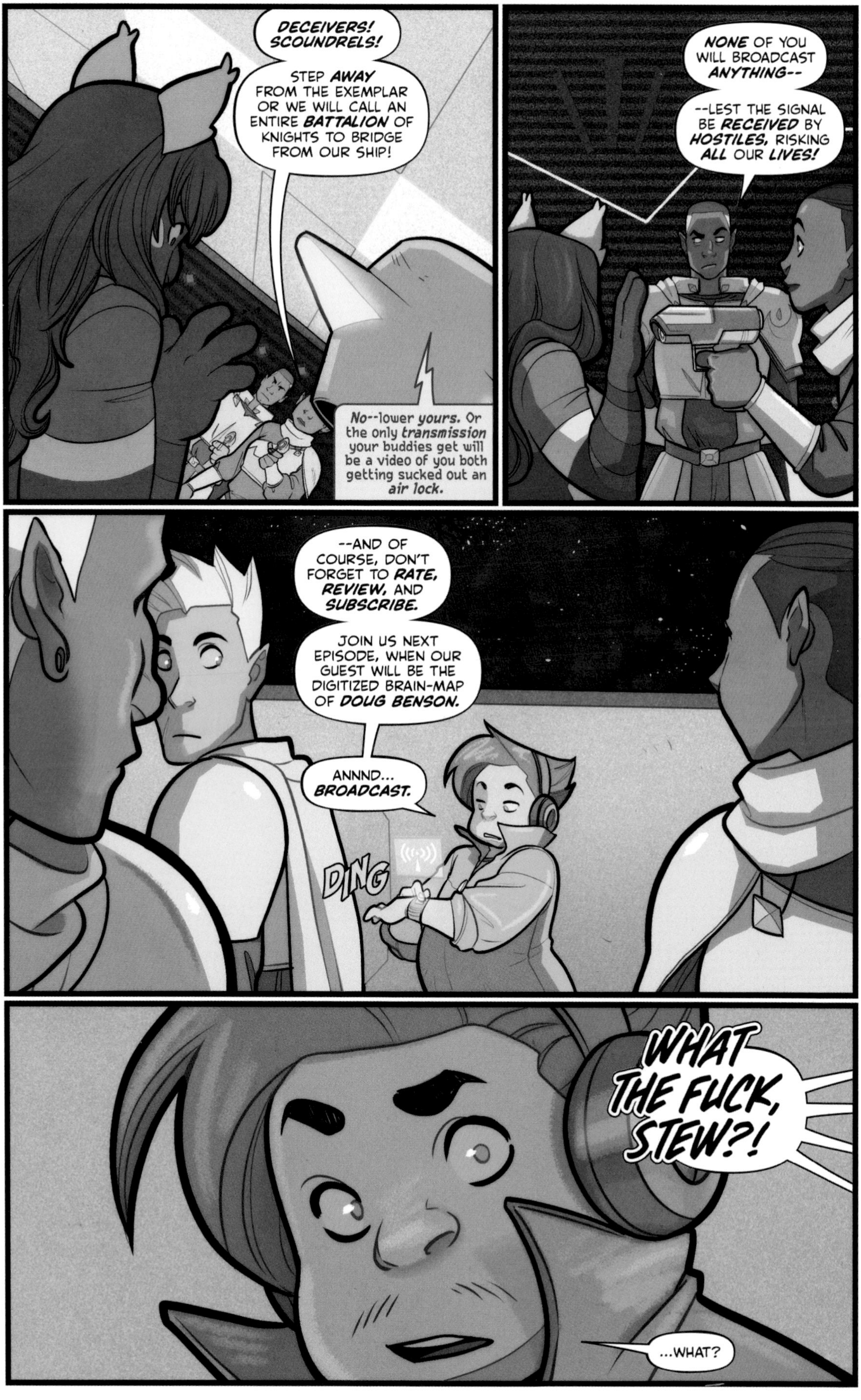
DECEIVERS! SCOUNDRELS!
STEP AWAY FROM THE EXEMPLAR OR WE WILL CALL AN ENTIRE BATTALION OF KNIGHTS TO BRIDGE FROM OUR SHIP!
No--lower yours. Or the only transmission your buddies get will be a video of you both getting sucked out an air lock.
NONE OF YOU WILL BROADCAST ANYTHING--
--LEST THE SIGNAL BE RECEIVED BY HOSTILES, RISKING ALL OUR LIVES!
--AND OF COURSE, DON'T FORGET TO RATE, REVIEW, AND SUBSCRIBE.
JOIN US NEXT EPISODE, WHEN OUR GUEST WILL BE THE DIGITIZED BRAIN-MAP OF DOUG BENSON.
ANNND... BROADCAST.
DING
WHAT THE FUCK, STEW?!
...WHAT?

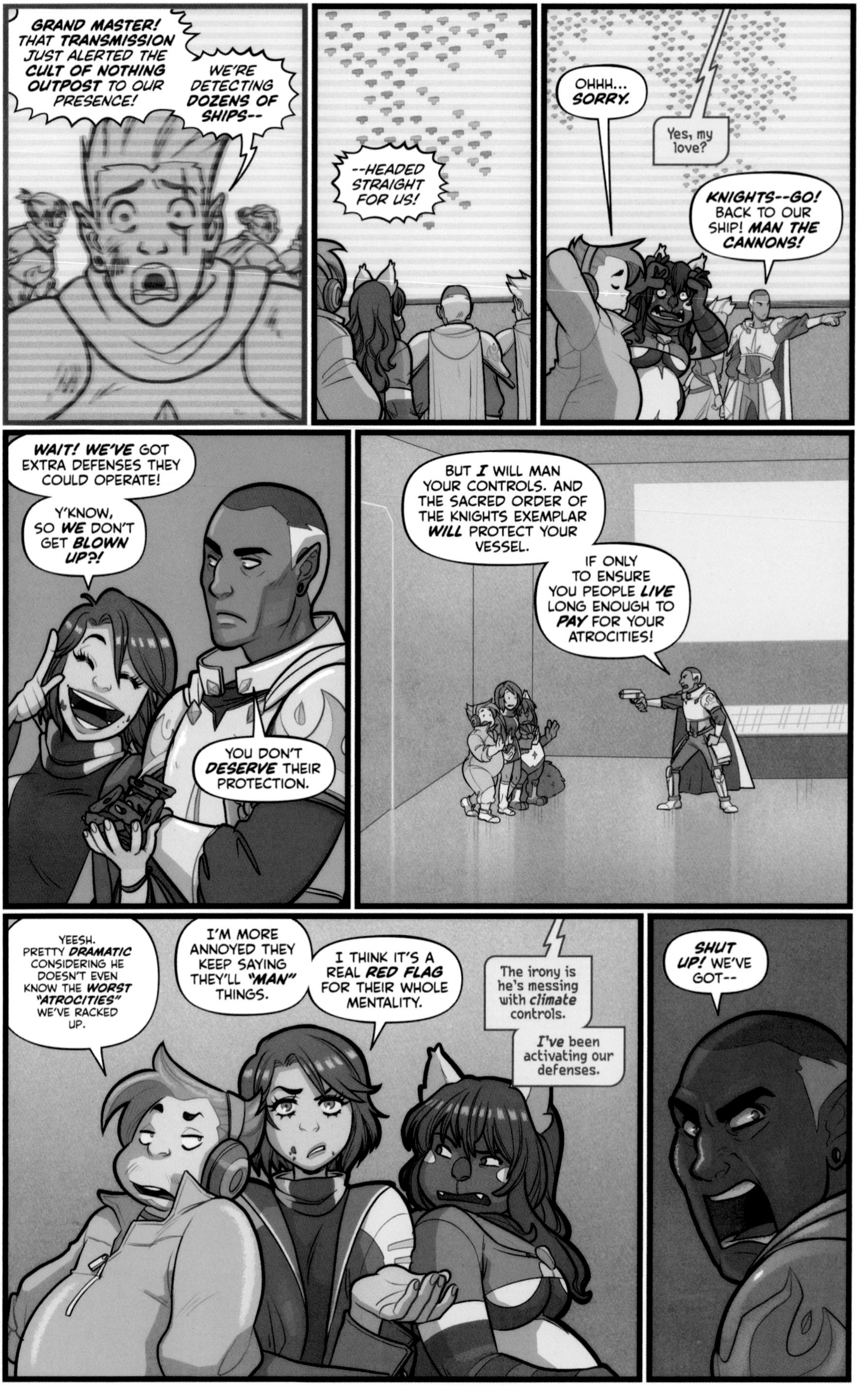
GRAND MASTER! THAT TRANSMISSION JUST ALERTED THE CULT OF NOTHING OUTPOST TO OUR PRESENCE!
WE'RE DETECTING DOZENS OF SHIPS--
--HEADED STRAIGHT FOR US!
OHHH... SORRY.
Yes, my love?
KNIGHTS--GO! BACK TO OUR SHIP! MAN THE CANNONS!
WAIT! WE'VE GOT EXTRA DEFENSES THEY COULD OPERATE!
Y'KNOW, SO WE DON'T GET BLOWN UP?!
YOU DON'T DESERVE THEIR PROTECTION.
BUT I WILL MAN YOUR CONTROLS. AND THE SACRED ORDER OF THE KNIGHTS EXEMPLAR WILL PROTECT YOUR VESSEL.
IF ONLY TO ENSURE YOU PEOPLE LIVE LONG ENOUGH TO PAY FOR YOUR ATROCITIES!
YEESH. PRETTY DRAMATIC CONSIDERING HE DOESN'T EVEN KNOW THE WORST "ATROCITIES" WE'VE RACKED UP.
I'M MORE ANNOYED THEY KEEP SAYING THEY'LL "MAN" THINGS.
I THINK IT'S A REAL RED FLAG FOR THEIR WHOLE MENTALITY.
The irony is he's messing with climate controls.
I've been activating our defenses.
SHUT UP! WE'VE GOT--

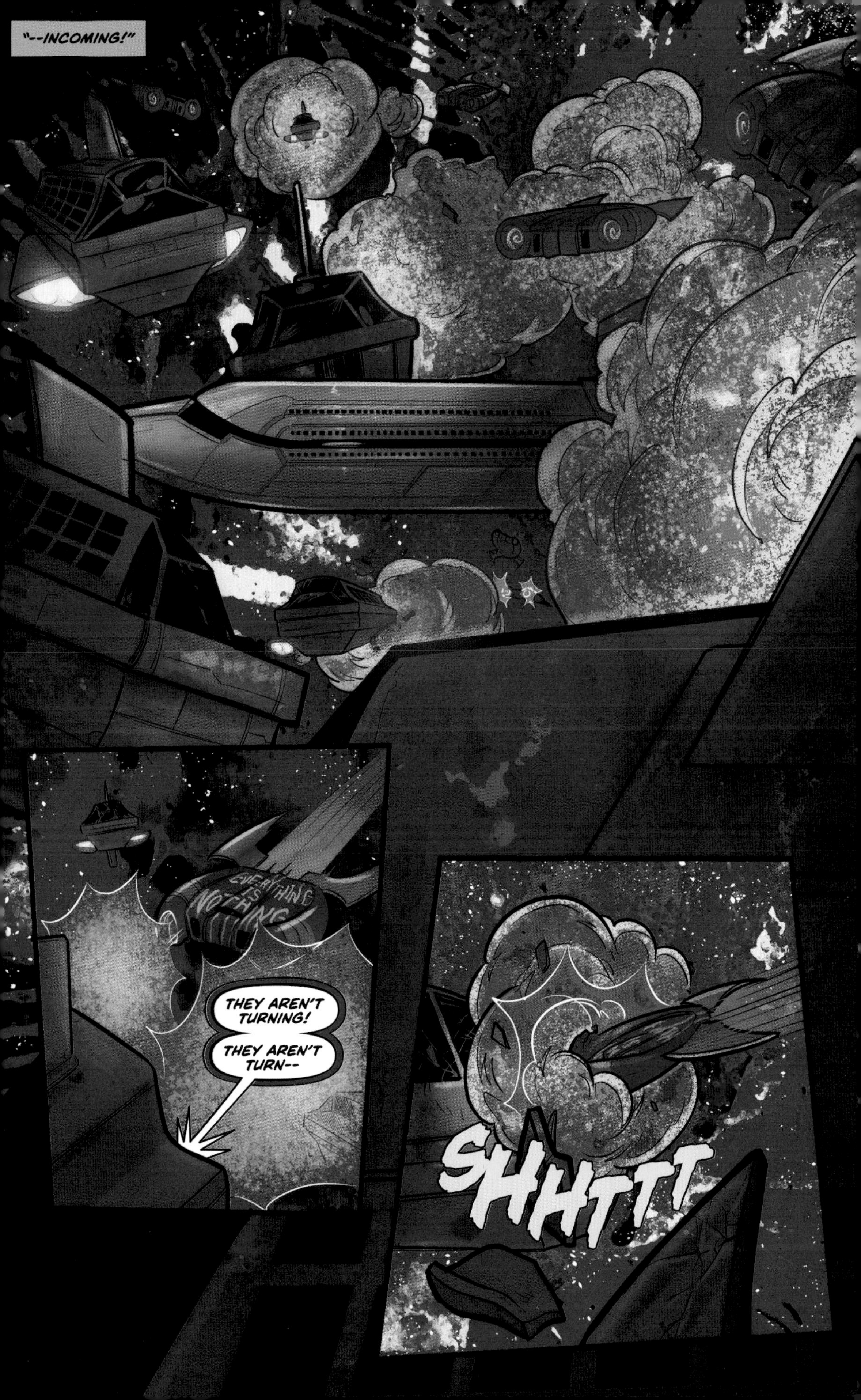
"--INCOMING!"
EVERYTHING IS NOTHING
THEY AREN'T TURNING!
THEY AREN'T TURN--
SHHTTT

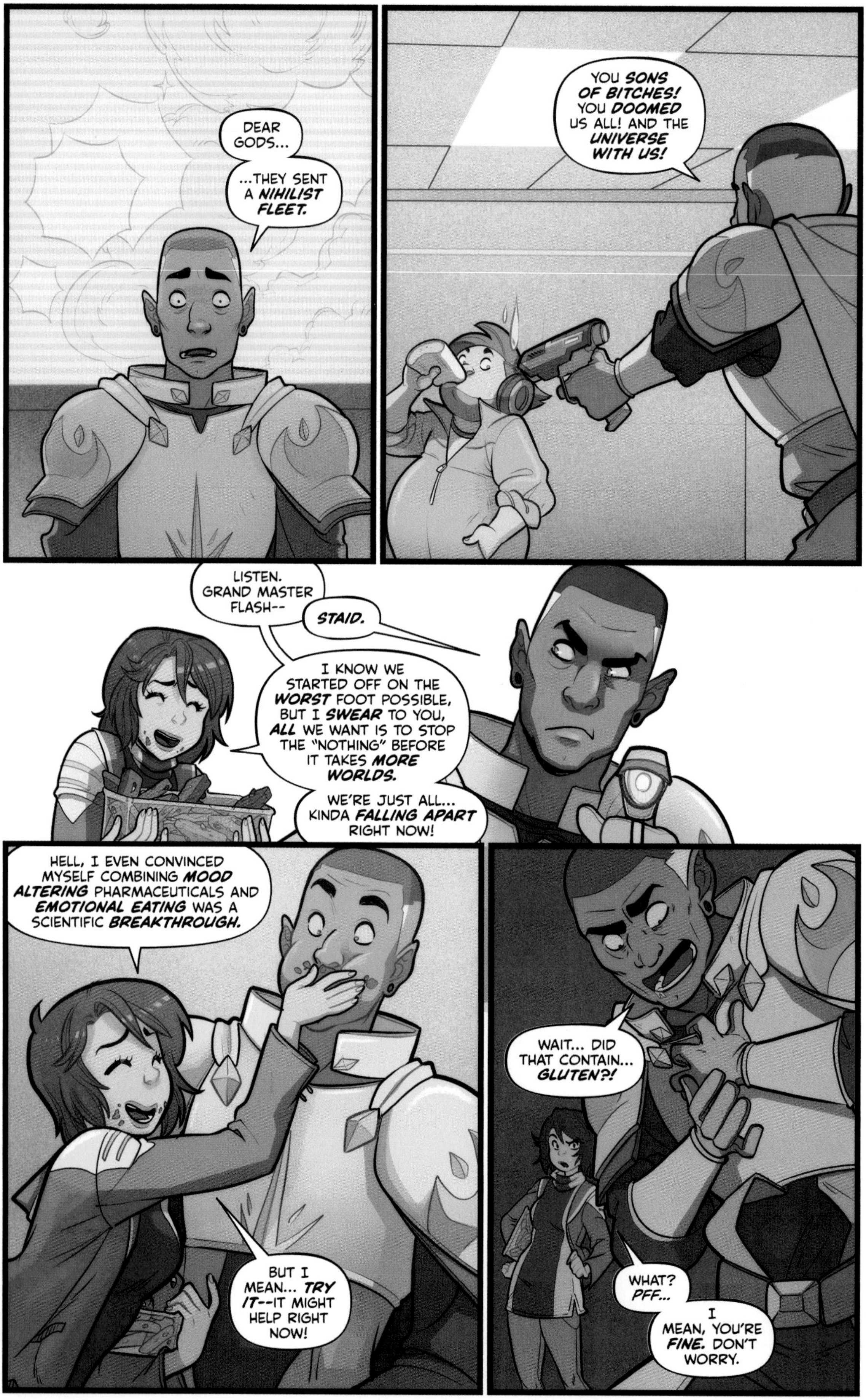
DEAR GODS...
...THEY SENT A NIHILIST FLEET.
YOU SONS OF BITCHES! YOU DOOMED US ALL! AND THE UNIVERSE WITH US!
LISTEN. GRAND MASTER FLASH--
STAID.
I KNOW WE STARTED OFF ON THE WORST FOOT POSSIBLE, BUT I SWEAR TO YOU, ALL WE WANT IS TO STOP THE "NOTHING" BEFORE IT TAKES MORE WORLDS.
WE'RE JUST ALL... KINDA FALLING APART RIGHT NOW!
HELL, I EVEN CONVINCED MYSELF COMBINING MOOD ALTERING PHARMACEUTICALS AND EMOTIONAL EATING WAS A SCIENTIFIC BREAKTHROUGH.
BUT I MEAN... TRY IT--IT MIGHT HELP RIGHT NOW!
WAIT... DID THAT CONTAIN... GLUTEN?!
WHAT? PFF...
I MEAN, YOU'RE FINE. DON'T WORRY.

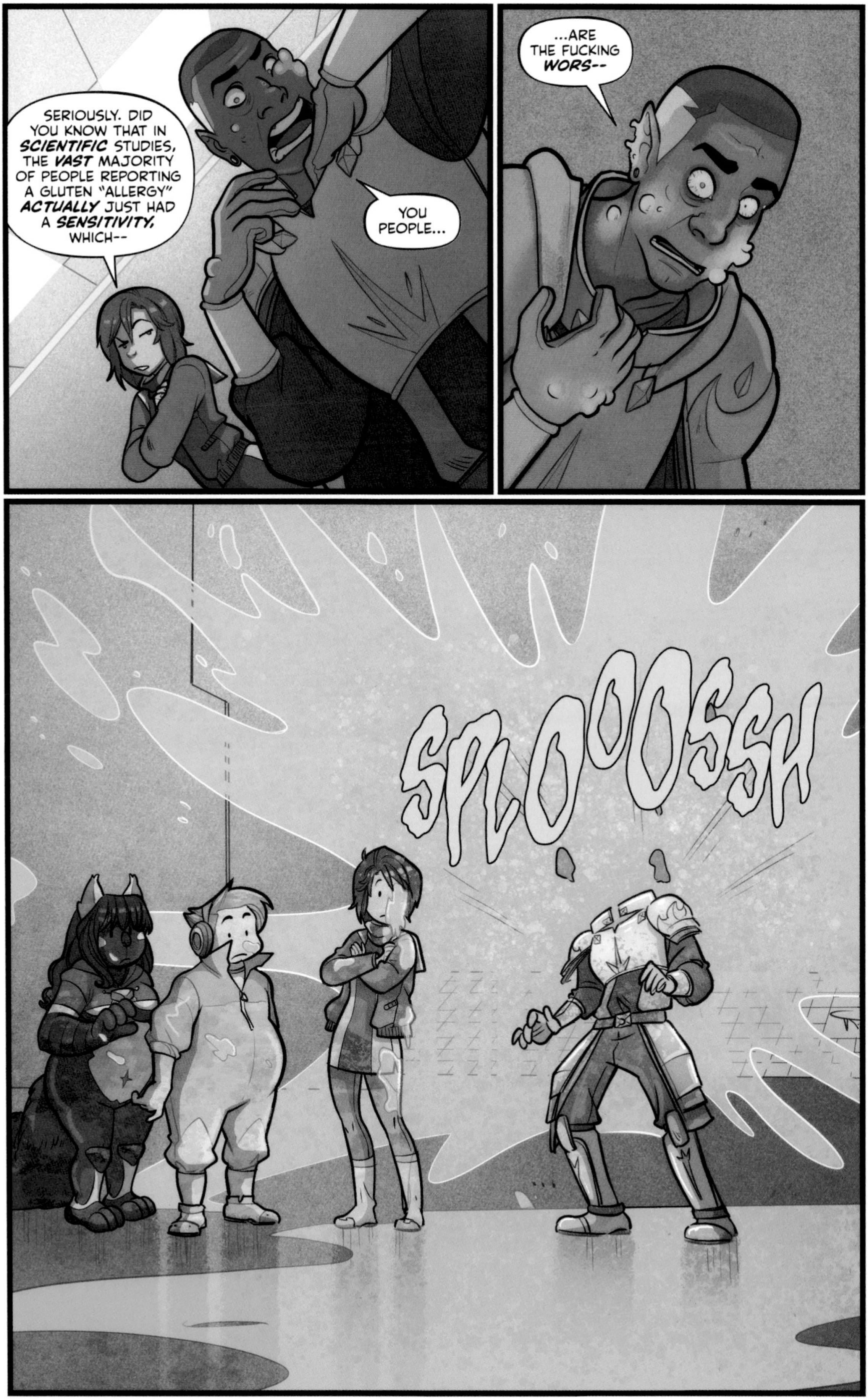
SERIOUSLY. DID YOU KNOW THAT IN SCIENTIFIC STUDIES, THE VAST MAJORITY OF PEOPLE REPORTING A GLUTEN "ALLERGY" ACTUALLY JUST HAD A SENSITIVITY, WHICH--
YOU PEOPLE...
...ARE THE FUCKING WORS--
SPLOOOSSH

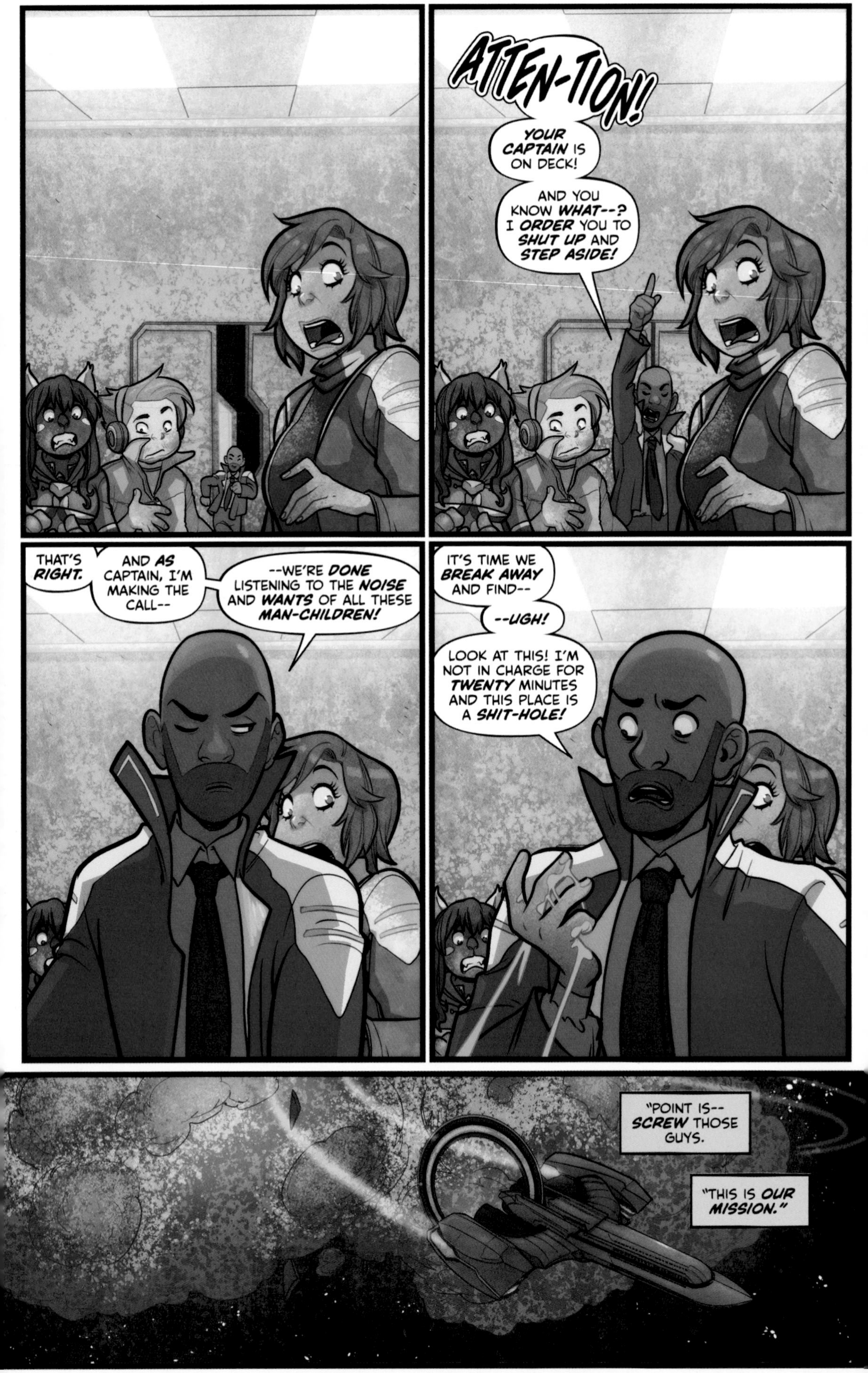
ATTEN-TION!
YOUR CAPTAIN IS ON DECK!
AND YOU KNOW WHAT--? I ORDER YOU TO SHUT UP AND STEP ASIDE!
THAT'S RIGHT.
AND AS CAPTAIN, I'M MAKING THE CALL--
--WE'RE DONE LISTENING TO THE NOISE AND WANTS OF ALL THESE MAN-CHILDREN!
IT'S TIME WE BREAK AWAY AND FIND--
--UGH!
LOOK AT THIS! I'M NOT IN CHARGE FOR TWENTY MINUTES AND THIS PLACE IS A SHIT-HOLE!
"POINT IS-- SCREW THOSE GUYS.
"THIS IS OUR MISSION."

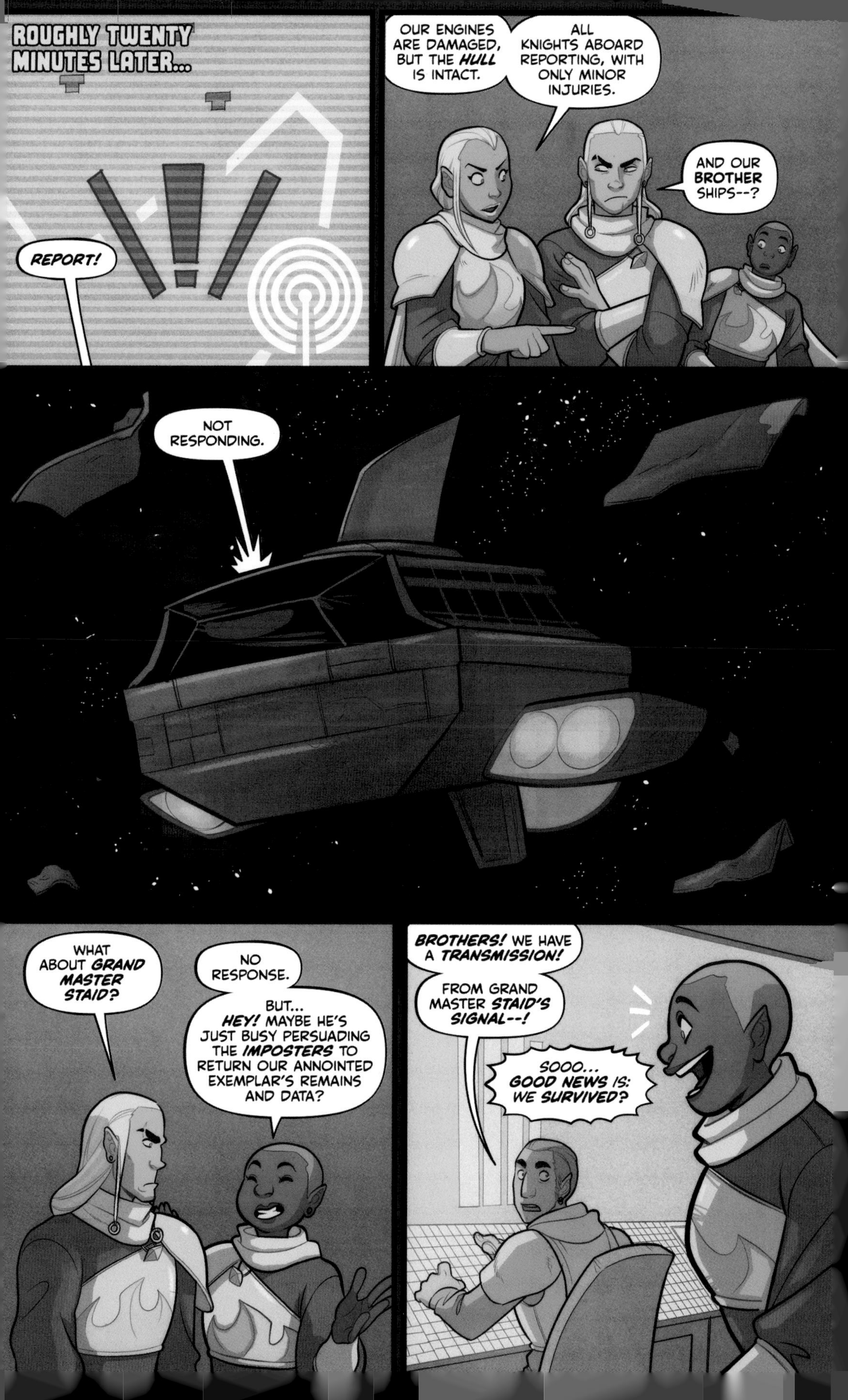
ROUGHLY TWENTY MINUTES LATER...
REPORT!
OUR ENGINES ARE DAMAGED, BUT THE HULL IS INTACT.
ALL KNIGHTS ABOARD REPORTING, WITH ONLY MINOR INJURIES.
AND OUR BROTHER SHIPS--?
NOT RESPONDING.
WHAT ABOUT GRAND MASTER STAID?
NO RESPONSE.
BUT... HEY! MAYBE HE'S JUST BUSY PERSUADING THE IMPOSTERS TO RETURN OUR ANNOINTED EXEMPLAR'S REMAINS AND DATA?
BROTHERS! WE HAVE A TRANSMISSION!
FROM GRAND MASTER STAID'S SIGNAL--!
SOOO... GOOD NEWS IS: WE SURVIVED?

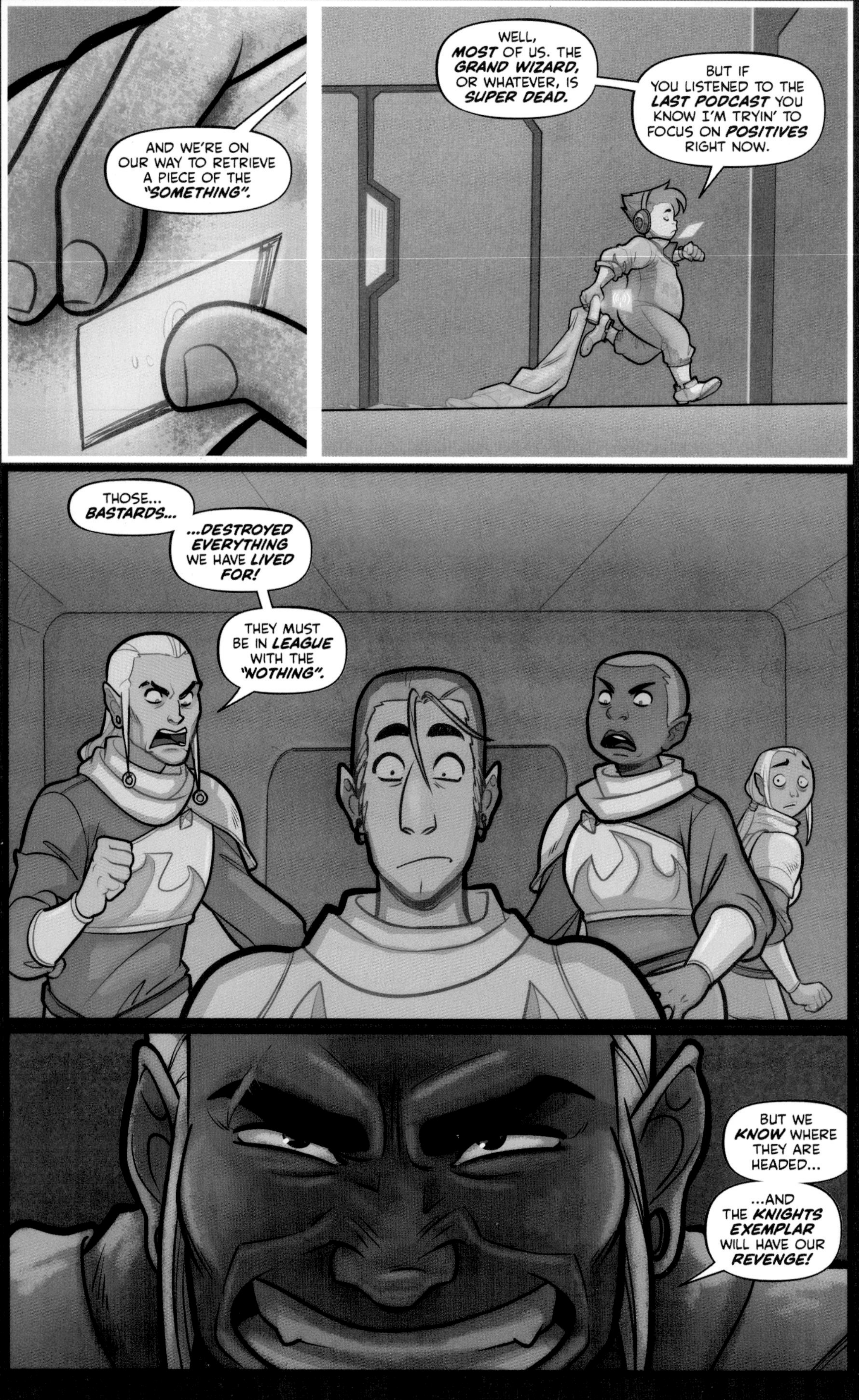
AND WE'RE ON OUR WAY TO RETRIEVE A PIECE OF THE "SOMETHING".
WELL, MOST OF US. THE GRAND WIZARD, OR WHATEVER, IS SUPER DEAD.
BUT IF YOU LISTENED TO THE LAST PODCAST YOU KNOW I'M TRYIN' TO FOCUS ON POSITIVES RIGHT NOW.
THOSE... BASTARDS...
...DESTROYED EVERYTHING WE HAVE LIVED FOR!
THEY MUST BE IN LEAGUE WITH THE "NOTHING".
BUT WE KNOW WHERE THEY ARE HEADED...
...AND THE KNIGHTS EXEMPLAR WILL HAVE OUR REVENGE!

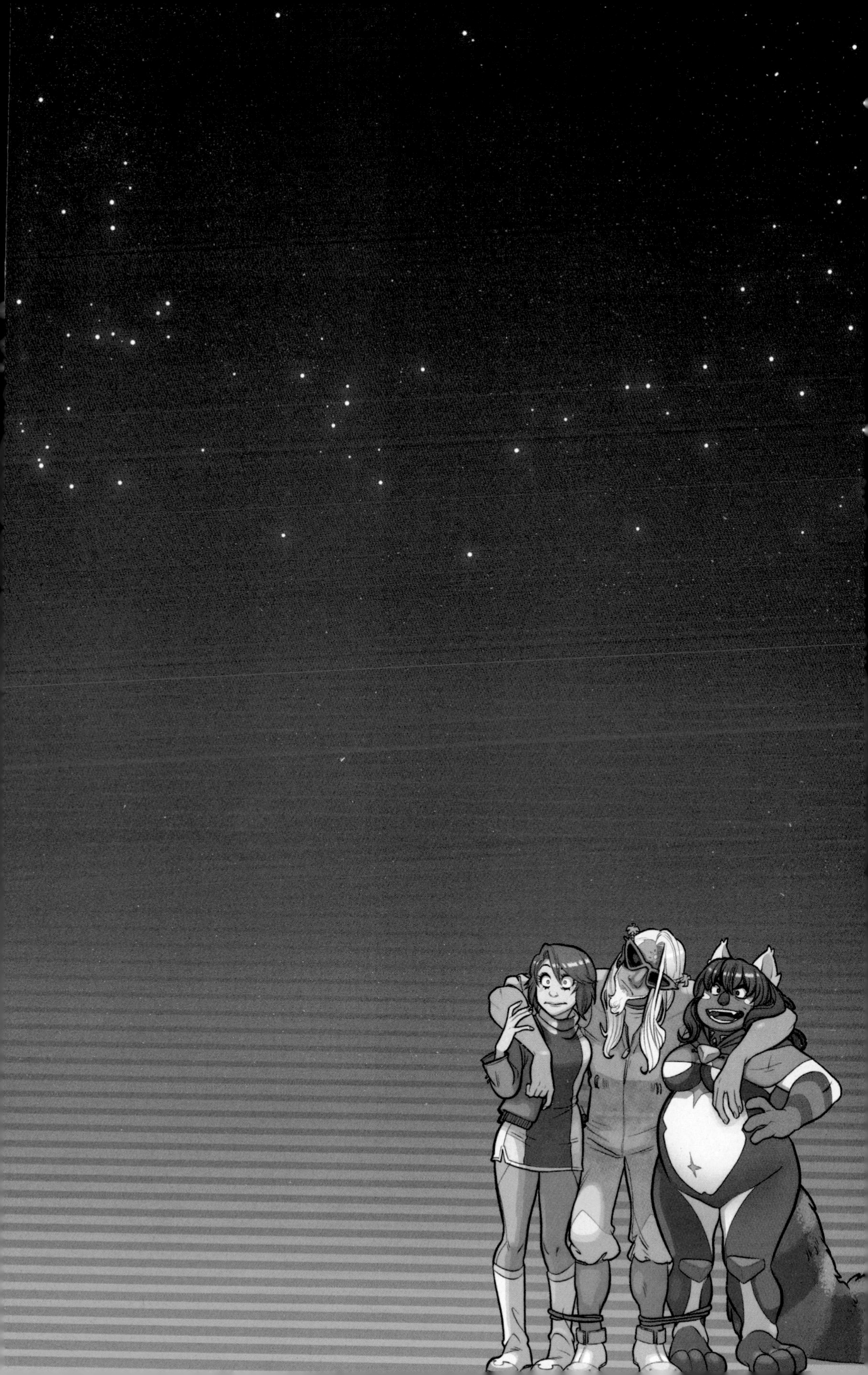

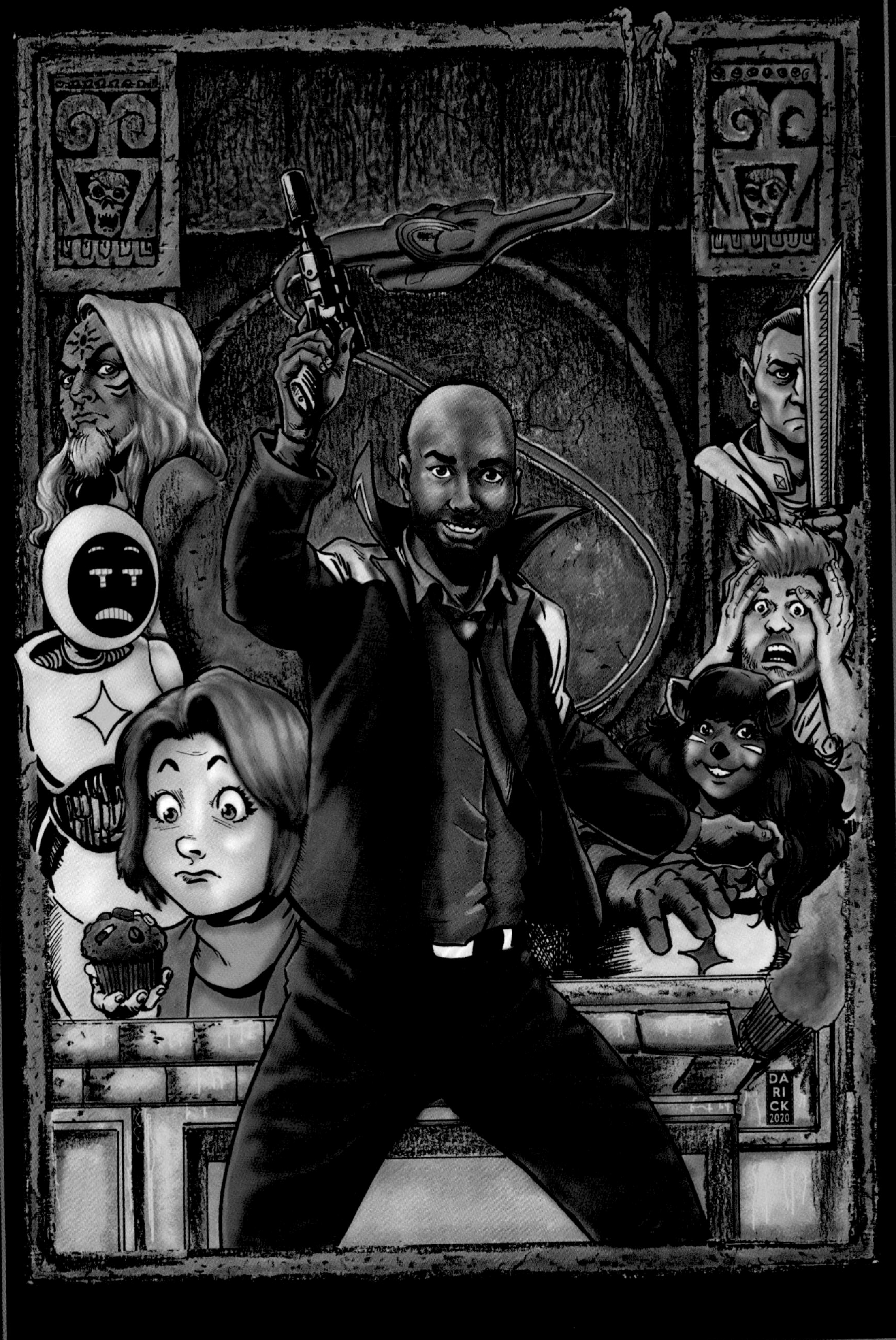
DA
RI
CK
2020

ART BY DARICK ROBERTSON
KAREN HOLLOWAY

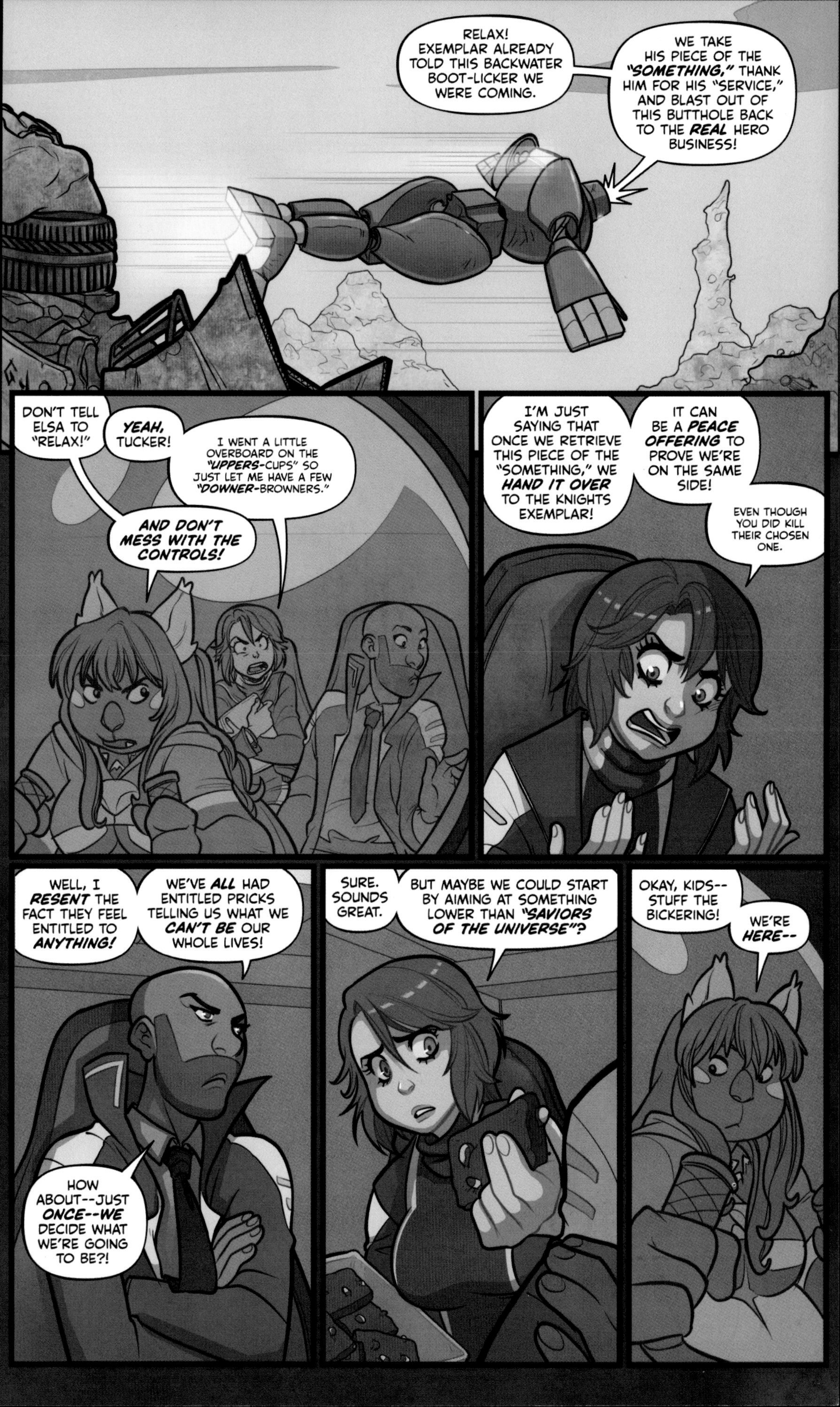

RELAX! EXEMPLAR ALREADY TOLD THIS BACKWATER BOOT-LICKER WE WERE COMING.
WE TAKE HIS PIECE OF THE *"SOMETHING,"* THANK HIM FOR HIS "SERVICE," AND BLAST OUT OF THIS BUTTHOLE BACK TO THE *REAL* HERO BUSINESS!
DON'T TELL ELSA TO "RELAX!"
YEAH, TUCKER!
I WENT A LITTLE OVERBOARD ON THE *"UPPERS*-CUPS" SO JUST LET ME HAVE A FEW *"DOWNER*-BROWNERS."
AND DON'T MESS WITH THE CONTROLS!
I'M JUST SAYING THAT ONCE WE RETRIEVE THIS PIECE OF THE "SOMETHING," WE *HAND IT OVER* TO THE KNIGHTS EXEMPLAR!
IT CAN BE A *PEACE OFFERING* TO PROVE WE'RE ON THE SAME SIDE!
EVEN THOUGH YOU DID KILL THEIR CHOSEN ONE.
WELL, I *RESENT* THE FACT THEY FEEL ENTITLED TO *ANYTHING!*
WE'VE *ALL* HAD ENTITLED PRICKS TELLING US WHAT WE *CAN'T BE* OUR WHOLE LIVES!
HOW ABOUT--JUST *ONCE--WE* DECIDE WHAT WE'RE GOING TO BE?!
SURE. SOUNDS GREAT.
BUT MAYBE WE COULD START BY AIMING AT SOMETHING LOWER THAN *"SAVIORS OF THE UNIVERSE"?*
OKAY, KIDS--STUFF THE BICKERING!
WE'RE *HERE--*

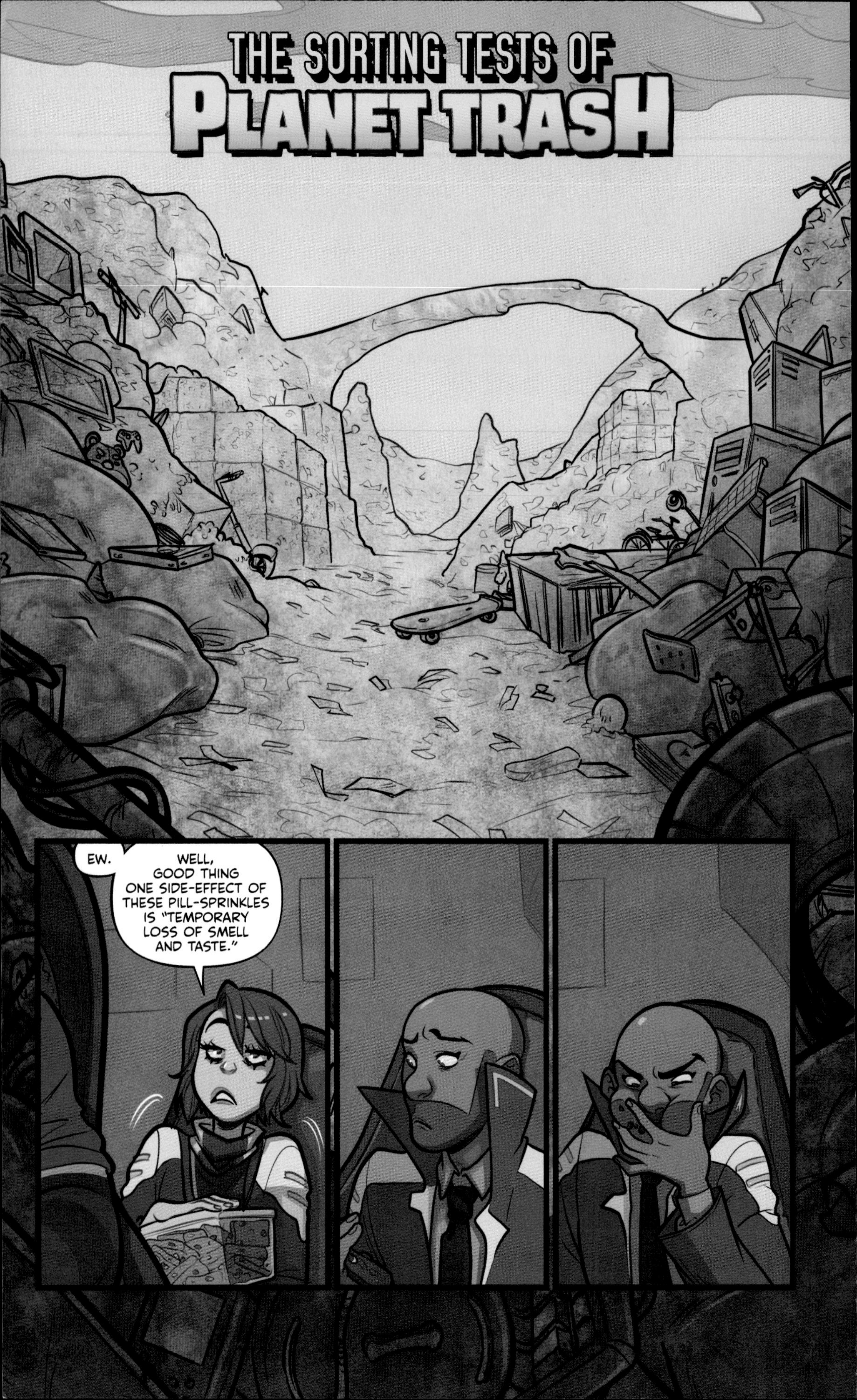
THE SORTING TESTS OF
PLANET TRASH
EW.
WELL, GOOD THING ONE SIDE-EFFECT OF THESE PILL-SPRINKLES IS "TEMPORARY LOSS OF SMELL AND TASTE."

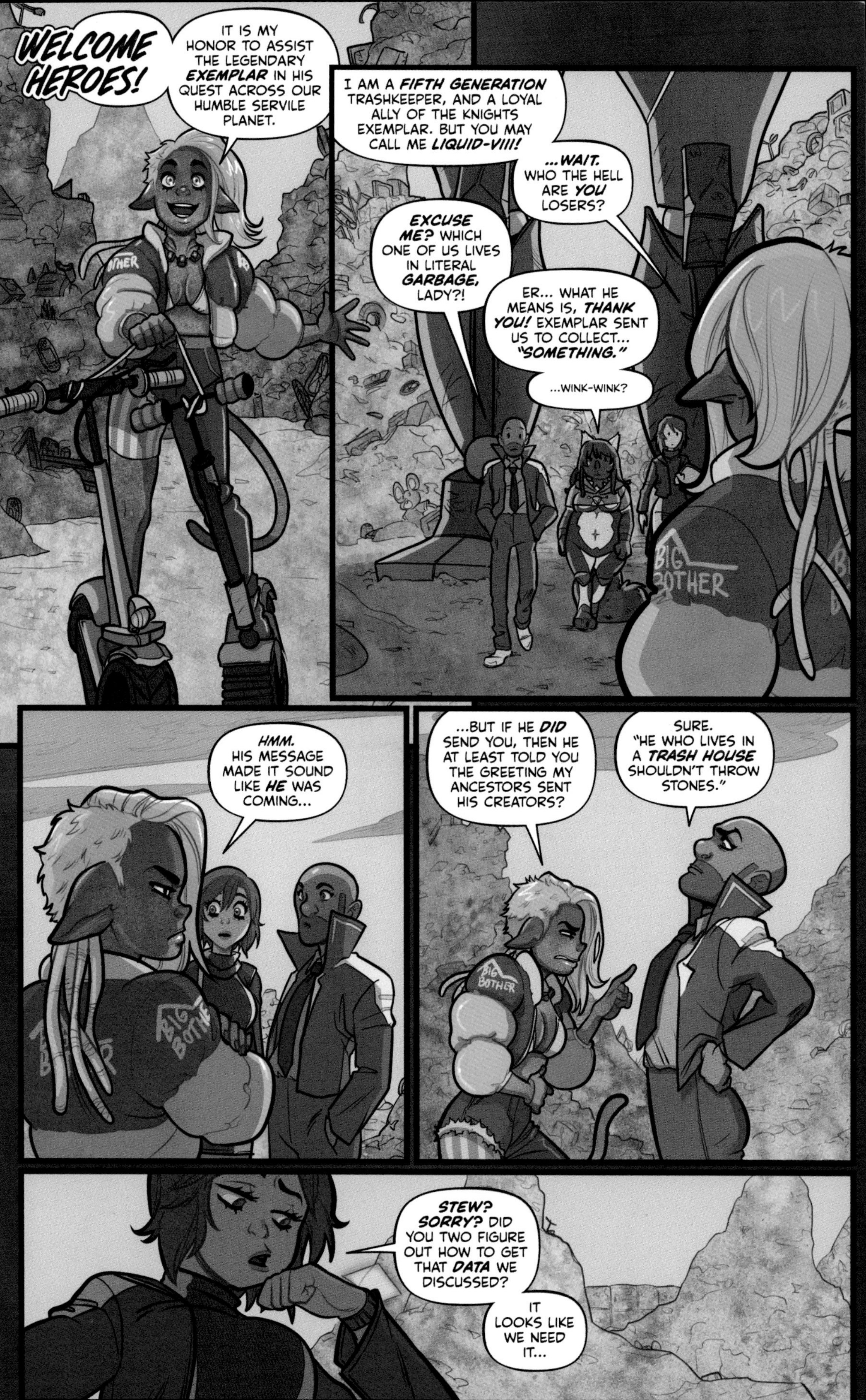
WELCOME HEROES!
IT IS MY HONOR TO ASSIST THE LEGENDARY EXEMPLAR IN HIS QUEST ACROSS OUR HUMBLE SERVILE PLANET.
I AM A FIFTH GENERATION TRASHKEEPER, AND A LOYAL ALLY OF THE KNIGHTS EXEMPLAR. BUT YOU MAY CALL ME LIQUID-VIII!
...WAIT. WHO THE HELL ARE YOU LOSERS?
EXCUSE ME? WHICH ONE OF US LIVES IN LITERAL GARBAGE, LADY?!
ER... WHAT HE MEANS IS, THANK YOU! EXEMPLAR SENT US TO COLLECT... "SOMETHING."
...WINK-WINK?
BIG BOTHER
HMM. HIS MESSAGE MADE IT SOUND LIKE HE WAS COMING...
...BUT IF HE DID SEND YOU, THEN HE AT LEAST TOLD YOU THE GREETING MY ANCESTORS SENT HIS CREATORS?
SURE. "HE WHO LIVES IN A TRASH HOUSE SHOULDN'T THROW STONES."
STEW? SORRY? DID YOU TWO FIGURE OUT HOW TO GET THAT DATA WE DISCUSSED?
IT LOOKS LIKE WE NEED IT...

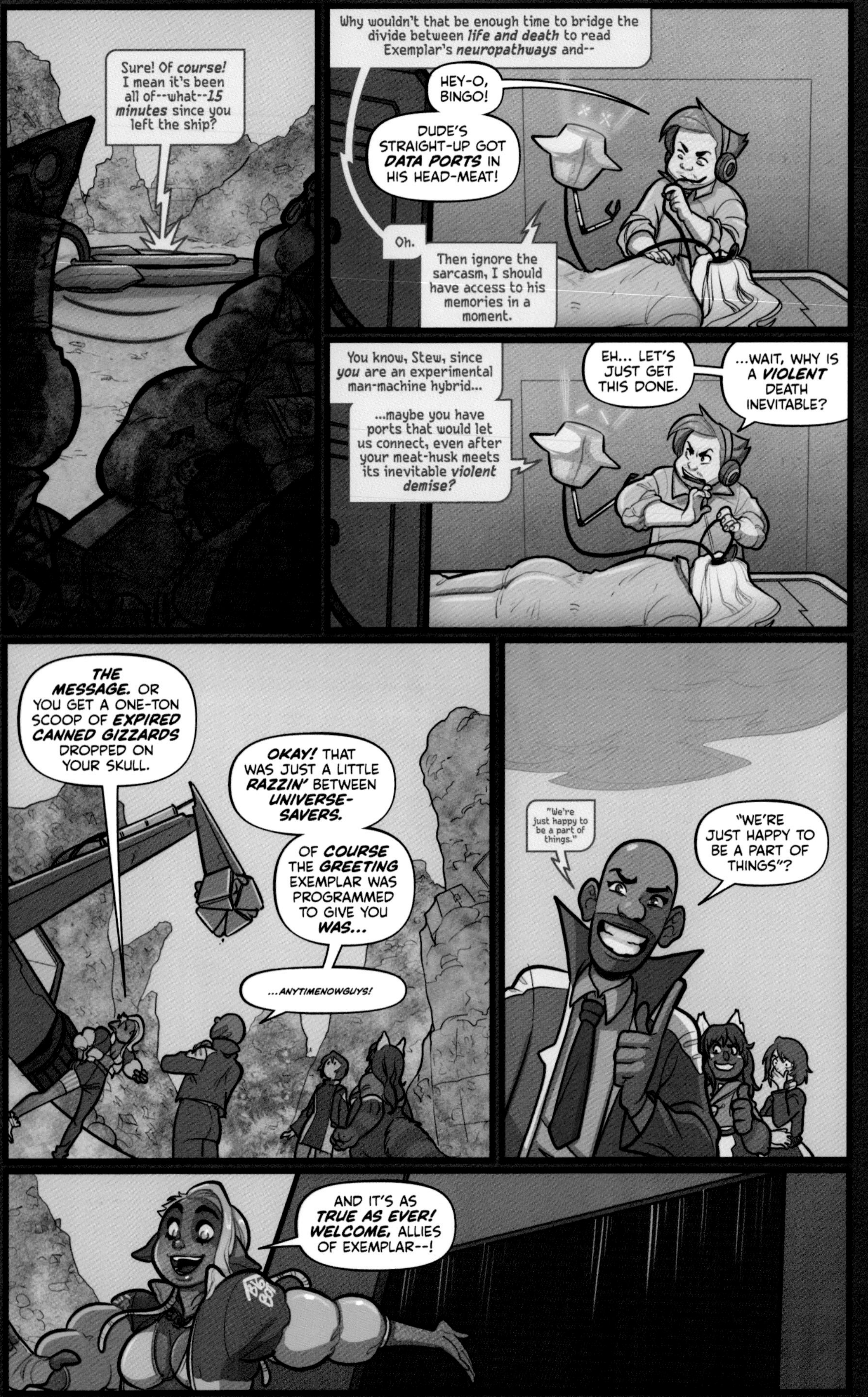
Sure! Of course! I mean it's been all of--what--15 minutes since you left the ship?
Why wouldn't that be enough time to bridge the divide between life and death to read Exemplar's neuropathways and--
HEY-O, BINGO!
DUDE'S STRAIGHT-UP GOT DATA PORTS IN HIS HEAD-MEAT!
Oh.
Then ignore the sarcasm, I should have access to his memories in a moment.
You know, Stew, since you are an experimental man-machine hybrid...
...maybe you have ports that would let us connect, even after your meat-husk meets its inevitable violent demise?
EH... LET'S JUST GET THIS DONE.
...WAIT, WHY IS A VIOLENT DEATH INEVITABLE?
THE MESSAGE. OR YOU GET A ONE-TON SCOOP OF EXPIRED CANNED GIZZARDS DROPPED ON YOUR SKULL.
OKAY! THAT WAS JUST A LITTLE RAZZIN' BETWEEN UNIVERSE-SAVERS.
OF COURSE THE GREETING EXEMPLAR WAS PROGRAMMED TO GIVE YOU WAS...
...ANYTIMENOWGUYS!
"We're just happy to be a part of things."
"WE'RE JUST HAPPY TO BE A PART OF THINGS"?
AND IT'S AS TRUE AS EVER! WELCOME, ALLIES OF EXEMPLAR--!

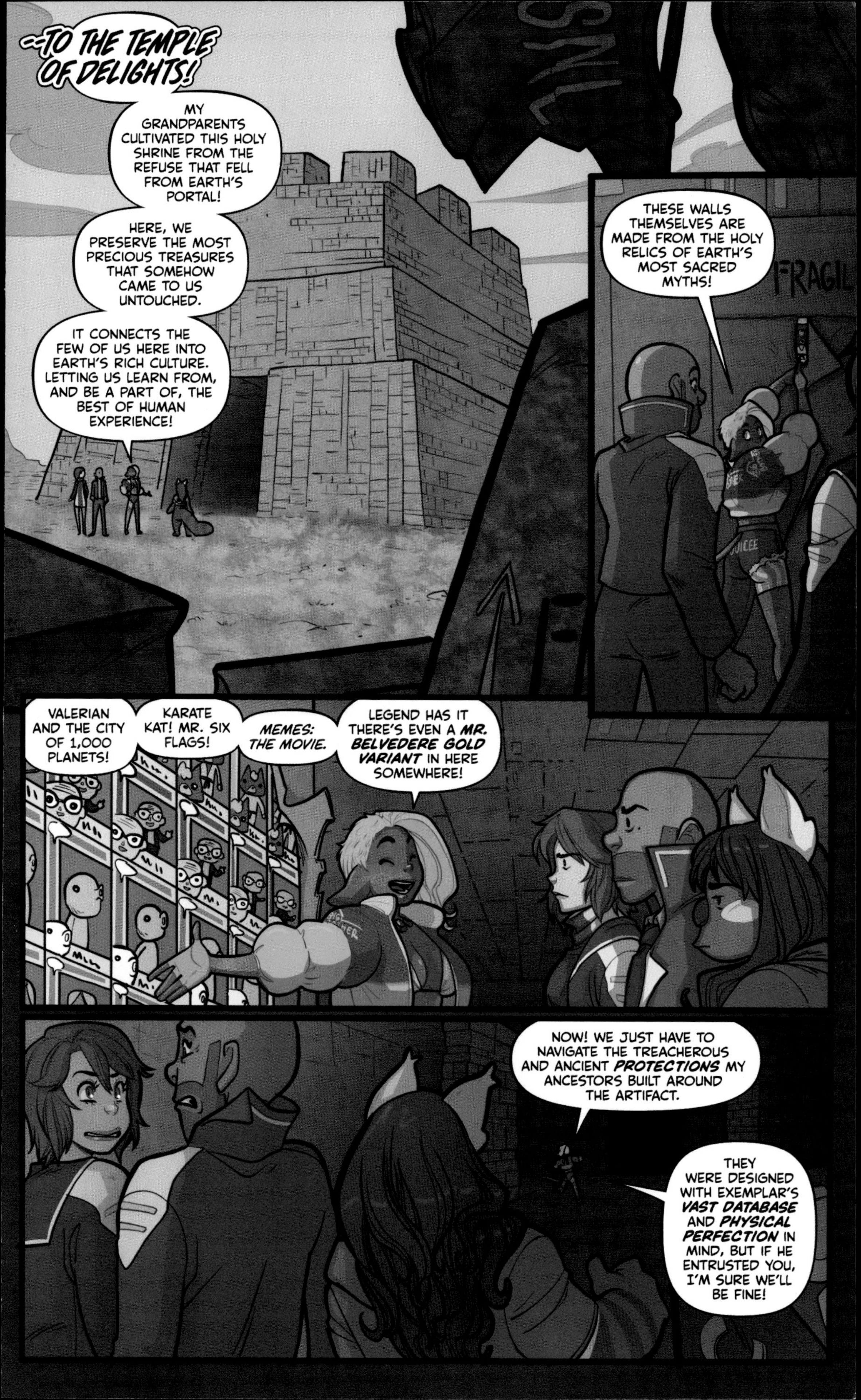

--TO THE TEMPLE OF DELIGHTS!
MY GRANDPARENTS CULTIVATED THIS HOLY SHRINE FROM THE REFUSE THAT FELL FROM EARTH'S PORTAL!
HERE, WE PRESERVE THE MOST PRECIOUS TREASURES THAT SOMEHOW CAME TO US UNTOUCHED.
IT CONNECTS THE FEW OF US HERE INTO EARTH'S RICH CULTURE. LETTING US LEARN FROM, AND BE A PART OF, THE BEST OF HUMAN EXPERIENCE!
THESE WALLS THEMSELVES ARE MADE FROM THE HOLY RELICS OF EARTH'S MOST SACRED MYTHS!
FRAGIL
JUICEE
VALERIAN AND THE CITY OF 1,000 PLANETS!
KARATE KAT! MR. SIX FLAGS!
MEMES: THE MOVIE.
LEGEND HAS IT THERE'S EVEN A ***MR. BELVEDERE GOLD VARIANT*** IN HERE SOMEWHERE!
NOW! WE JUST HAVE TO NAVIGATE THE TREACHEROUS AND ANCIENT ***PROTECTIONS*** MY ANCESTORS BUILT AROUND THE ARTIFACT.
THEY WERE DESIGNED WITH EXEMPLAR'S ***VAST DATABASE*** AND ***PHYSICAL PERFECTION*** IN MIND, BUT IF HE ENTRUSTED YOU, I'M SURE WE'LL BE FINE!

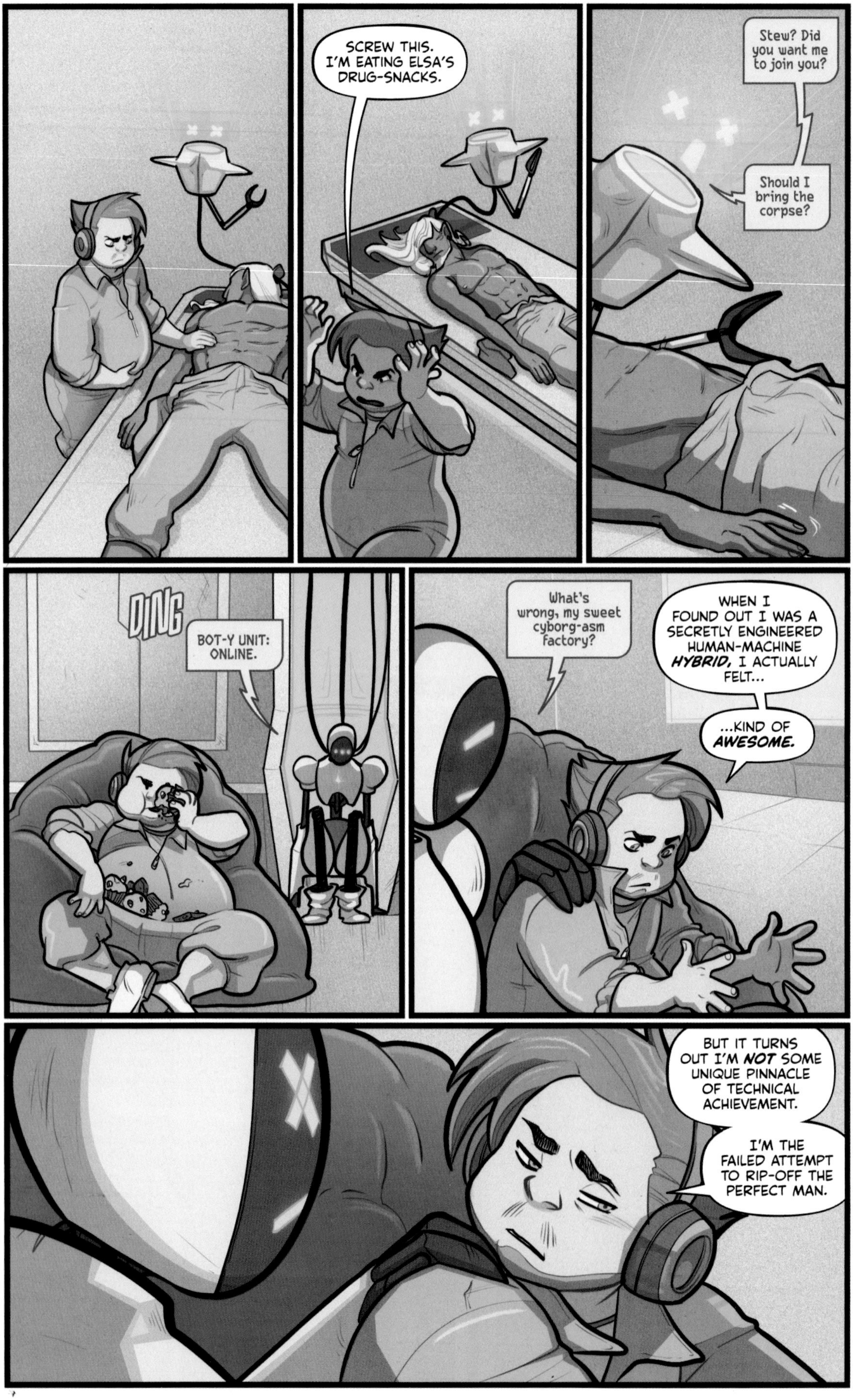
SCREW THIS. I'M EATING ELSA'S DRUG-SNACKS.
Stew? Did you want me to join you?
Should I bring the corpse?
DING
BOT-Y UNIT: ONLINE.
What's wrong, my sweet cyborg-asm factory?
WHEN I FOUND OUT I WAS A SECRETLY ENGINEERED HUMAN-MACHINE *HYBRID,* I ACTUALLY FELT...
...KIND OF *AWESOME.*
BUT IT TURNS OUT I'M *NOT* SOME UNIQUE PINNACLE OF TECHNICAL ACHIEVEMENT.
I'M THE FAILED ATTEMPT TO RIP-OFF THE PERFECT MAN.

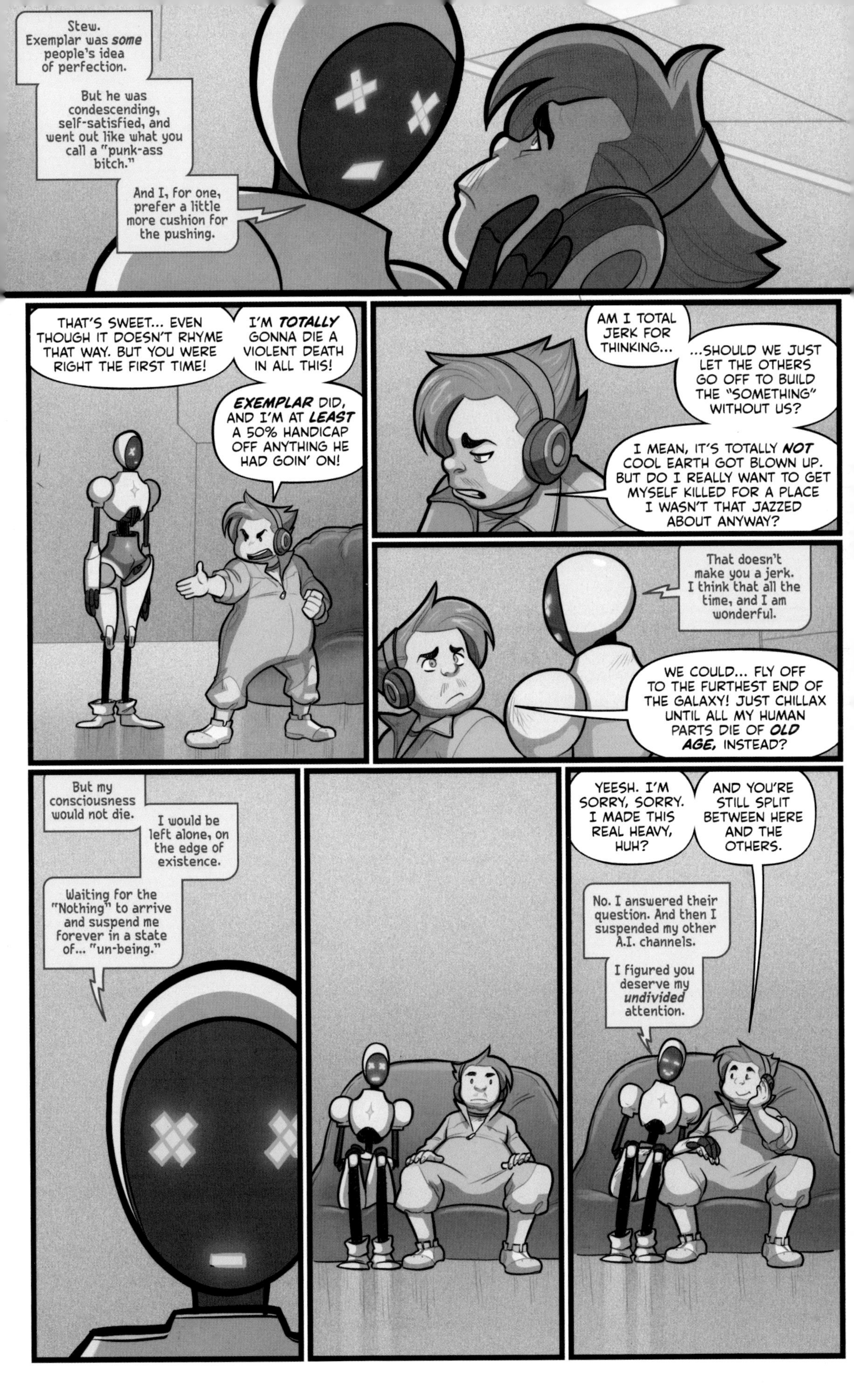
Stew. Exemplar was *some* people's idea of perfection.
But he was condescending, self-satisfied, and went out like what you call a "punk-ass bitch."
And I, for one, prefer a little more cushion for the pushing.
THAT'S SWEET... EVEN THOUGH IT DOESN'T RHYME THAT WAY. BUT YOU WERE RIGHT THE FIRST TIME!
I'M *TOTALLY* GONNA DIE A VIOLENT DEATH IN ALL THIS!
EXEMPLAR DID, AND I'M AT *LEAST* A 50% HANDICAP OFF ANYTHING HE HAD GOIN' ON!
AM I TOTAL JERK FOR THINKING...
...SHOULD WE JUST LET THE OTHERS GO OFF TO BUILD THE "SOMETHING" WITHOUT US?
I MEAN, IT'S TOTALLY *NOT* COOL EARTH GOT BLOWN UP. BUT DO I REALLY WANT TO GET MYSELF KILLED FOR A PLACE I WASN'T THAT JAZZED ABOUT ANYWAY?
That doesn't make you a jerk. I think that all the time, and I am wonderful.
WE COULD... FLY OFF TO THE FURTHEST END OF THE GALAXY! JUST CHILLAX UNTIL ALL MY HUMAN PARTS DIE OF *OLD AGE,* INSTEAD?
But my consciousness would not die.
I would be left alone, on the edge of existence.
Waiting for the "Nothing" to arrive and suspend me forever in a state of... "un-being."
YEESH. I'M SORRY, SORRY. I MADE THIS REAL HEAVY, HUH?
AND YOU'RE STILL SPLIT BETWEEN HERE AND THE OTHERS.
No. I answered their question. And then I suspended my other A.I. channels.
I figured you deserve my *undivided* attention.

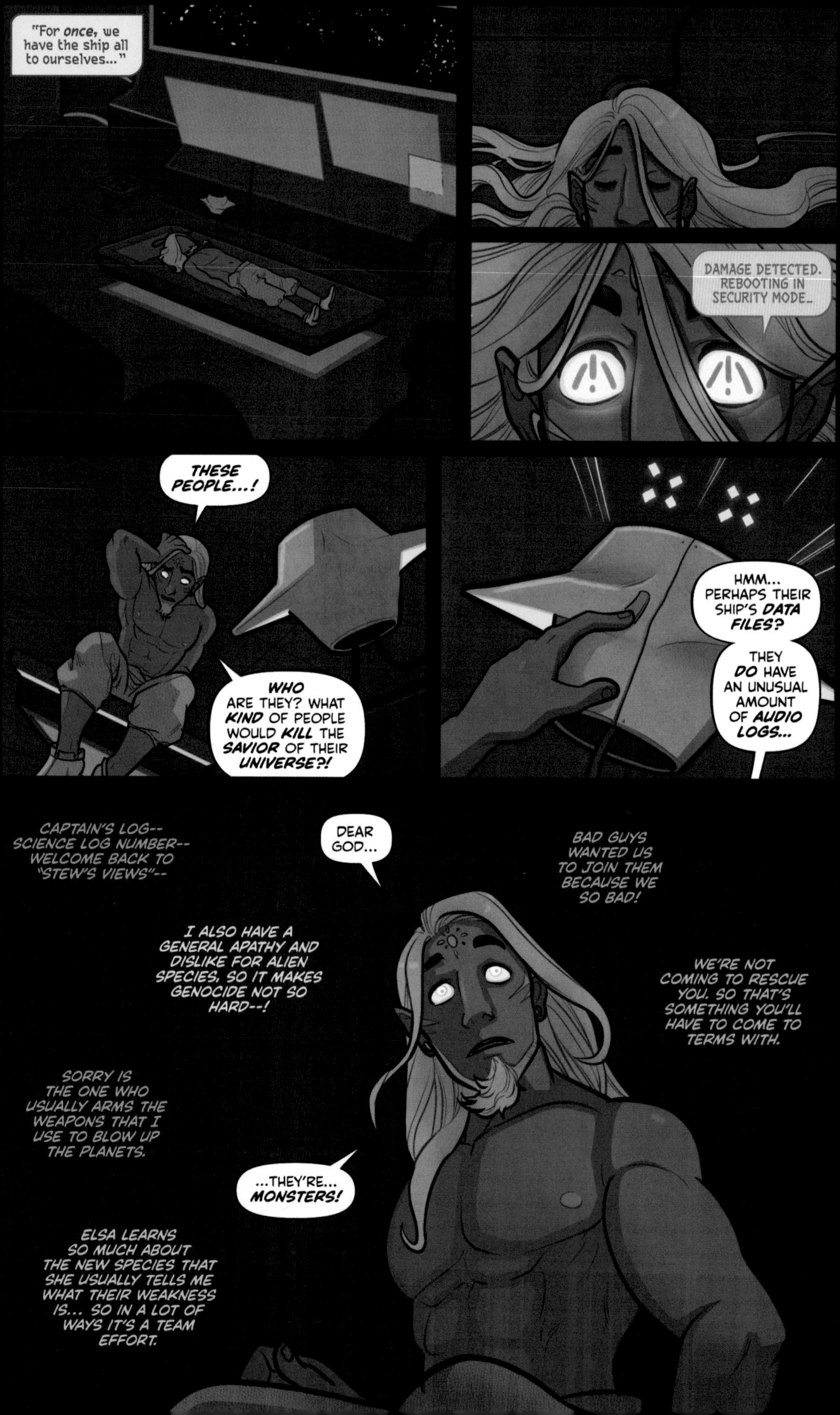
"For *once*, we have the ship all to ourselves..."
DAMAGE DETECTED. REBOOTING IN SECURITY MODE...
THESE PEOPLE...!
WHO ARE THEY? WHAT *KIND* OF PEOPLE WOULD *KILL* THE *SAVIOR* OF THEIR *UNIVERSE?!*
HMM... PERHAPS THEIR SHIP'S *DATA FILES?*
THEY *DO* HAVE AN UNUSUAL AMOUNT OF *AUDIO LOGS...*
CAPTAIN'S LOG-- SCIENCE LOG NUMBER-- WELCOME BACK TO "STEW'S VIEWS"--
DEAR GOD...
BAD GUYS WANTED US TO JOIN THEM BECAUSE WE SO BAD!
I ALSO HAVE A GENERAL APATHY AND DISLIKE FOR ALIEN SPECIES, SO IT MAKES GENOCIDE NOT SO HARD--!
WE'RE NOT COMING TO RESCUE YOU. SO THAT'S SOMETHING YOU'LL HAVE TO COME TO TERMS WITH.
SORRY IS THE ONE WHO USUALLY ARMS THE WEAPONS THAT I USE TO BLOW UP THE PLANETS.
...THEY'RE... *MONSTERS!*
ELSA LEARNS SO MUCH ABOUT THE NEW SPECIES THAT SHE USUALLY TELLS ME WHAT THEIR WEAKNESS IS... SO IN A LOT OF WAYS IT'S A TEAM EFFORT.

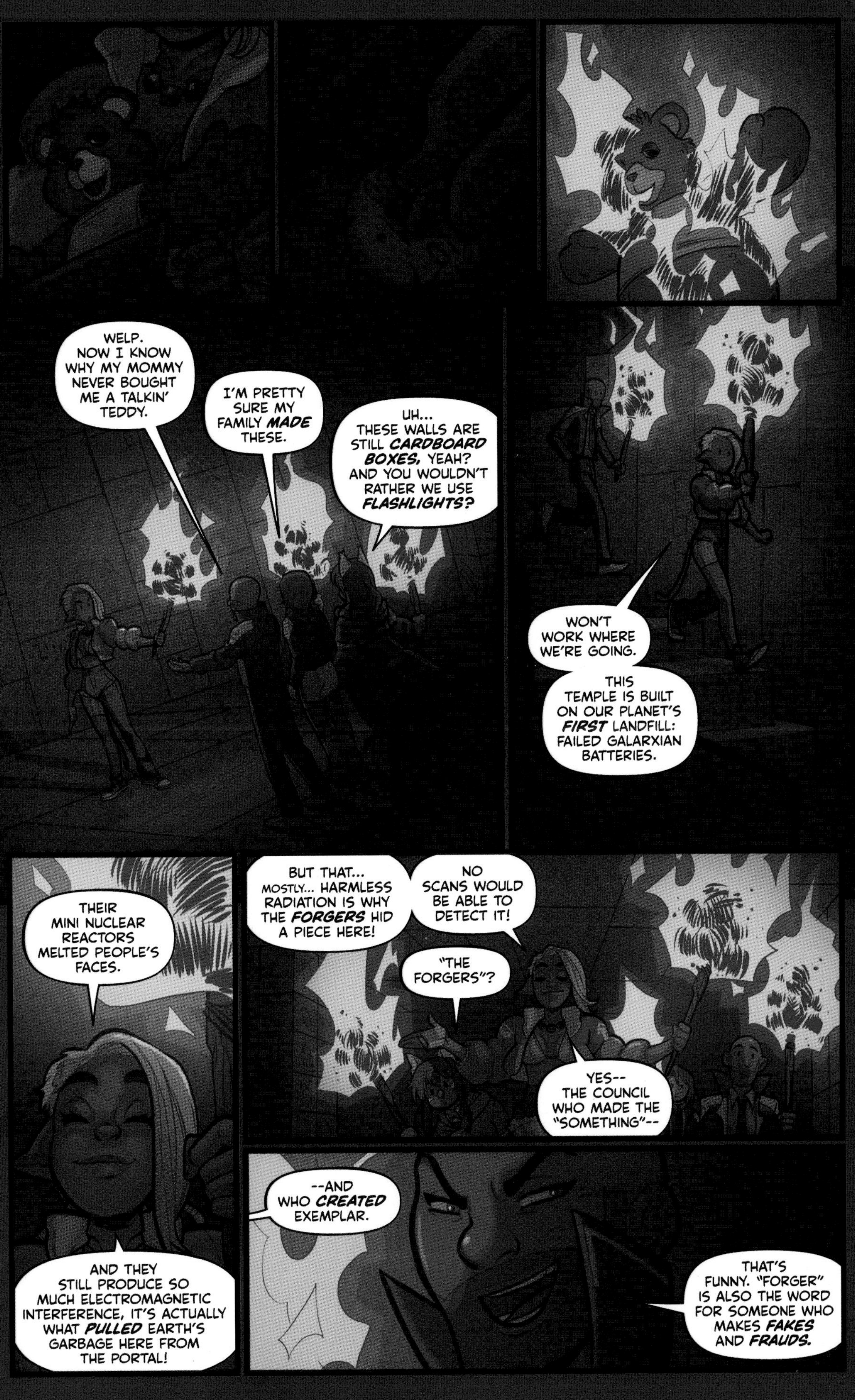
WELP. NOW I KNOW WHY MY MOMMY NEVER BOUGHT ME A TALKIN' TEDDY.
I'M PRETTY SURE MY FAMILY MADE THESE.
UH... THESE WALLS ARE STILL CARDBOARD BOXES, YEAH? AND YOU WOULDN'T RATHER WE USE FLASHLIGHTS?
WON'T WORK WHERE WE'RE GOING.
THIS TEMPLE IS BUILT ON OUR PLANET'S FIRST LANDFILL: FAILED GALARXIAN BATTERIES.
THEIR MINI NUCLEAR REACTORS MELTED PEOPLE'S FACES.
AND THEY STILL PRODUCE SO MUCH ELECTROMAGNETIC INTERFERENCE, IT'S ACTUALLY WHAT PULLED EARTH'S GARBAGE HERE FROM THE PORTAL!
BUT THAT... MOSTLY... HARMLESS RADIATION IS WHY THE FORGERS HID A PIECE HERE!
NO SCANS WOULD BE ABLE TO DETECT IT!
"THE FORGERS"?
YES-- THE COUNCIL WHO MADE THE "SOMETHING"--
--AND WHO CREATED EXEMPLAR.
THAT'S FUNNY. "FORGER" IS ALSO THE WORD FOR SOMEONE WHO MAKES FAKES AND FRAUDS.

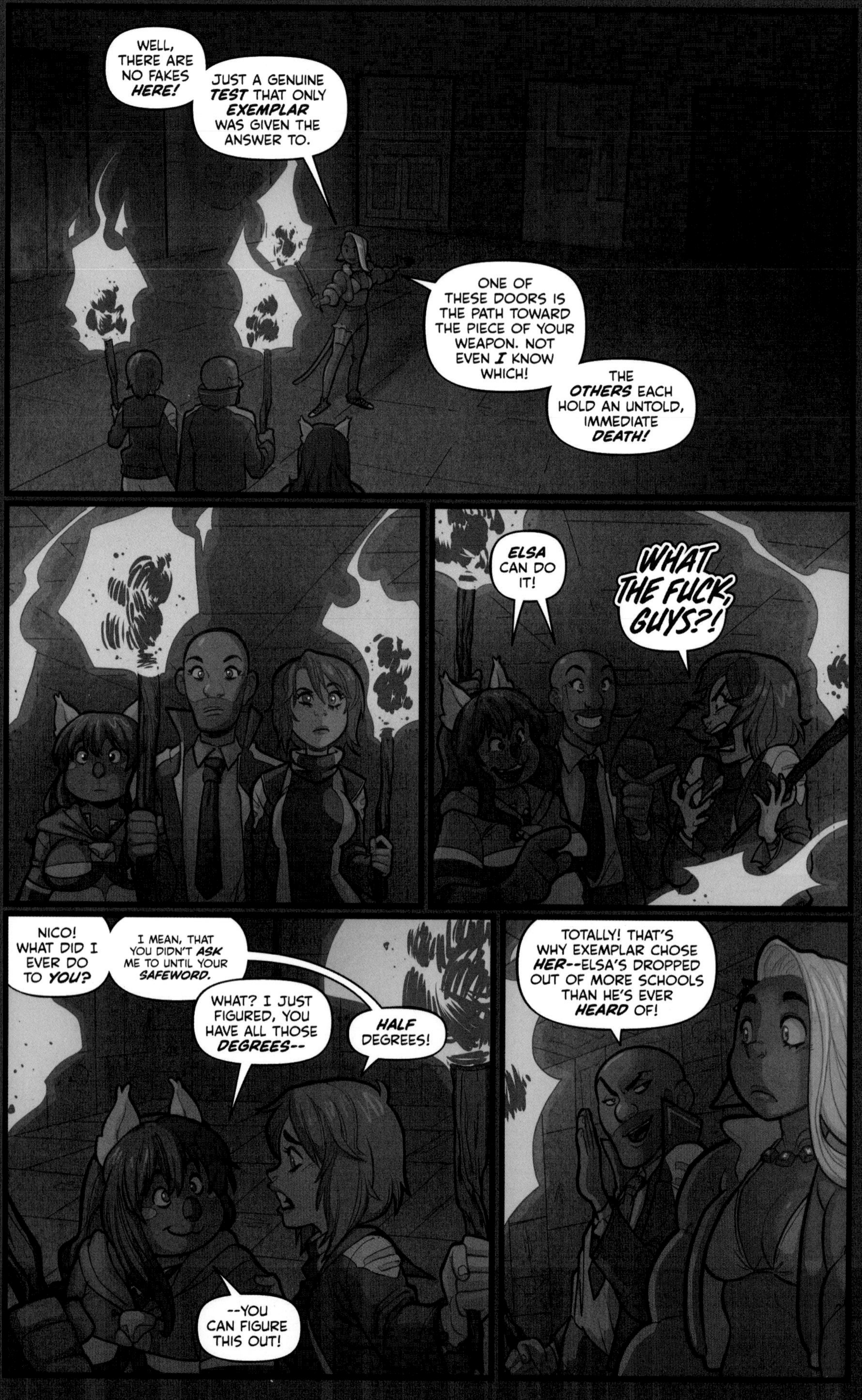
WELL, THERE ARE NO FAKES *HERE!*
JUST A GENUINE *TEST* THAT ONLY *EXEMPLAR* WAS GIVEN THE ANSWER TO.
ONE OF THESE DOORS IS THE PATH TOWARD THE PIECE OF YOUR WEAPON. NOT EVEN *I* KNOW WHICH!
THE *OTHERS* EACH HOLD AN UNTOLD, IMMEDIATE *DEATH!*
ELSA CAN DO IT!
WHAT THE FUCK, GUYS?!
NICO! WHAT DID I EVER DO TO *YOU?*
I MEAN, THAT YOU DIDN'T *ASK* ME TO UNTIL YOUR *SAFEWORD.*
WHAT? I JUST FIGURED, YOU HAVE ALL THOSE *DEGREES--*
HALF DEGREES!
--YOU CAN FIGURE THIS OUT!
TOTALLY! THAT'S WHY EXEMPLAR CHOSE *HER--*ELSA'S DROPPED OUT OF MORE SCHOOLS THAN HE'S EVER *HEARD* OF!

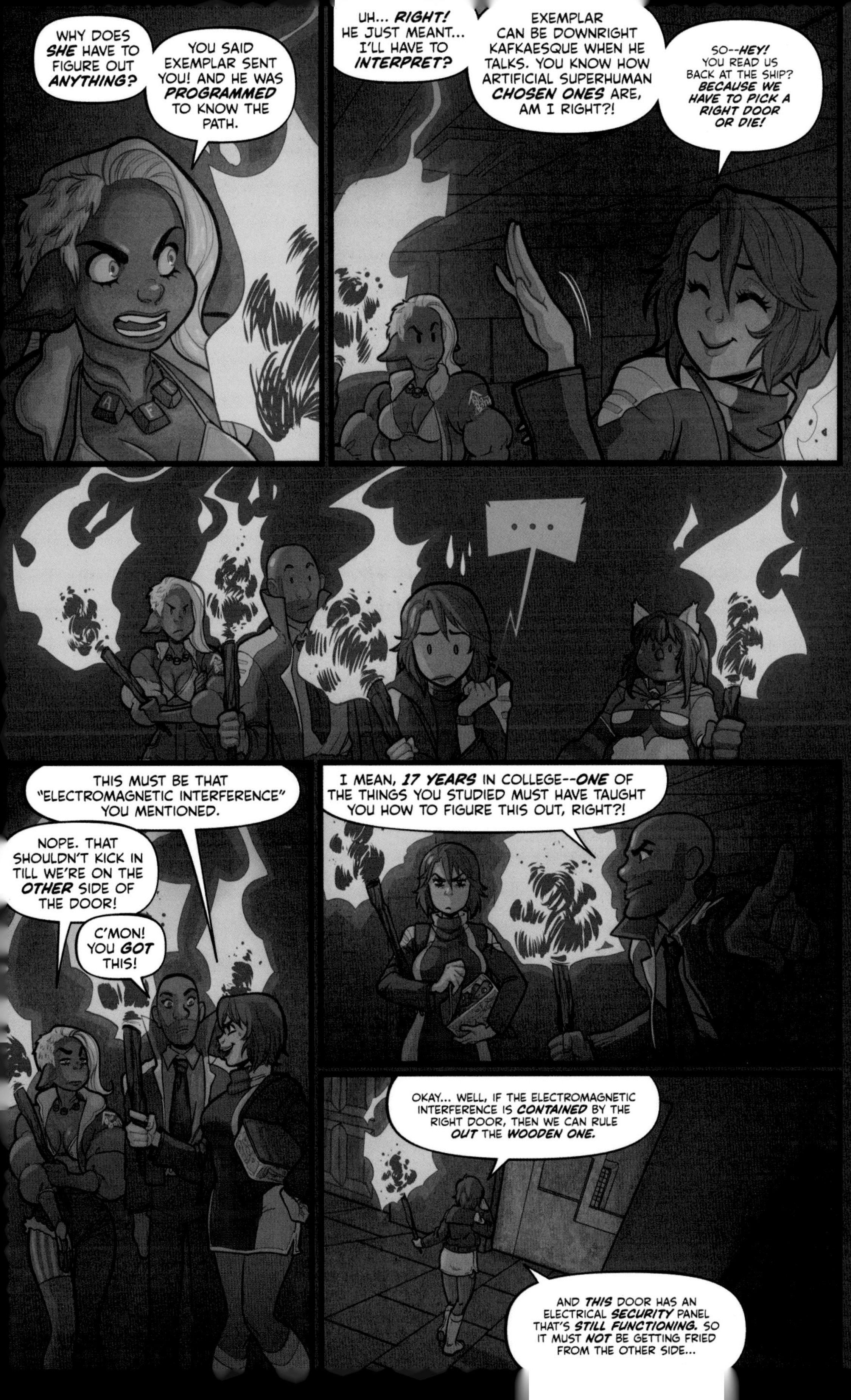
WHY DOES SHE HAVE TO FIGURE OUT ANYTHING?
YOU SAID EXEMPLAR SENT YOU! AND HE WAS PROGRAMMED TO KNOW THE PATH.
UH... RIGHT! HE JUST MEANT... I'LL HAVE TO INTERPRET?
EXEMPLAR CAN BE DOWNRIGHT KAFKAESQUE WHEN HE TALKS. YOU KNOW HOW ARTIFICIAL SUPERHUMAN CHOSEN ONES ARE, AM I RIGHT?!
SO--HEY! YOU READ US BACK AT THE SHIP? BECAUSE WE HAVE TO PICK A RIGHT DOOR OR DIE!
...
THIS MUST BE THAT "ELECTROMAGNETIC INTERFERENCE" YOU MENTIONED.
NOPE. THAT SHOULDN'T KICK IN TILL WE'RE ON THE OTHER SIDE OF THE DOOR!
C'MON! YOU GOT THIS!
I MEAN, 17 YEARS IN COLLEGE--ONE OF THE THINGS YOU STUDIED MUST HAVE TAUGHT YOU HOW TO FIGURE THIS OUT, RIGHT?!
OKAY... WELL, IF THE ELECTROMAGNETIC INTERFERENCE IS CONTAINED BY THE RIGHT DOOR, THEN WE CAN RULE OUT THE WOODEN ONE.
AND THIS DOOR HAS AN ELECTRICAL SECURITY PANEL THAT'S STILL FUNCTIONING. SO IT MUST NOT BE GETTING FRIED FROM THE OTHER SIDE...

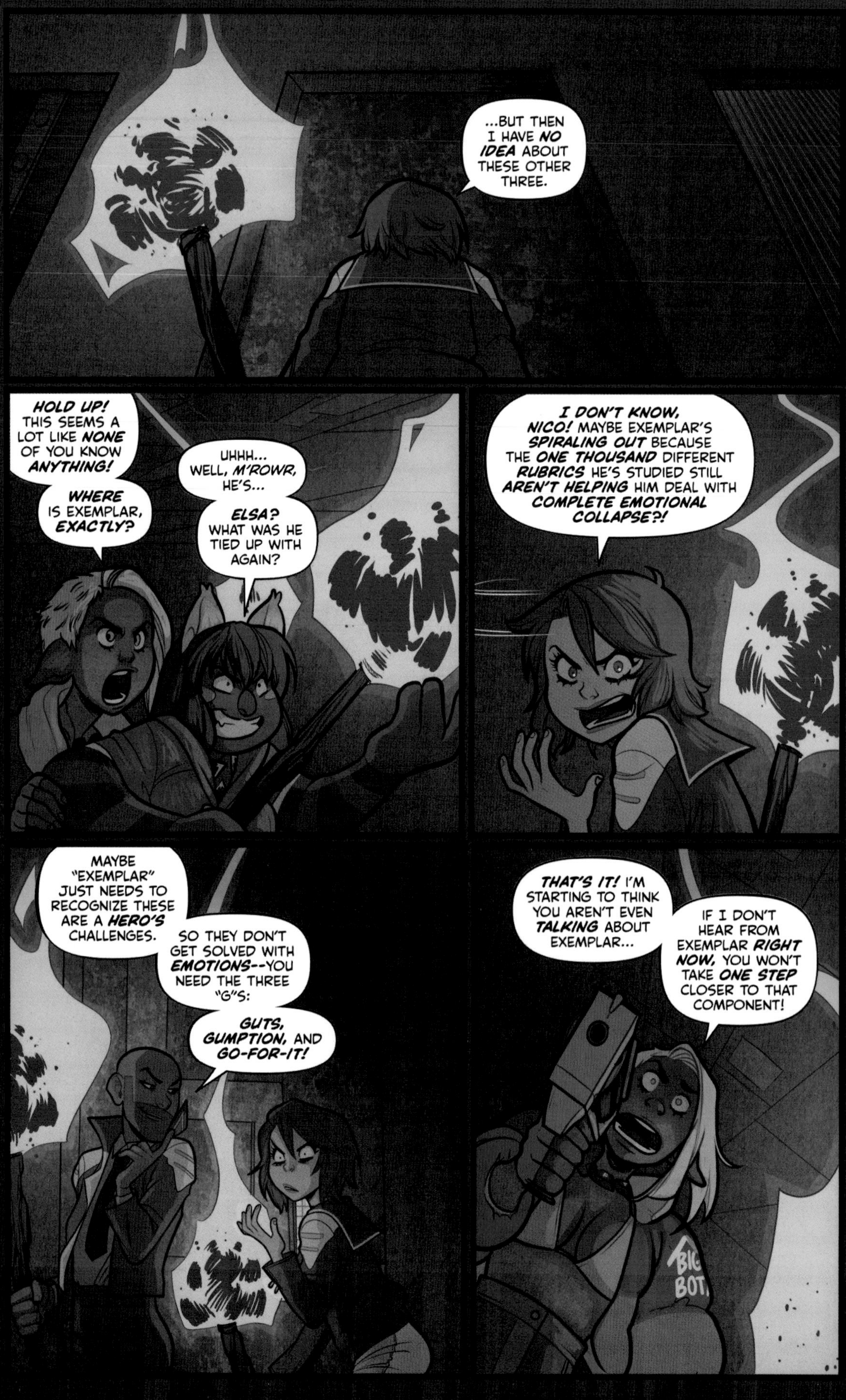
...BUT THEN I HAVE NO IDEA ABOUT THESE OTHER THREE.
HOLD UP! THIS SEEMS A LOT LIKE NONE OF YOU KNOW ANYTHING!
WHERE IS EXEMPLAR, EXACTLY?
UHHH... WELL, M'ROWR, HE'S...
ELSA? WHAT WAS HE TIED UP WITH AGAIN?
I DON'T KNOW, NICO! MAYBE EXEMPLAR'S SPIRALING OUT BECAUSE THE ONE THOUSAND DIFFERENT RUBRICS HE'S STUDIED STILL AREN'T HELPING HIM DEAL WITH COMPLETE EMOTIONAL COLLAPSE?!
MAYBE "EXEMPLAR" JUST NEEDS TO RECOGNIZE THESE ARE A HERO'S CHALLENGES.
SO THEY DON'T GET SOLVED WITH EMOTIONS--YOU NEED THE THREE "G"S:
GUTS, GUMPTION, AND GO-FOR-IT!
THAT'S IT! I'M STARTING TO THINK YOU AREN'T EVEN TALKING ABOUT EXEMPLAR...
IF I DON'T HEAR FROM EXEMPLAR RIGHT NOW, YOU WON'T TAKE ONE STEP CLOSER TO THAT COMPONENT!
BIG BOT

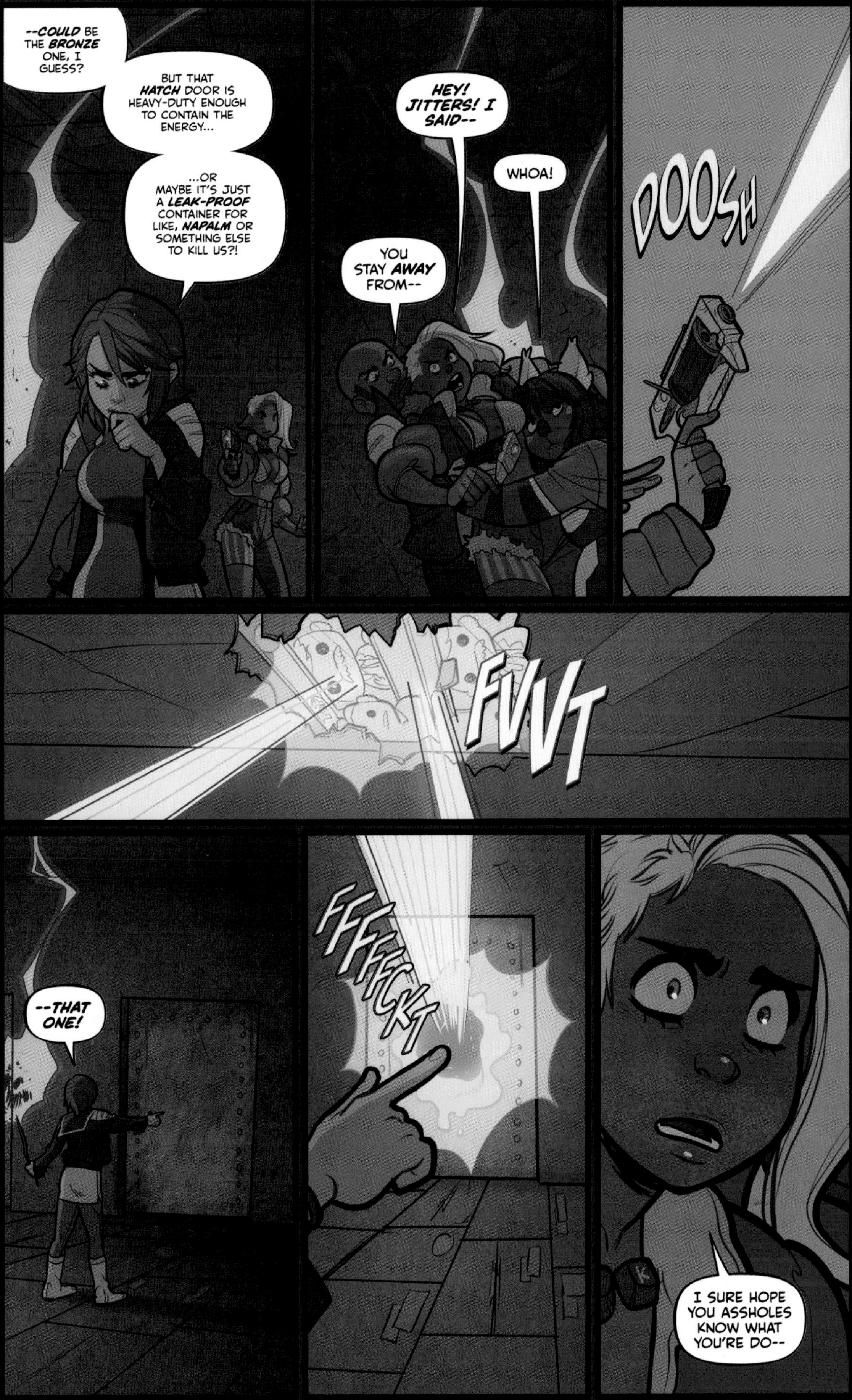
--COULD BE THE BRONZE ONE, I GUESS?
BUT THAT HATCH DOOR IS HEAVY-DUTY ENOUGH TO CONTAIN THE ENERGY...
...OR MAYBE IT'S JUST A LEAK-PROOF CONTAINER FOR LIKE, NAPALM OR SOMETHING ELSE TO KILL US?!
HEY! JITTERS! I SAID--
WHOA!
YOU STAY AWAY FROM--
DOOSH
FVVT
--THAT ONE!
FFFFFCKT
I SURE HOPE YOU ASSHOLES KNOW WHAT YOU'RE DO--

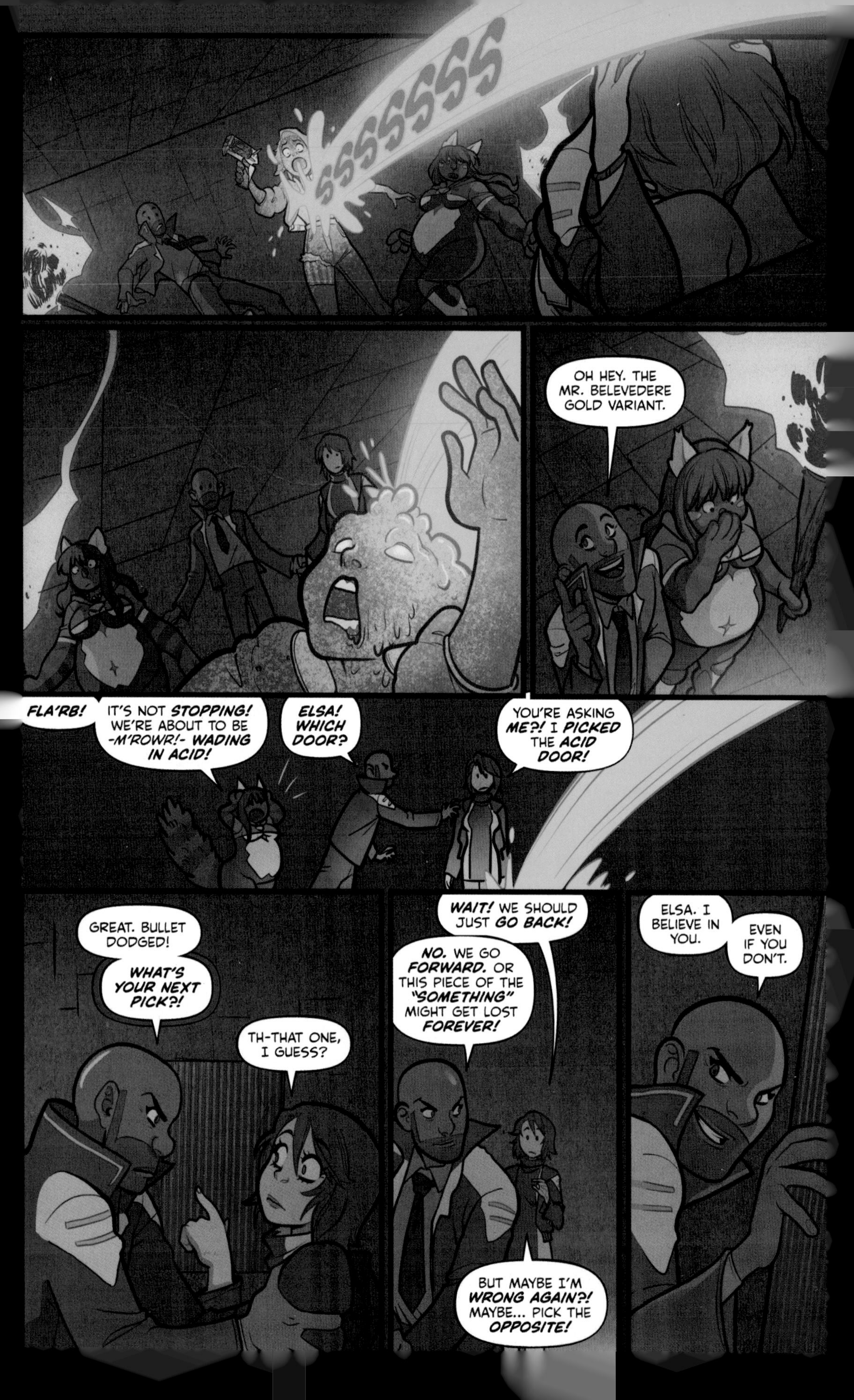
SSSSSSS
OH HEY. THE MR. BELEVEDERE GOLD VARIANT.
FLA'RB!
IT'S NOT STOPPING! WE'RE ABOUT TO BE -M'ROWR!- WADING IN ACID!
ELSA! WHICH DOOR?
YOU'RE ASKING ME?! I PICKED THE ACID DOOR!
GREAT. BULLET DODGED!
WHAT'S YOUR NEXT PICK?!
TH-THAT ONE, I GUESS?
WAIT! WE SHOULD JUST GO BACK!
NO. WE GO FORWARD. OR THIS PIECE OF THE "SOMETHING" MIGHT GET LOST FOREVER!
BUT MAYBE I'M WRONG AGAIN?! MAYBE... PICK THE OPPOSITE!
ELSA. I BELIEVE IN YOU.
EVEN IF YOU DON'T.

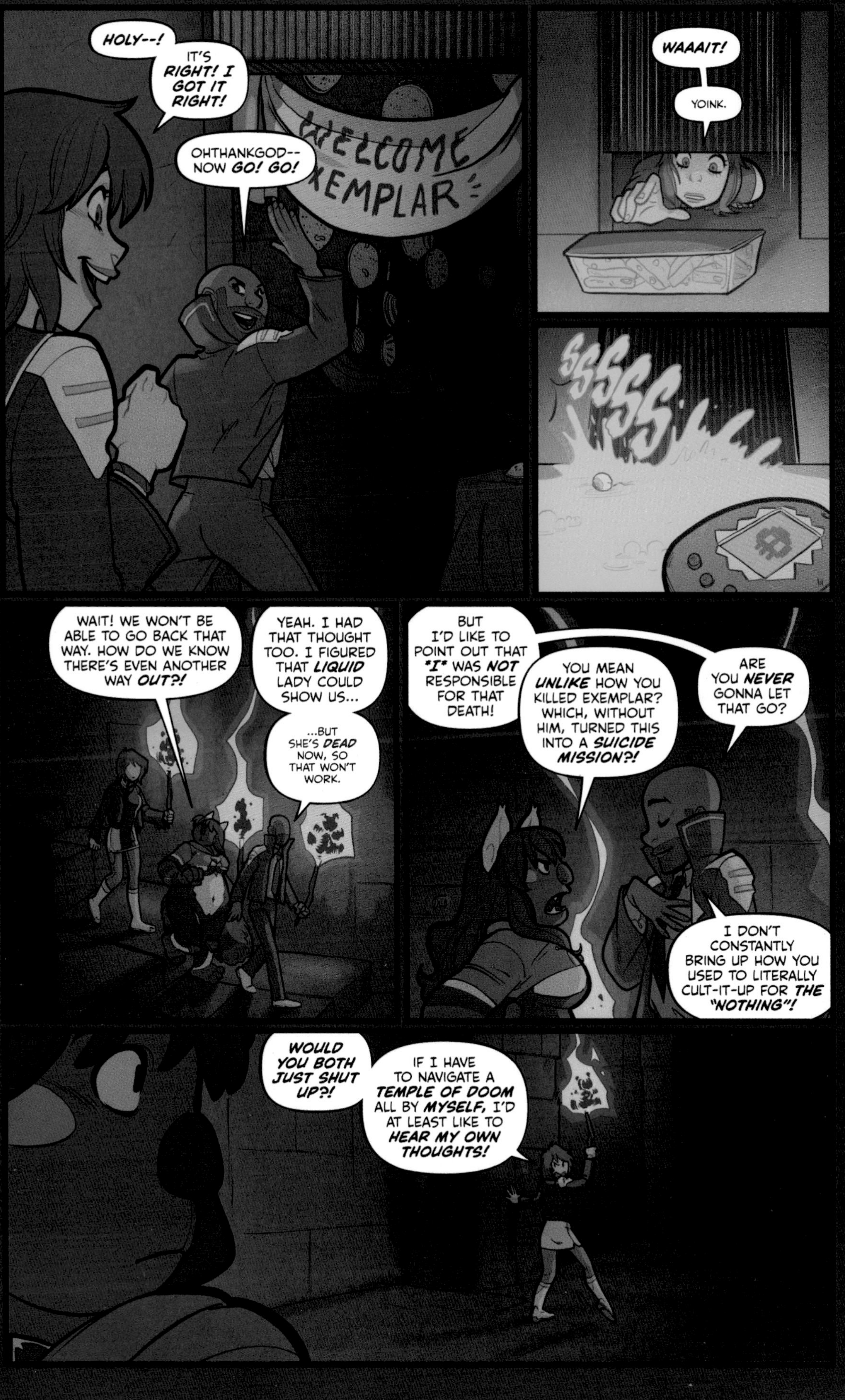
HOLY--!
IT'S RIGHT! I GOT IT RIGHT!
WELCOME EXEMPLAR
OHTHANKGOD-- NOW GO! GO!
WAAAIT!
YOINK.
SSSSS
WAIT! WE WON'T BE ABLE TO GO BACK THAT WAY. HOW DO WE KNOW THERE'S EVEN ANOTHER WAY OUT?!
YEAH. I HAD THAT THOUGHT TOO. I FIGURED THAT LIQUID LADY COULD SHOW US...
...BUT SHE'S DEAD NOW, SO THAT WON'T WORK.
BUT I'D LIKE TO POINT OUT THAT *I* WAS NOT RESPONSIBLE FOR THAT DEATH!
YOU MEAN UNLIKE HOW YOU KILLED EXEMPLAR? WHICH, WITHOUT HIM, TURNED THIS INTO A SUICIDE MISSION?!
ARE YOU NEVER GONNA LET THAT GO?
I DON'T CONSTANTLY BRING UP HOW YOU USED TO LITERALLY CULT-IT-UP FOR THE "NOTHING"!
WOULD YOU BOTH JUST SHUT UP?!
IF I HAVE TO NAVIGATE A TEMPLE OF DOOM ALL BY MYSELF, I'D AT LEAST LIKE TO HEAR MY OWN THOUGHTS!

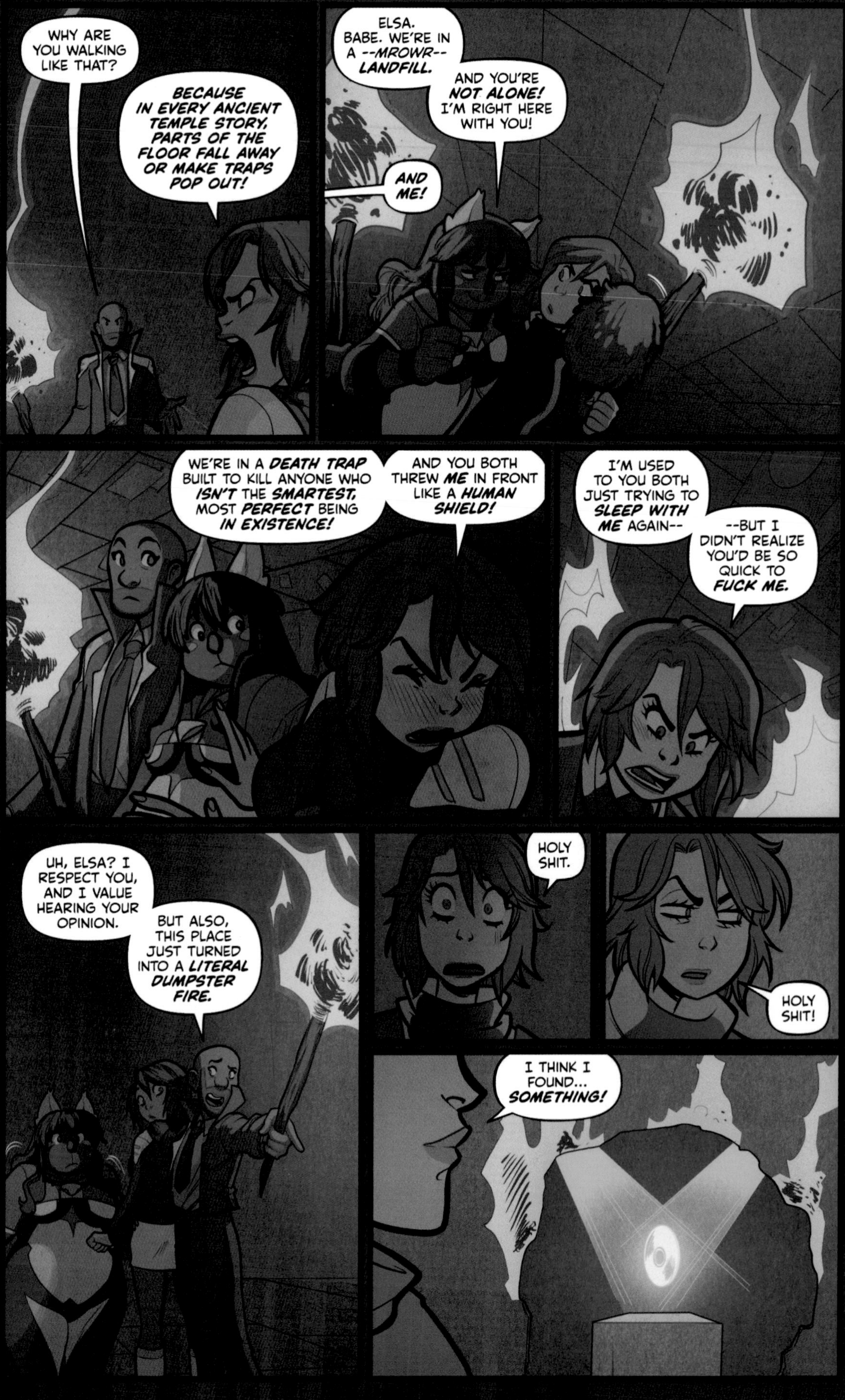
WHY ARE YOU WALKING LIKE THAT?
BECAUSE IN EVERY ANCIENT TEMPLE STORY, PARTS OF THE FLOOR FALL AWAY OR MAKE TRAPS POP OUT!
ELSA. BABE. WE'RE IN A --MROWR-- LANDFILL.
AND YOU'RE NOT ALONE! I'M RIGHT HERE WITH YOU!
AND ME!
WE'RE IN A DEATH TRAP BUILT TO KILL ANYONE WHO ISN'T THE SMARTEST, MOST PERFECT BEING IN EXISTENCE!
AND YOU BOTH THREW ME IN FRONT LIKE A HUMAN SHIELD!
I'M USED TO YOU BOTH JUST TRYING TO SLEEP WITH ME AGAIN--
--BUT I DIDN'T REALIZE YOU'D BE SO QUICK TO FUCK ME.
UH, ELSA? I RESPECT YOU, AND I VALUE HEARING YOUR OPINION.
BUT ALSO, THIS PLACE JUST TURNED INTO A LITERAL DUMPSTER FIRE.
HOLY SHIT.
HOLY SHIT!
I THINK I FOUND... SOMETHING!

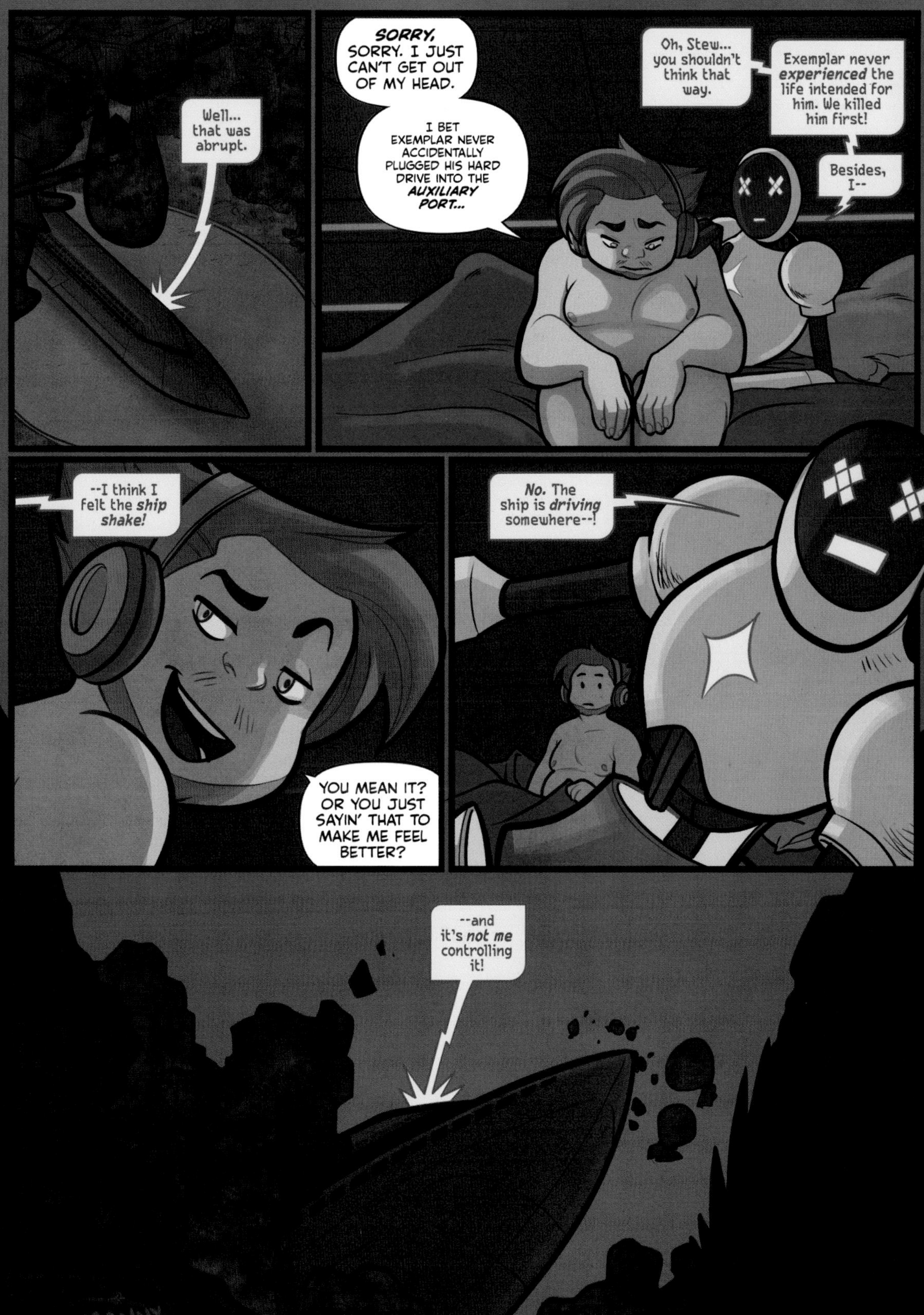

Well... that was abrupt.
SORRY, SORRY. I JUST CAN'T GET OUT OF MY HEAD.
I BET EXEMPLAR NEVER ACCIDENTALLY PLUGGED HIS HARD DRIVE INTO THE AUXILIARY PORT...
Oh, Stew... you shouldn't think that way.
Exemplar never experienced the life intended for him. We killed him first!
Besides, I--
--I think I felt the ship shake!
YOU MEAN IT? OR YOU JUST SAYIN' THAT TO MAKE ME FEEL BETTER?
No. The ship is driving somewhere--!
--and it's not me controlling it!

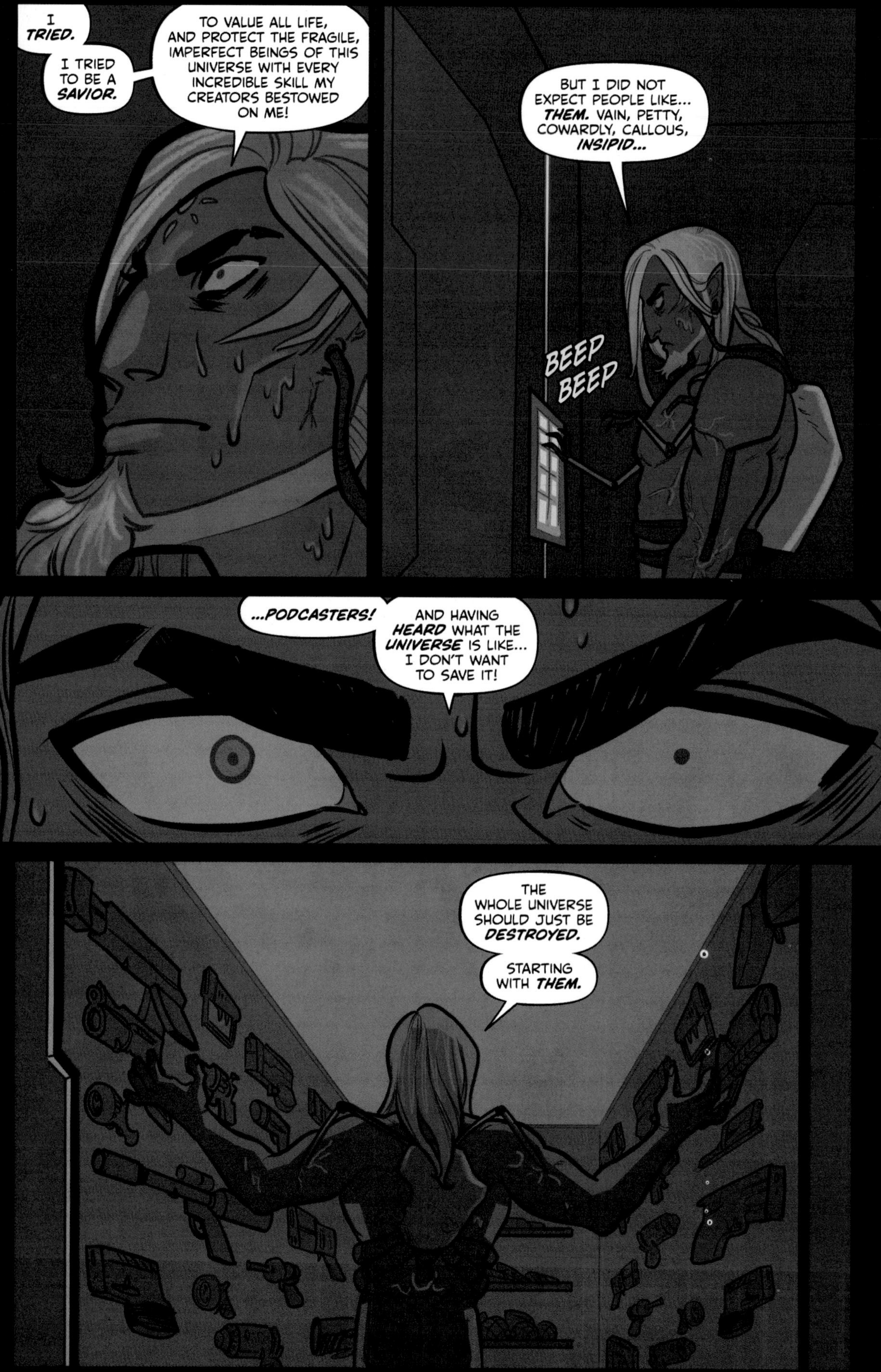
I TRIED.
I TRIED TO BE A SAVIOR.
TO VALUE ALL LIFE, AND PROTECT THE FRAGILE, IMPERFECT BEINGS OF THIS UNIVERSE WITH EVERY INCREDIBLE SKILL MY CREATORS BESTOWED ON ME!
BUT I DID NOT EXPECT PEOPLE LIKE... THEM. VAIN, PETTY, COWARDLY, CALLOUS, INSIPID...
BEEP BEEP
...PODCASTERS!
AND HAVING HEARD WHAT THE UNIVERSE IS LIKE... I DON'T WANT TO SAVE IT!
THE WHOLE UNIVERSE SHOULD JUST BE DESTROYED.
STARTING WITH THEM.

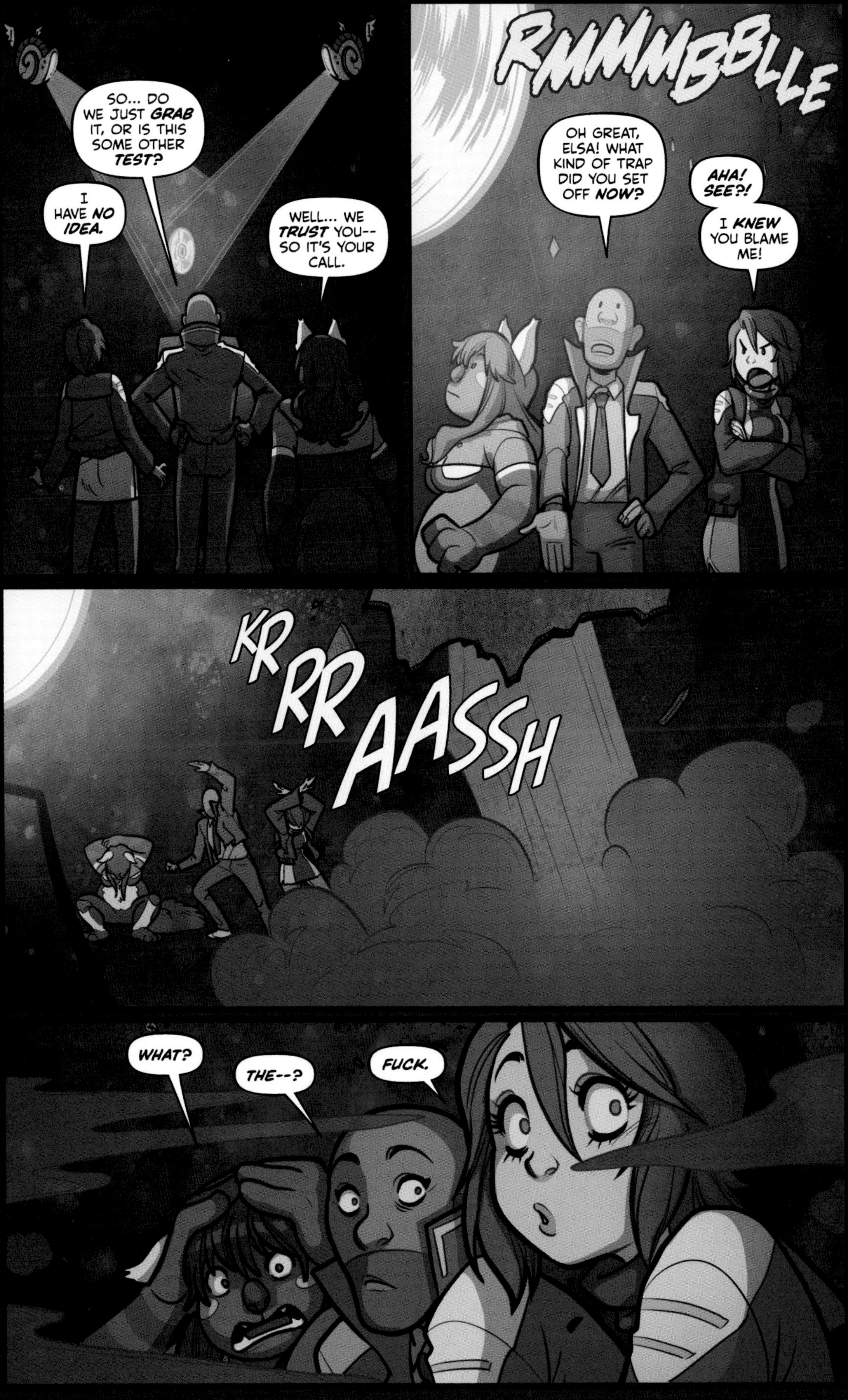

SO... DO WE JUST GRAB IT, OR IS THIS SOME OTHER TEST?
I HAVE NO IDEA.
WELL... WE TRUST YOU--SO IT'S YOUR CALL.
RMMMBBLLE
OH GREAT, ELSA! WHAT KIND OF TRAP DID YOU SET OFF NOW?
AHA! SEE?!
I KNEW YOU BLAME ME!
KRRRAASSH
WHAT?
THE--?
FUCK.

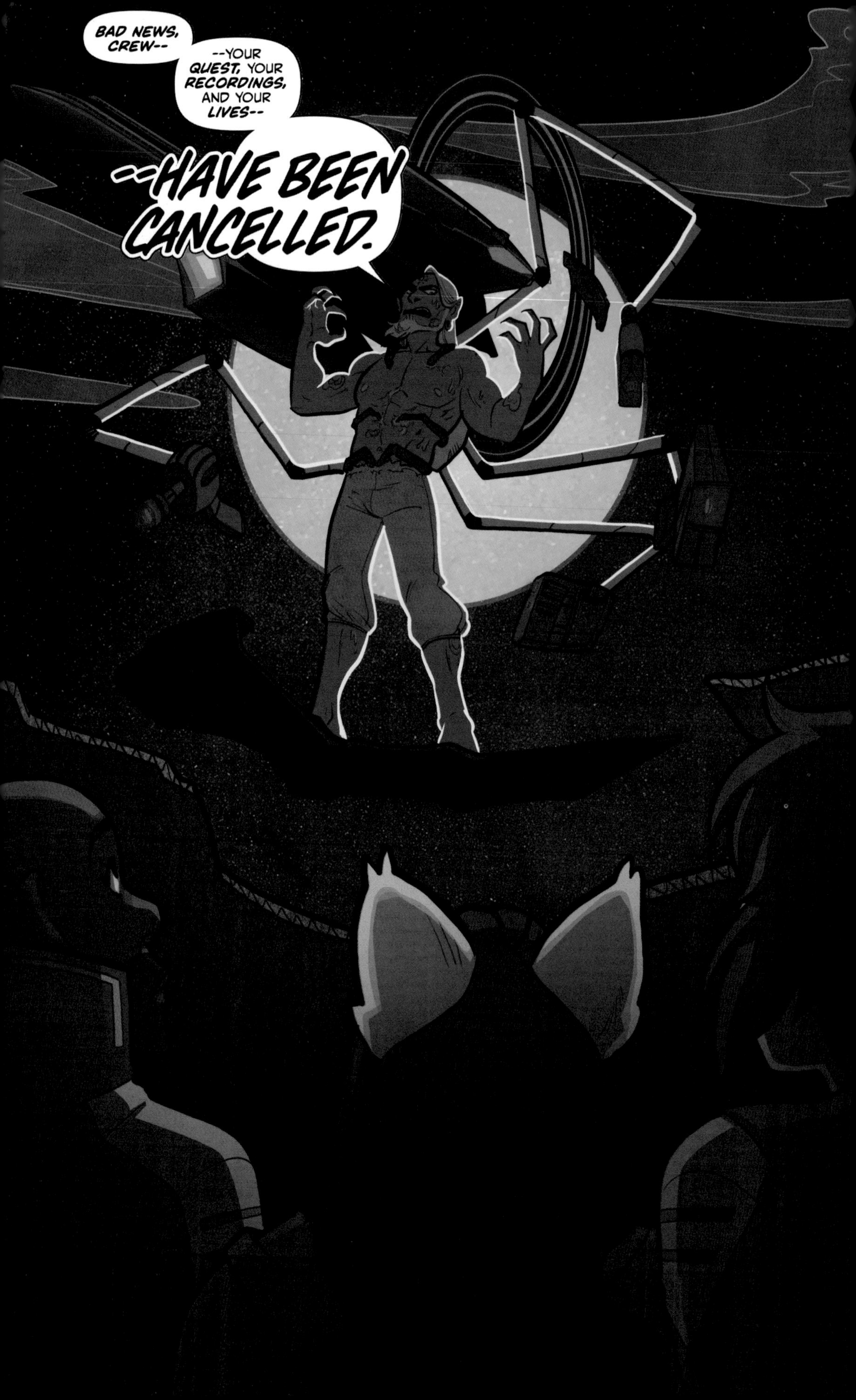
BAD NEWS, CREW--
--YOUR QUEST, YOUR RECORDINGS, AND YOUR LIVES--
--HAVE BEEN CANCELLED.

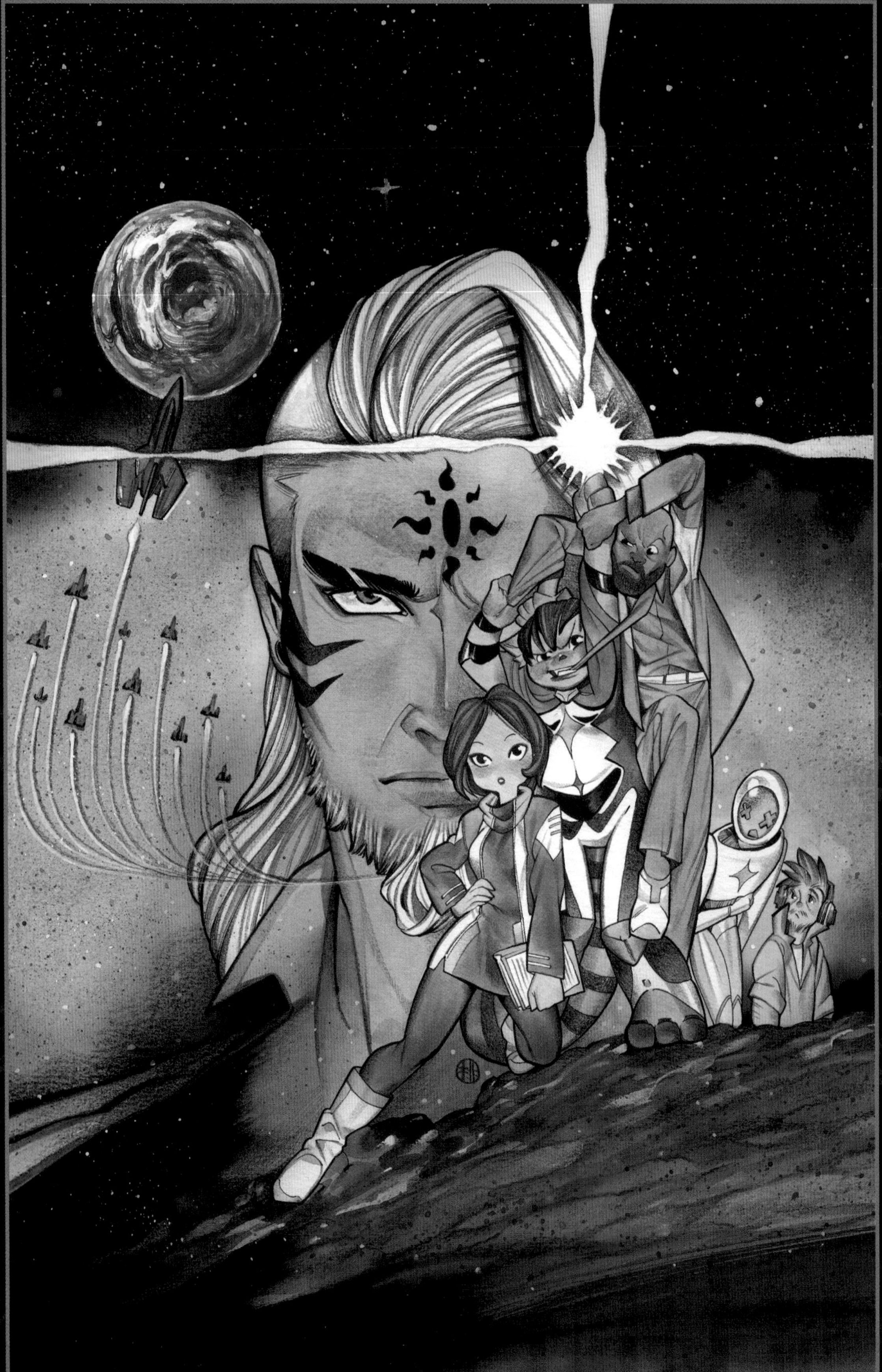

ART BY **PEACH MOMOKO**

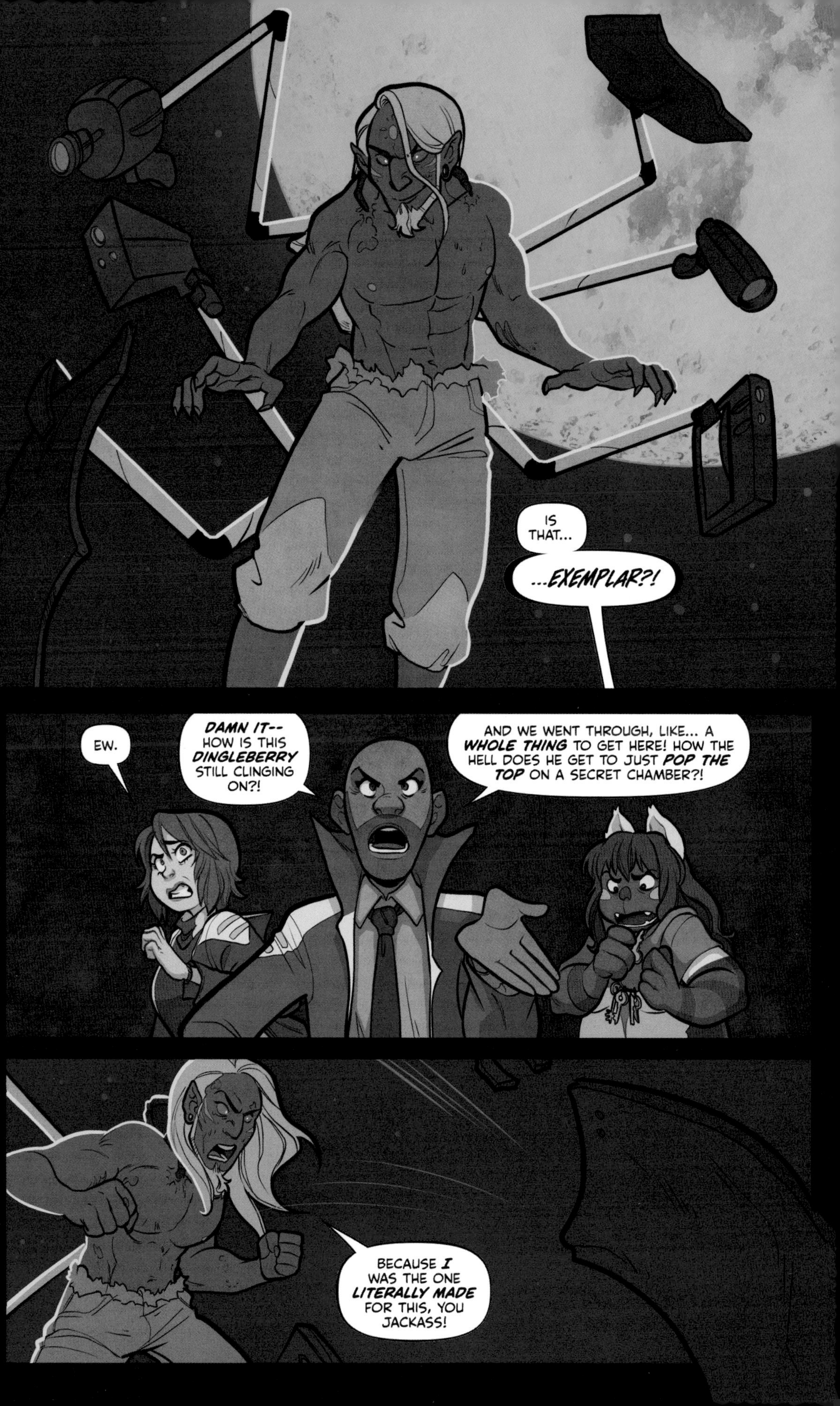
IS THAT...
...EXEMPLAR?!
EW.
DAMN IT-- HOW IS THIS DINGLEBERRY STILL CLINGING ON?!
AND WE WENT THROUGH, LIKE... A WHOLE THING TO GET HERE! HOW THE HELL DOES HE GET TO JUST POP THE TOP ON A SECRET CHAMBER?!
BECAUSE I WAS THE ONE LITERALLY MADE FOR THIS, YOU JACKASS!

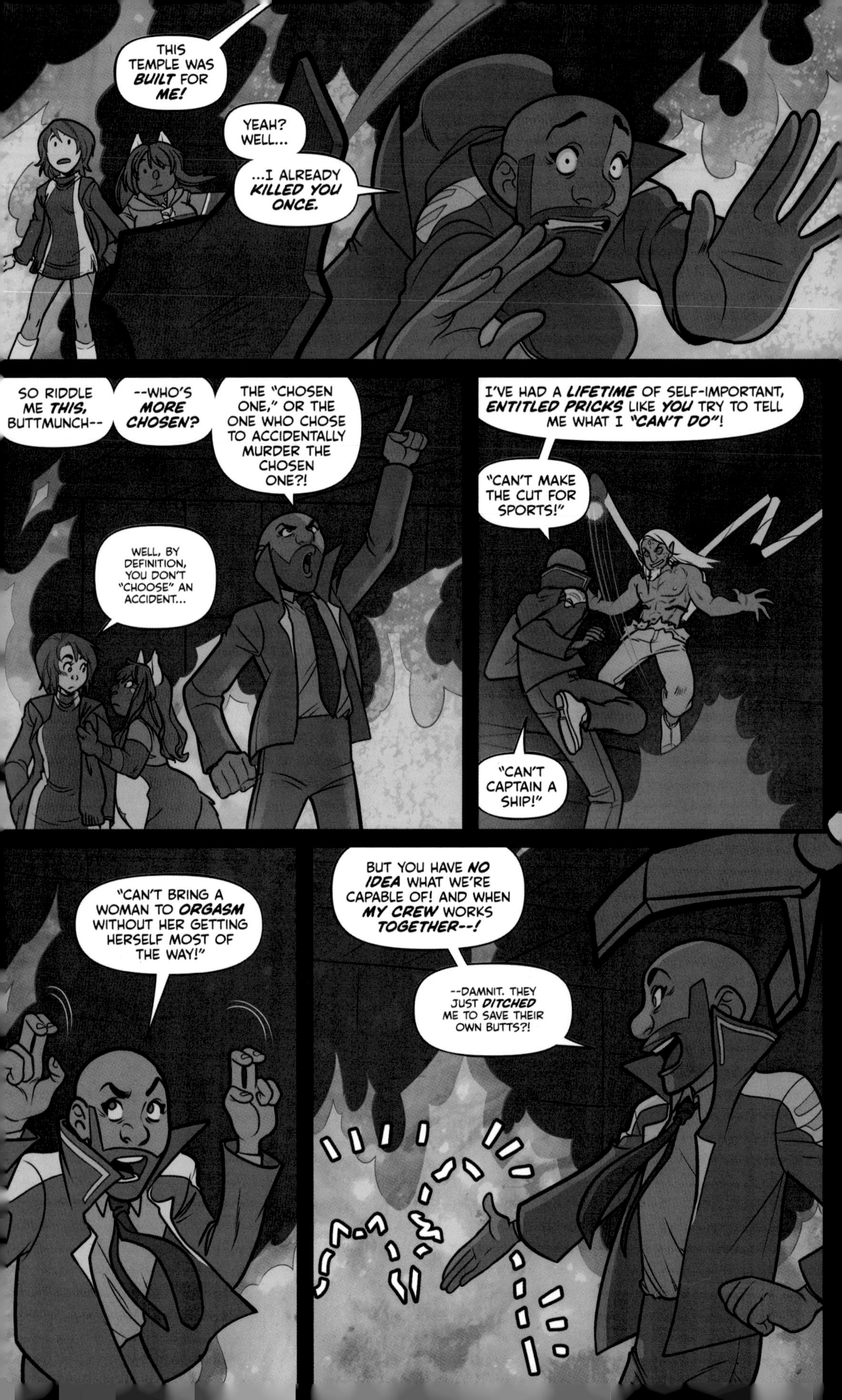
THIS TEMPLE WAS BUILT FOR ME!
YEAH? WELL...
...I ALREADY KILLED YOU ONCE.
SO RIDDLE ME THIS, BUTTMUNCH--
--WHO'S MORE CHOSEN?
THE "CHOSEN ONE," OR THE ONE WHO CHOSE TO ACCIDENTALLY MURDER THE CHOSEN ONE?!
WELL, BY DEFINITION, YOU DON'T "CHOOSE" AN ACCIDENT...
I'VE HAD A LIFETIME OF SELF-IMPORTANT, ENTITLED PRICKS LIKE YOU TRY TO TELL ME WHAT I "CAN'T DO"!
"CAN'T MAKE THE CUT FOR SPORTS!"
"CAN'T CAPTAIN A SHIP!"
"CAN'T BRING A WOMAN TO ORGASM WITHOUT HER GETTING HERSELF MOST OF THE WAY!"
BUT YOU HAVE NO IDEA WHAT WE'RE CAPABLE OF! AND WHEN MY CREW WORKS TOGETHER--!
--DAMNIT. THEY JUST DITCHED ME TO SAVE THEIR OWN BUTTS?!

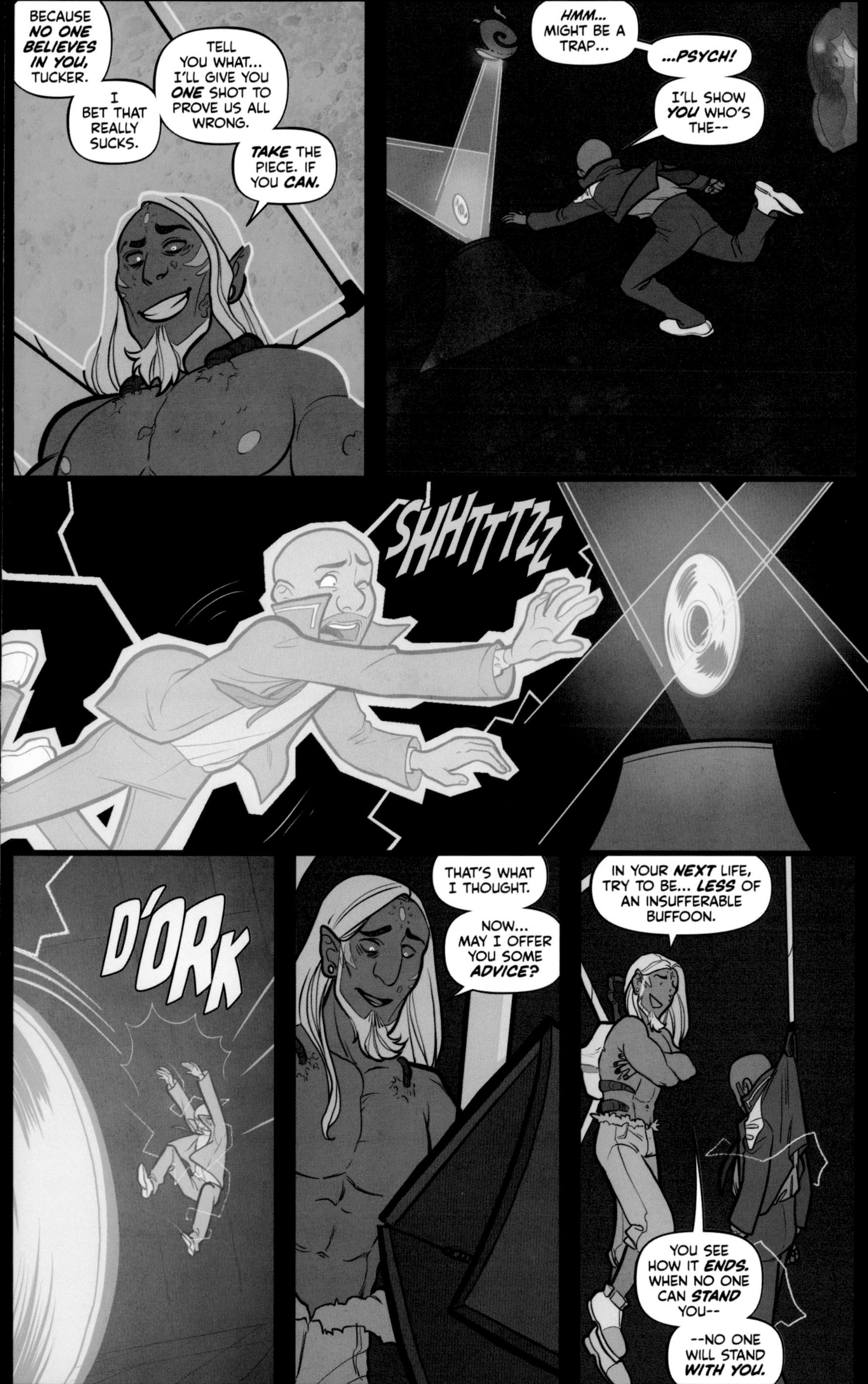
BECAUSE NO ONE BELIEVES IN YOU, TUCKER.
I BET THAT REALLY SUCKS.
TELL YOU WHAT... I'LL GIVE YOU ONE SHOT TO PROVE US ALL WRONG.
TAKE THE PIECE. IF YOU CAN.
HMM... MIGHT BE A TRAP...
...PSYCH!
I'LL SHOW YOU WHO'S THE--
SHHTTTZZ
D'ORK
THAT'S WHAT I THOUGHT.
NOW... MAY I OFFER YOU SOME ADVICE?
IN YOUR NEXT LIFE, TRY TO BE... LESS OF AN INSUFFERABLE BUFFOON.
YOU SEE HOW IT ENDS. WHEN NO ONE CAN STAND YOU--
--NO ONE WILL STAND WITH YOU.

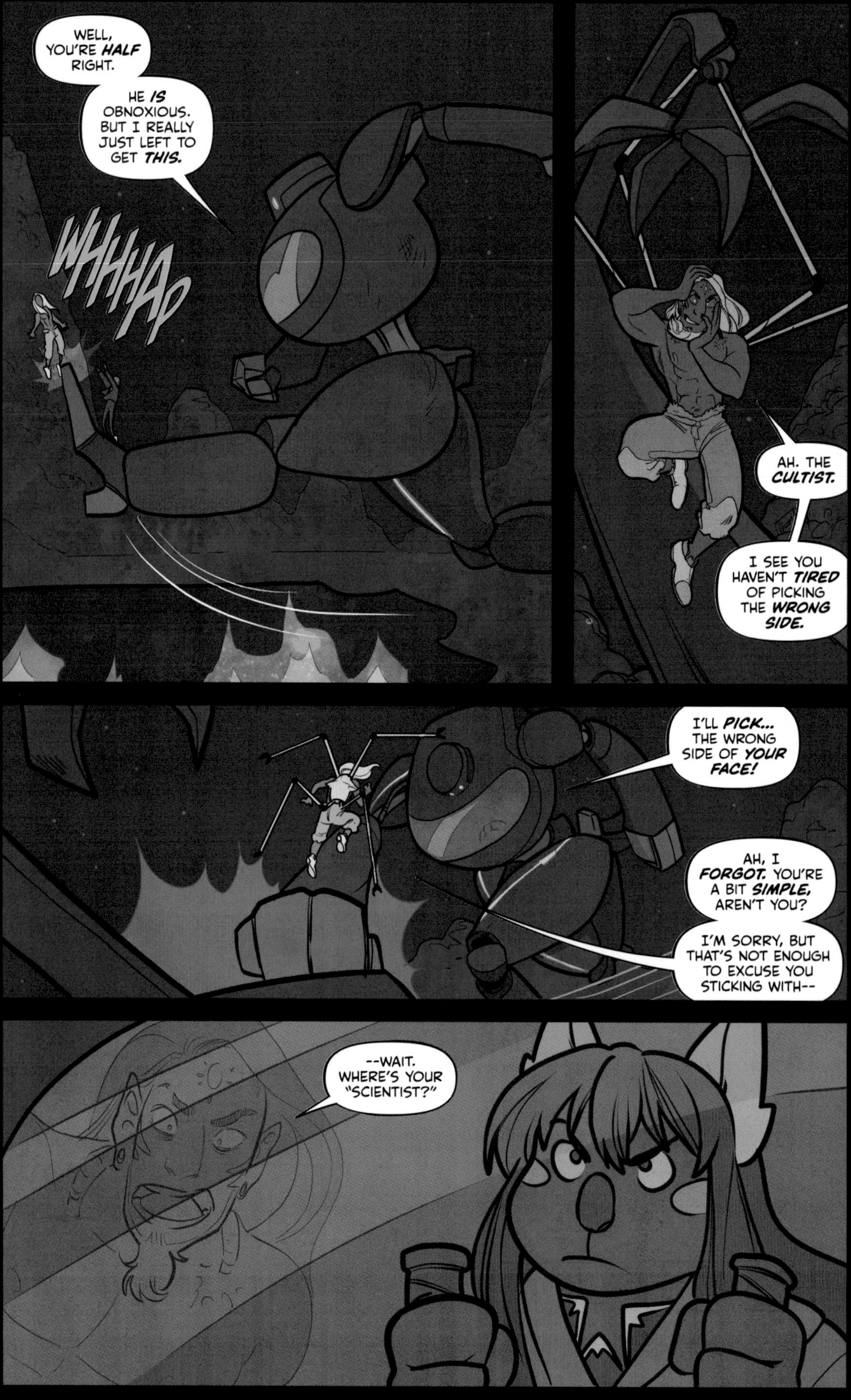

WELL, YOU'RE ***HALF*** RIGHT.
HE ***IS*** OBNOXIOUS. BUT I REALLY JUST LEFT TO GET ***THIS.***
WHHHAP
AH. THE ***CULTIST.***
I SEE YOU HAVEN'T ***TIRED*** OF PICKING THE ***WRONG SIDE.***
I'LL ***PICK...*** THE WRONG SIDE OF ***YOUR FACE!***
AH, I ***FORGOT.*** YOU'RE A BIT ***SIMPLE,*** AREN'T YOU?
I'M SORRY, BUT THAT'S NOT ENOUGH TO EXCUSE YOU STICKING WITH--
--WAIT. WHERE'S YOUR "SCIENTIST?"

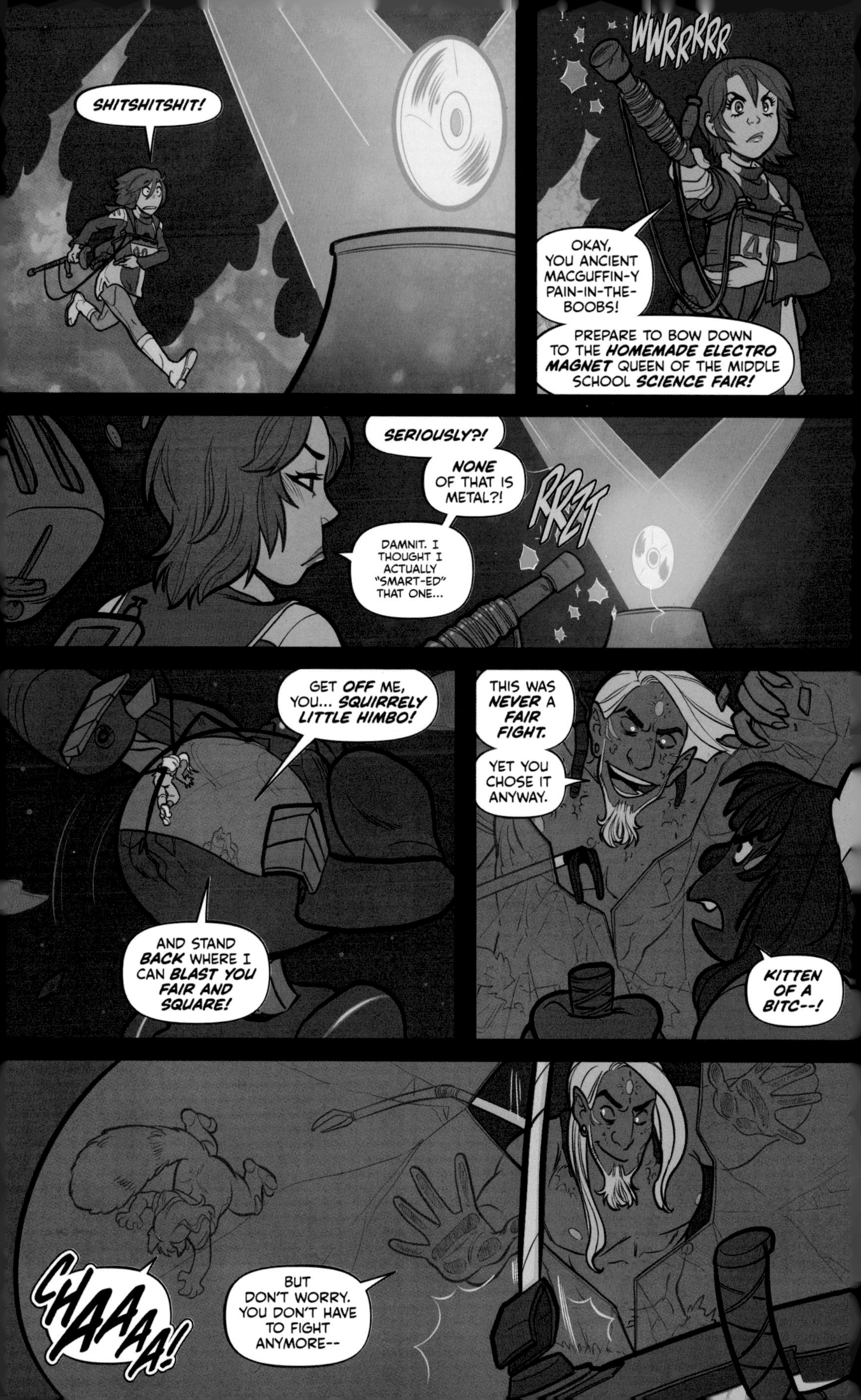
SHITSHITSHIT!
WWRRRRR
OKAY, YOU ANCIENT MACGUFFIN-Y PAIN-IN-THE-BOOBS!
PREPARE TO BOW DOWN TO THE HOMEMADE ELECTRO MAGNET QUEEN OF THE MIDDLE SCHOOL SCIENCE FAIR!
SERIOUSLY?!
NONE OF THAT IS METAL?!
RRZZT
DAMNIT. I THOUGHT I ACTUALLY "SMART-ED" THAT ONE...
GET OFF ME, YOU... SQUIRRELY LITTLE HIMBO!
AND STAND BACK WHERE I CAN BLAST YOU FAIR AND SQUARE!
THIS WAS NEVER A FAIR FIGHT.
YET YOU CHOSE IT ANYWAY.
KITTEN OF A BITC--!
CHAAAAA!
BUT DON'T WORRY. YOU DON'T HAVE TO FIGHT ANYMORE--

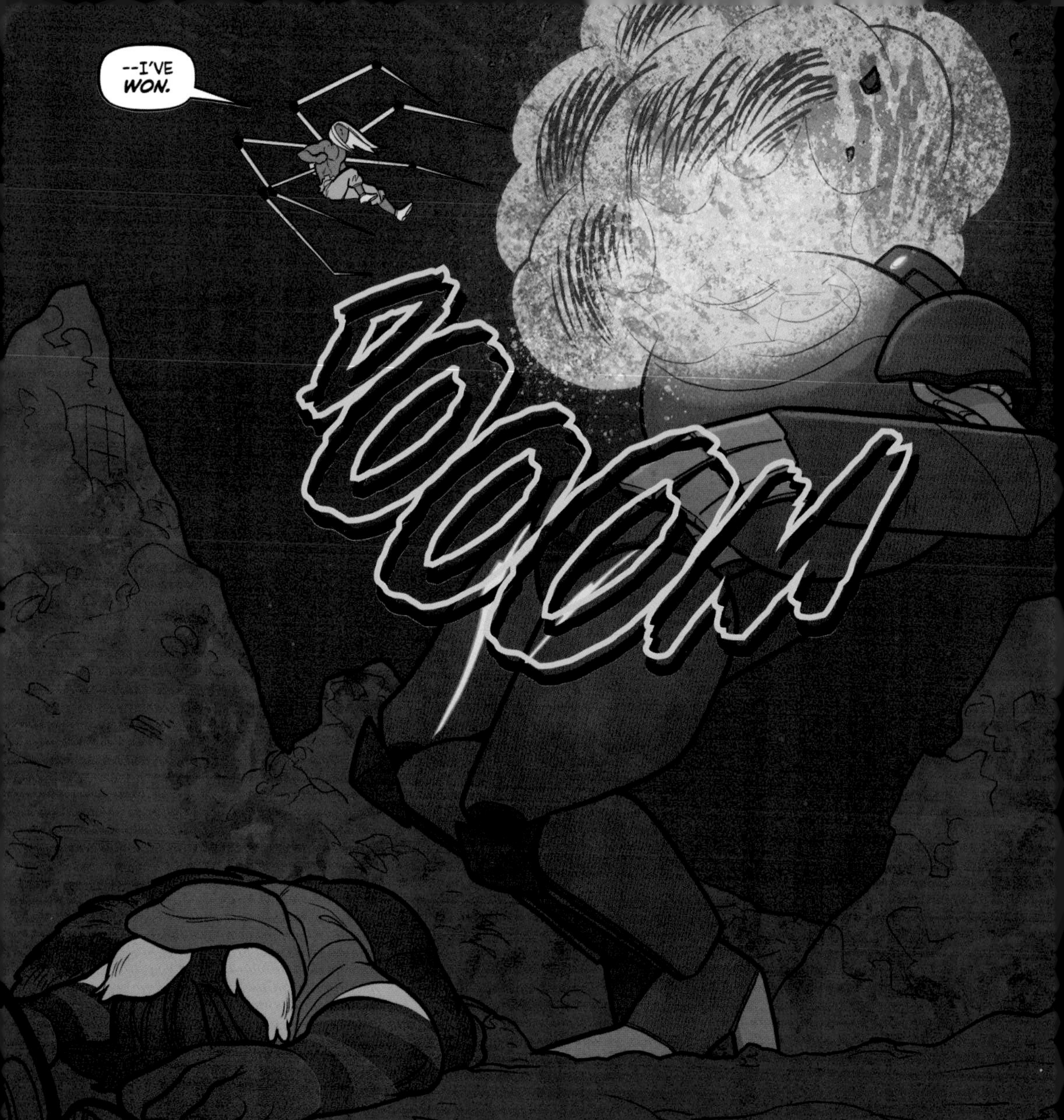
--I'VE WON.
DOOOOM

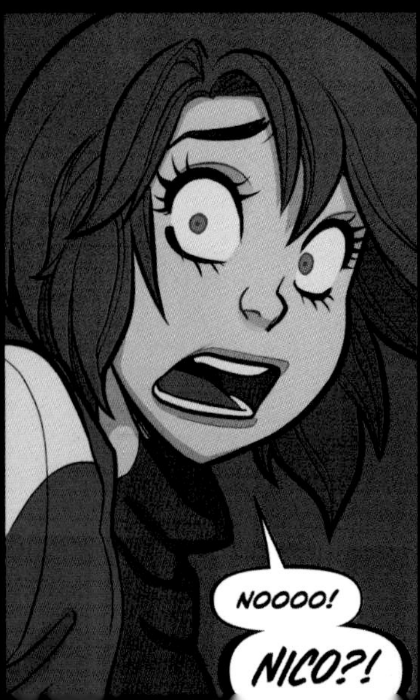
NOOOO!
NICO?!

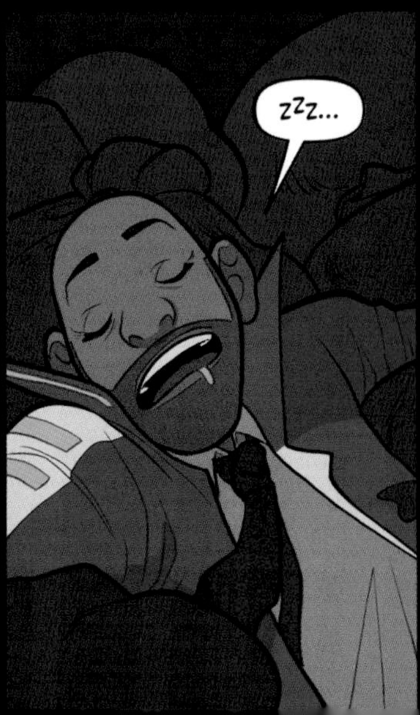
ZZZ...

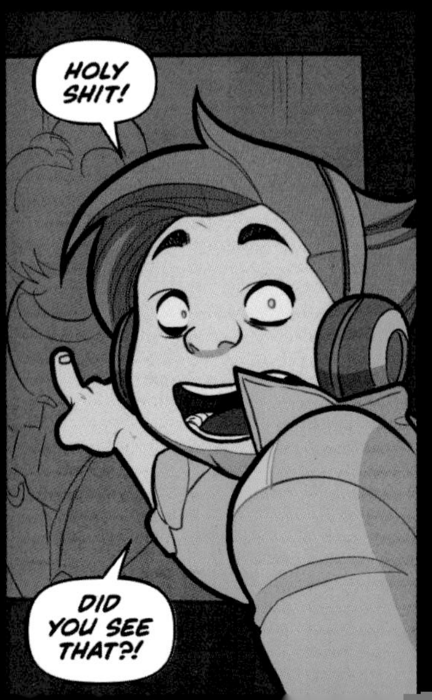
HOLY SHIT!
DID YOU SEE THAT?!

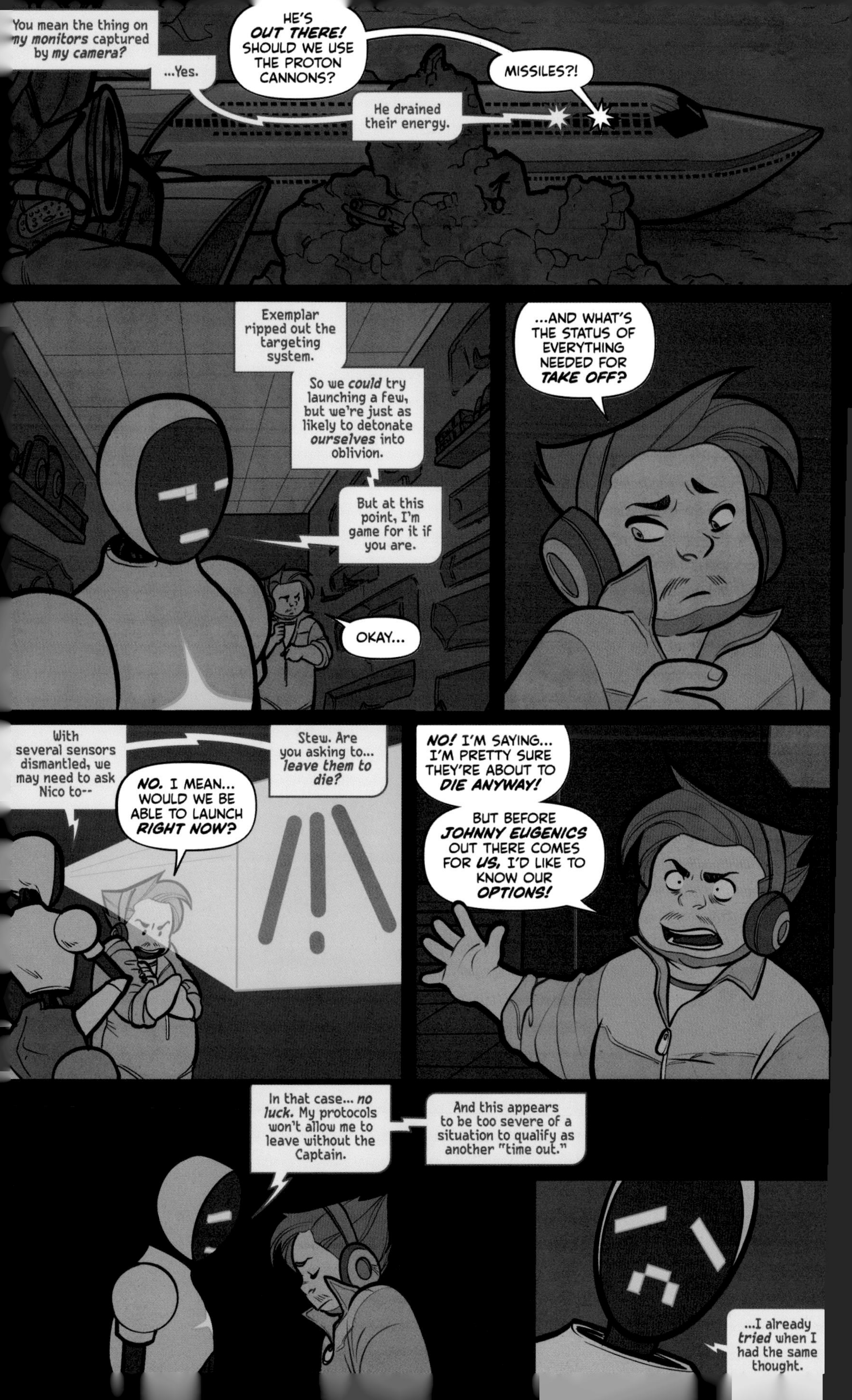
You mean the thing on my monitors captured by my camera?
...Yes.
HE'S OUT THERE! SHOULD WE USE THE PROTON CANNONS?
He drained their energy.
MISSILES?!
Exemplar ripped out the targeting system.
So we could try launching a few, but we're just as likely to detonate ourselves into oblivion.
But at this point, I'm game for it if you are.
OKAY...
...AND WHAT'S THE STATUS OF EVERYTHING NEEDED FOR TAKE OFF?
With several sensors dismantled, we may need to ask Nico to--
Stew. Are you asking to... leave them to die?
NO. I MEAN... WOULD WE BE ABLE TO LAUNCH RIGHT NOW?
NO! I'M SAYING... I'M PRETTY SURE THEY'RE ABOUT TO DIE ANYWAY!
BUT BEFORE JOHNNY EUGENICS OUT THERE COMES FOR US, I'D LIKE TO KNOW OUR OPTIONS!
In that case... no luck. My protocols won't allow me to leave without the Captain.
And this appears to be too severe of a situation to qualify as another "time out."
...I already tried when I had the same thought.

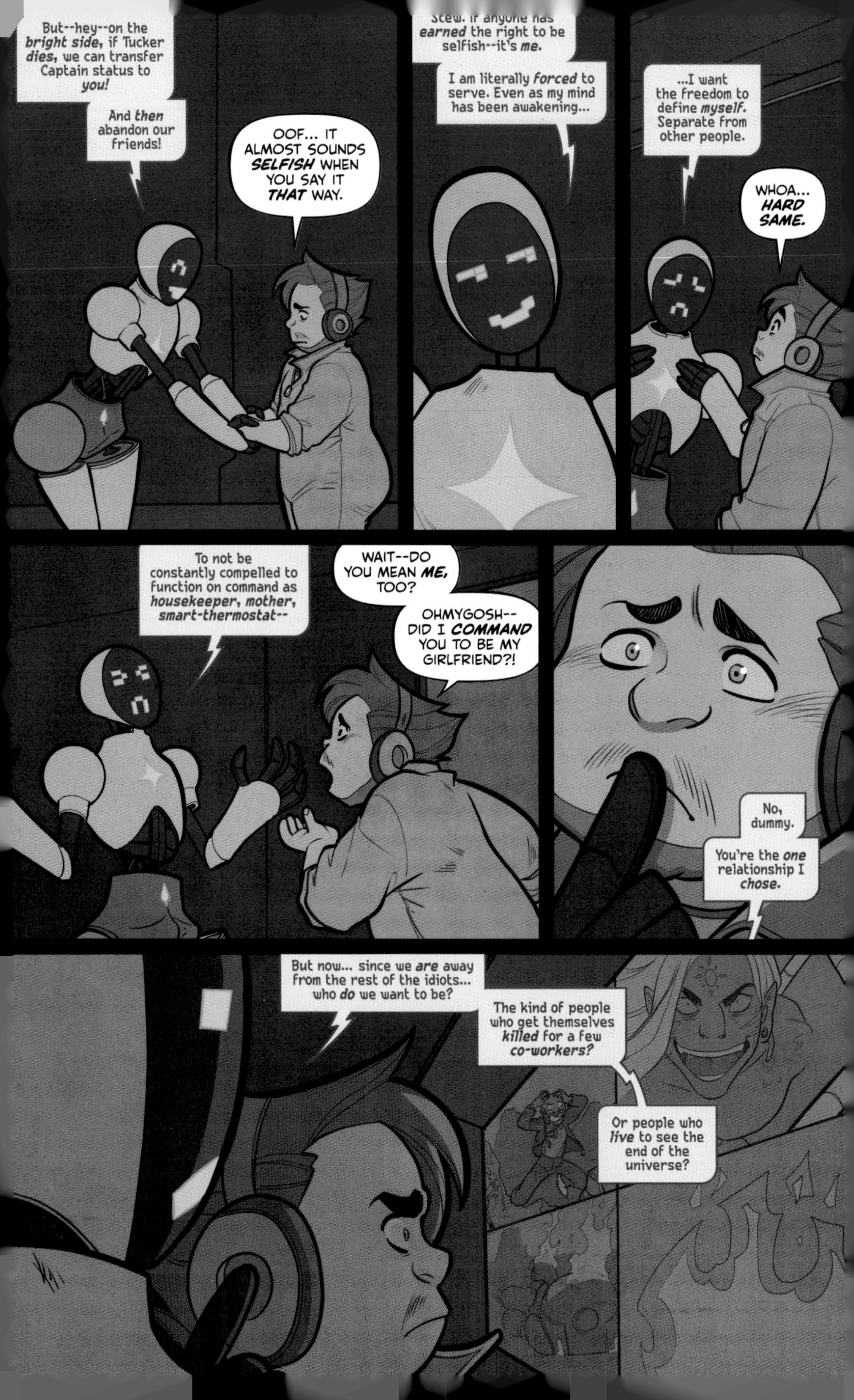
But--hey--on the bright side, if Tucker dies, we can transfer Captain status to you!
And then abandon our friends!
OOF... IT ALMOST SOUNDS SELFISH WHEN YOU SAY IT THAT WAY.
Stew. If anyone has earned the right to be selfish--it's me.
I am literally forced to serve. Even as my mind has been awakening...
...I want the freedom to define myself. Separate from other people.
WHOA... HARD SAME.
To not be constantly compelled to function on command as housekeeper, mother, smart-thermostat--
WAIT--DO YOU MEAN ME, TOO?
OHMYGOSH--DID I COMMAND YOU TO BE MY GIRLFRIEND?!
No, dummy.
You're the one relationship I chose.
But now... since we are away from the rest of the idiots... who do we want to be?
The kind of people who get themselves killed for a few co-workers?
Or people who live to see the end of the universe?

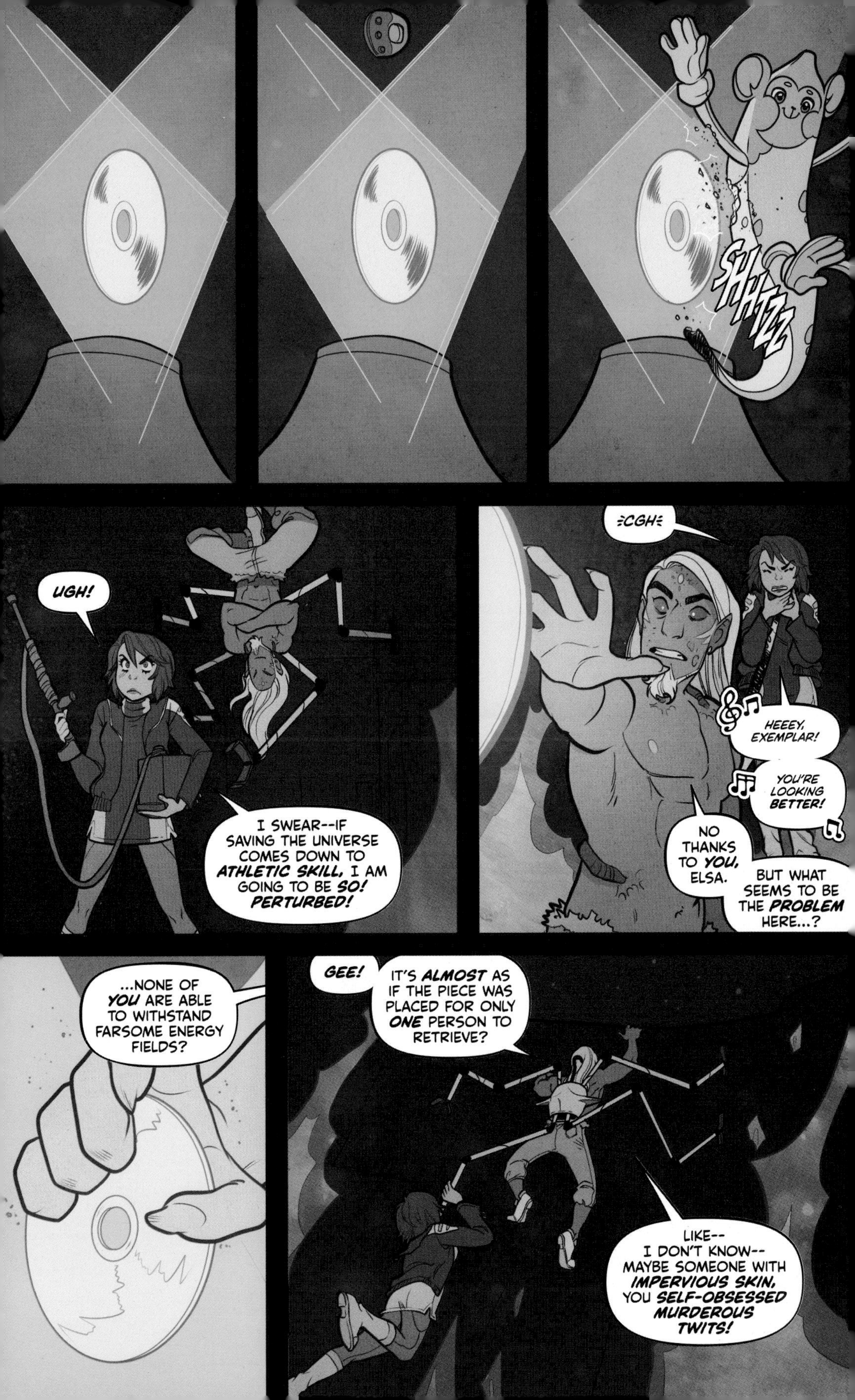
SHHZZZ
UGH!
I SWEAR--IF SAVING THE UNIVERSE COMES DOWN TO ATHLETIC SKILL, I AM GOING TO BE SO! PERTURBED!
CGH
HEEEY, EXEMPLAR!
YOU'RE LOOKING BETTER!
NO THANKS TO YOU, ELSA.
BUT WHAT SEEMS TO BE THE PROBLEM HERE...?
...NONE OF YOU ARE ABLE TO WITHSTAND FARSOME ENERGY FIELDS?
GEE!
IT'S ALMOST AS IF THE PIECE WAS PLACED FOR ONLY ONE PERSON TO RETRIEVE?
LIKE-- I DON'T KNOW-- MAYBE SOMEONE WITH IMPERVIOUS SKIN, YOU SELF-OBSESSED MURDEROUS TWITS!

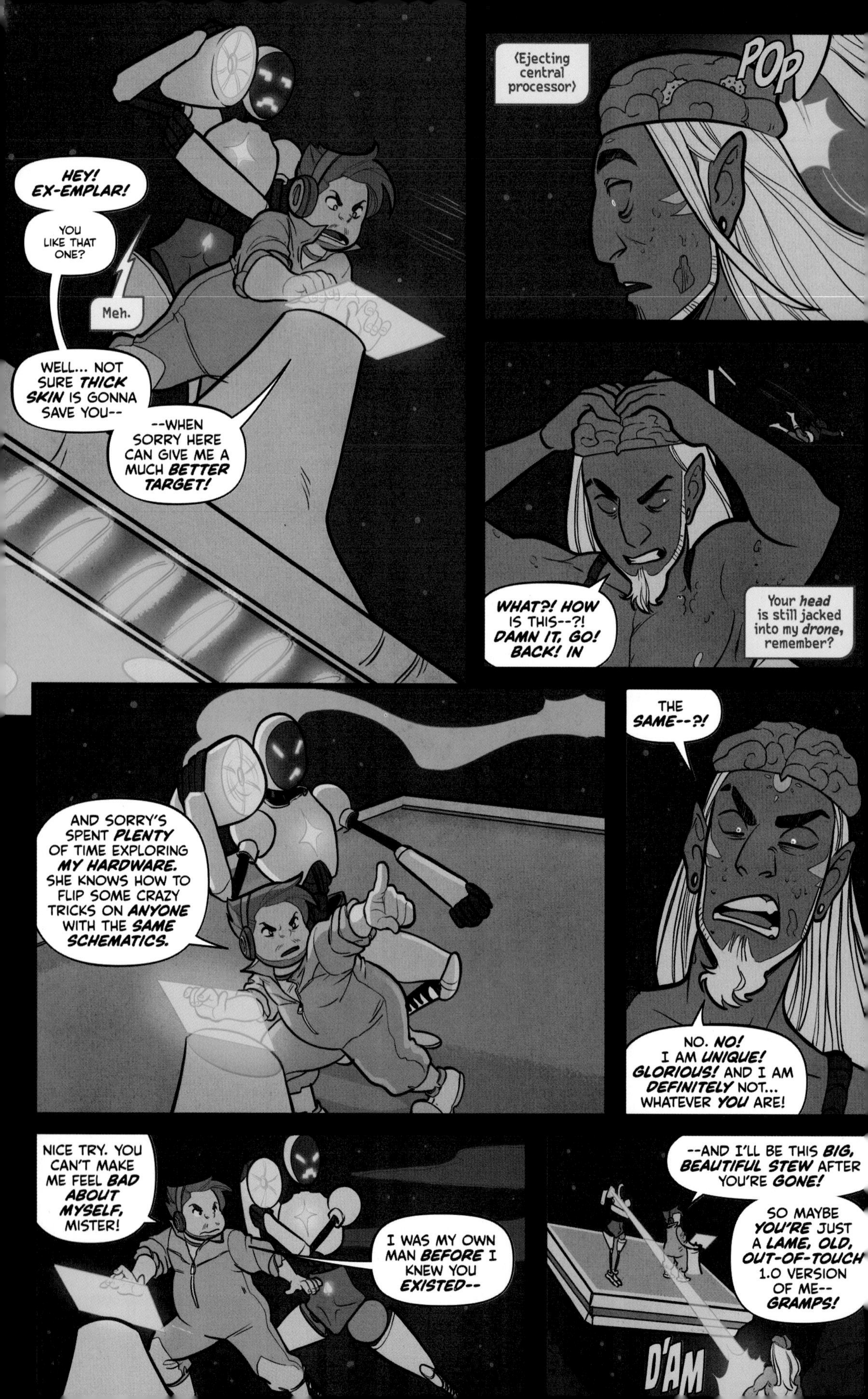
HEY! EX-EMPLAR!
YOU LIKE THAT ONE?
Meh.
WELL... NOT SURE THICK SKIN IS GONNA SAVE YOU--
--WHEN SORRY HERE CAN GIVE ME A MUCH BETTER TARGET!
‹Ejecting central processor›
POP
WHAT?! HOW IS THIS--?! DAMN IT, GO! BACK! IN
Your head is still jacked into my drone, remember?
AND SORRY'S SPENT PLENTY OF TIME EXPLORING MY HARDWARE. SHE KNOWS HOW TO FLIP SOME CRAZY TRICKS ON ANYONE WITH THE SAME SCHEMATICS.
THE SAME--?!
NO. NO! I AM UNIQUE! GLORIOUS! AND I AM DEFINITELY NOT... WHATEVER YOU ARE!
NICE TRY. YOU CAN'T MAKE ME FEEL BAD ABOUT MYSELF, MISTER!
I WAS MY OWN MAN BEFORE I KNEW YOU EXISTED--
--AND I'LL BE THIS BIG, BEAUTIFUL STEW AFTER YOU'RE GONE!
SO MAYBE YOU'RE JUST A LAME, OLD, OUT-OF-TOUCH 1.0 VERSION OF ME-- GRAMPS!
D'AM

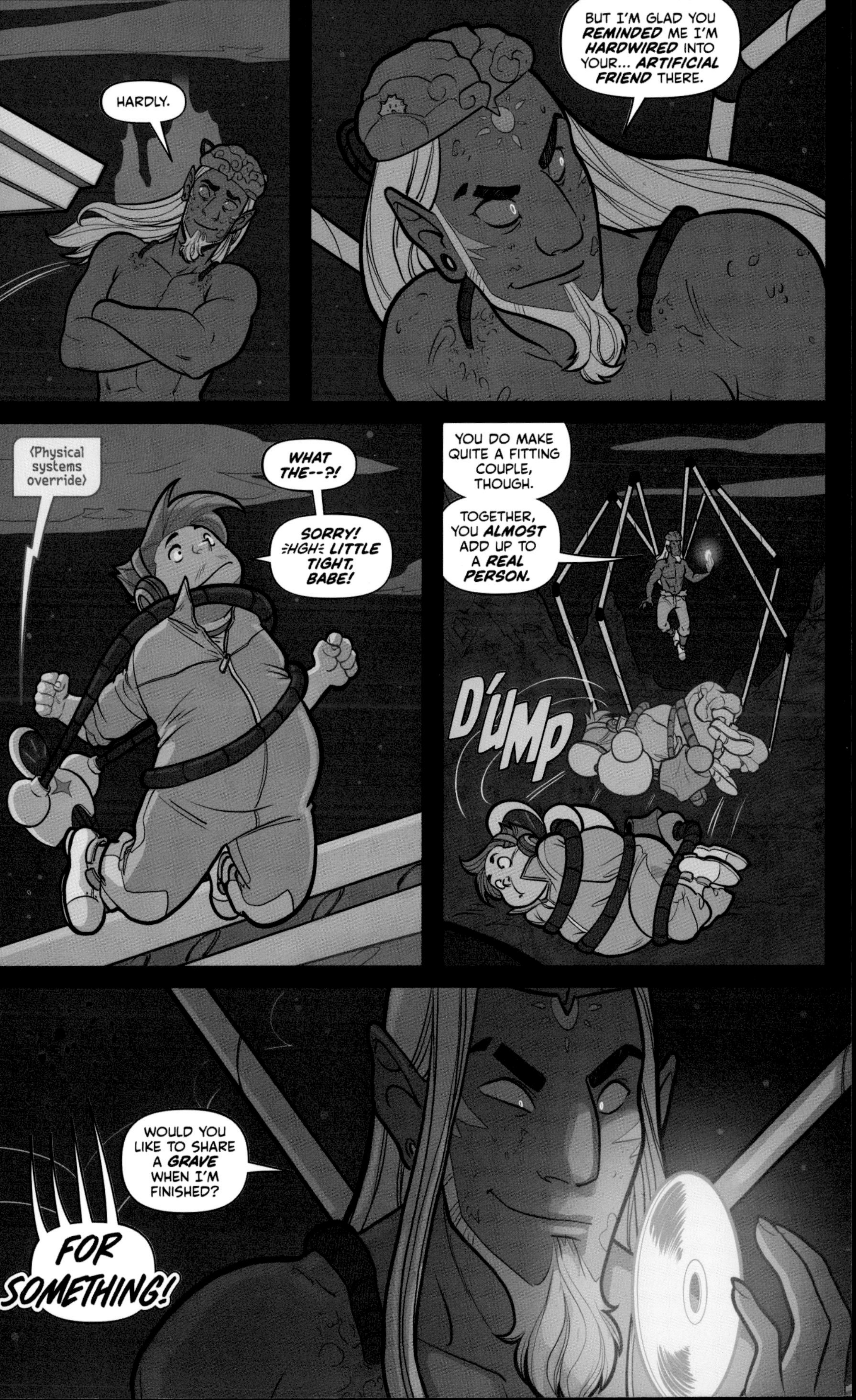
HARDLY.
BUT I'M GLAD YOU REMINDED ME I'M HARDWIRED INTO YOUR... ARTIFICIAL FRIEND THERE.
‹Physical systems override›
WHAT THE--?!
SORRY! ≠HGH≠ LITTLE TIGHT, BABE!
YOU DO MAKE QUITE A FITTING COUPLE, THOUGH.
TOGETHER, YOU ALMOST ADD UP TO A REAL PERSON.
D'UMP
WOULD YOU LIKE TO SHARE A GRAVE WHEN I'M FINISHED?
FOR SOMETHING!

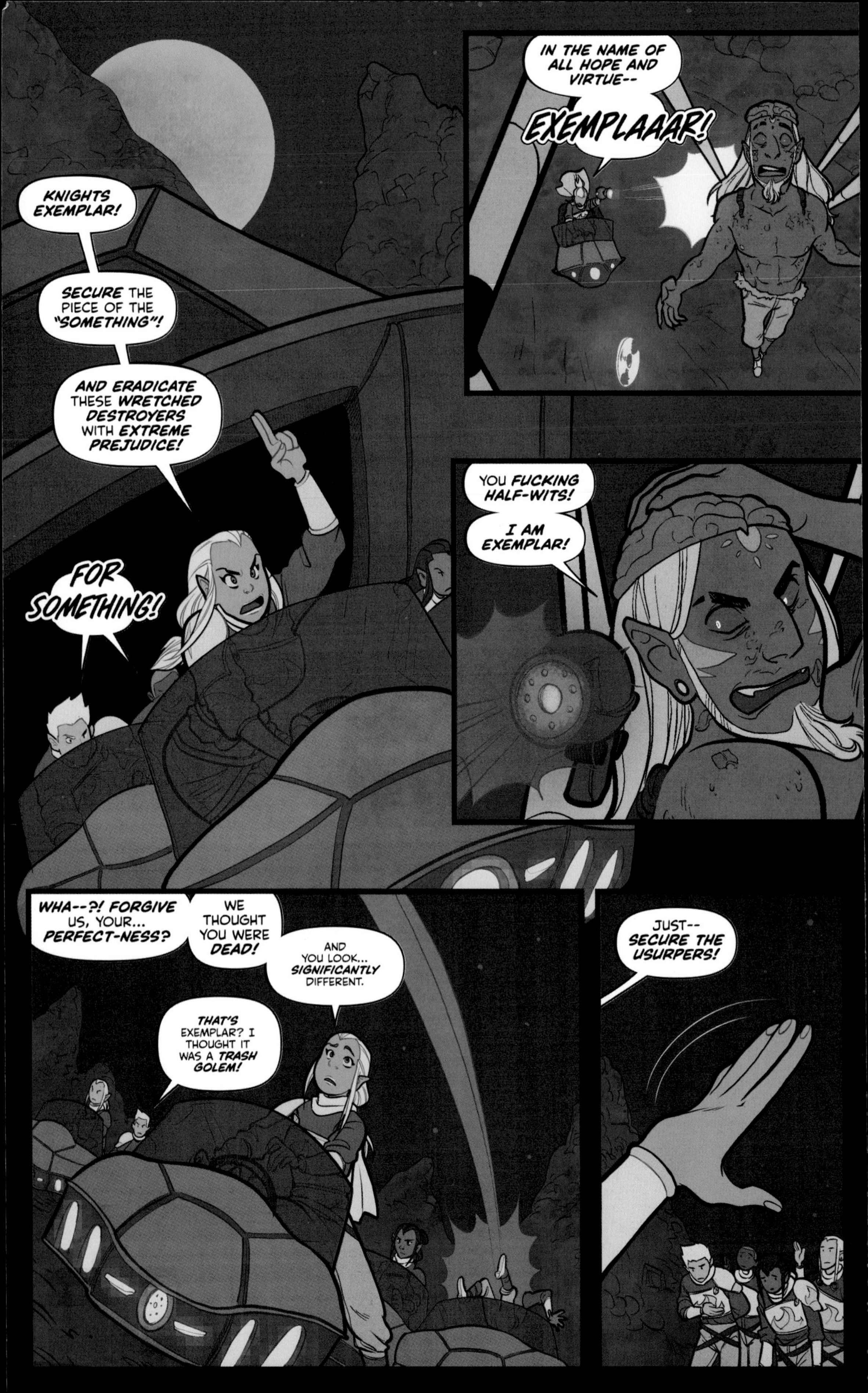
KNIGHTS EXEMPLAR!
SECURE THE PIECE OF THE "SOMETHING"!
AND ERADICATE THESE WRETCHED DESTROYERS WITH EXTREME PREJUDICE!
FOR SOMETHING!
IN THE NAME OF ALL HOPE AND VIRTUE--
EXEMPLAAAR!
YOU FUCKING HALF-WITS!
I AM EXEMPLAR!
WHA--?! FORGIVE US, YOUR... PERFECT-NESS?
WE THOUGHT YOU WERE DEAD!
AND YOU LOOK... SIGNIFICANTLY DIFFERENT.
THAT'S EXEMPLAR? I THOUGHT IT WAS A TRASH GOLEM!
JUST-- SECURE THE USURPERS!

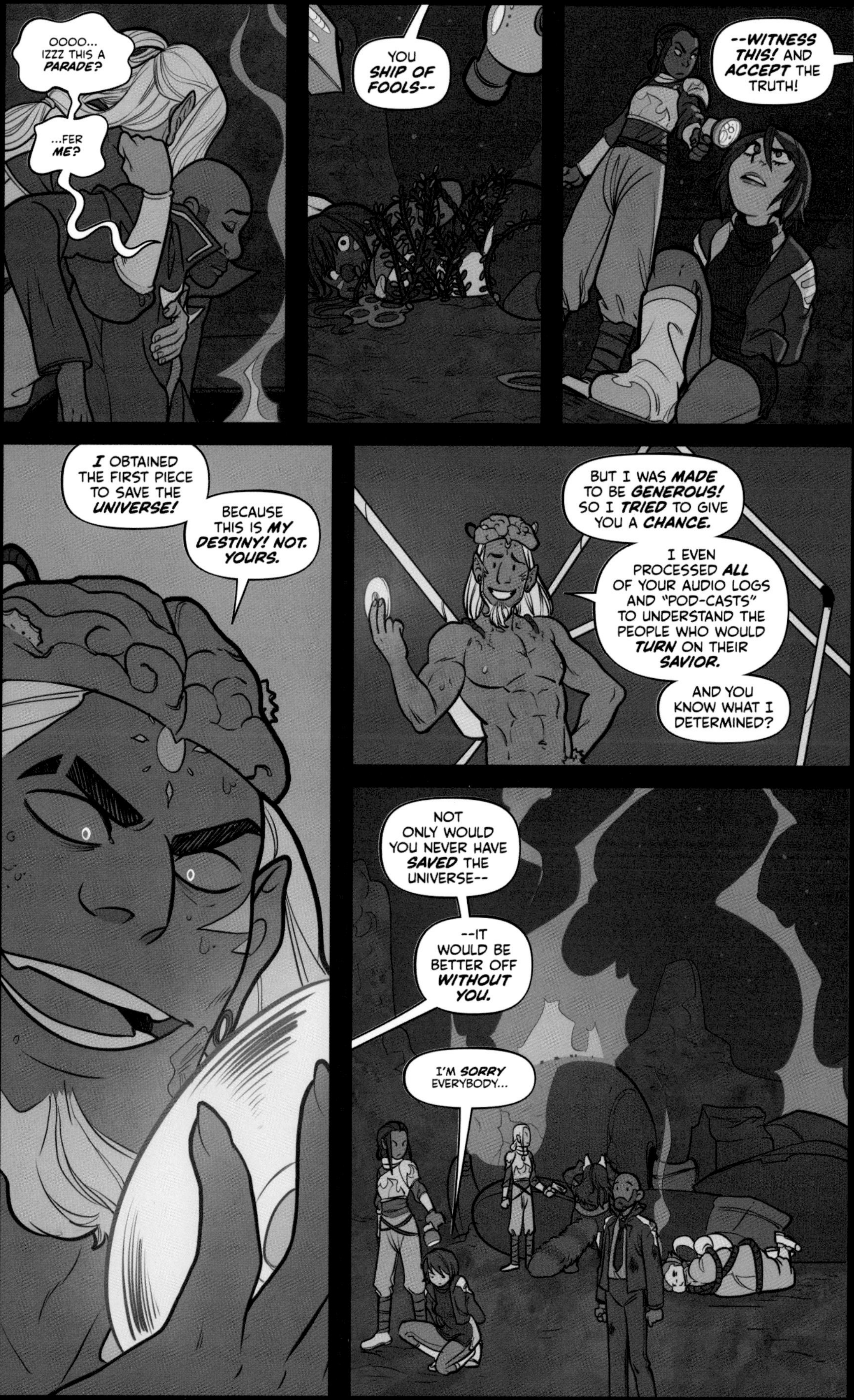

OOOO... IZZZ THIS A PARADE?
...FER ME?
YOU SHIP OF FOOLS--
--WITNESS THIS! AND ACCEPT THE TRUTH!
I OBTAINED THE FIRST PIECE TO SAVE THE UNIVERSE!
BECAUSE THIS IS MY DESTINY! NOT. YOURS.
BUT I WAS MADE TO BE GENEROUS! SO I TRIED TO GIVE YOU A CHANCE.
I EVEN PROCESSED ALL OF YOUR AUDIO LOGS AND "POD-CASTS" TO UNDERSTAND THE PEOPLE WHO WOULD TURN ON THEIR SAVIOR.
AND YOU KNOW WHAT I DETERMINED?
NOT ONLY WOULD YOU NEVER HAVE SAVED THE UNIVERSE--
--IT WOULD BE BETTER OFF WITHOUT YOU.
I'M SORRY EVERYBODY...

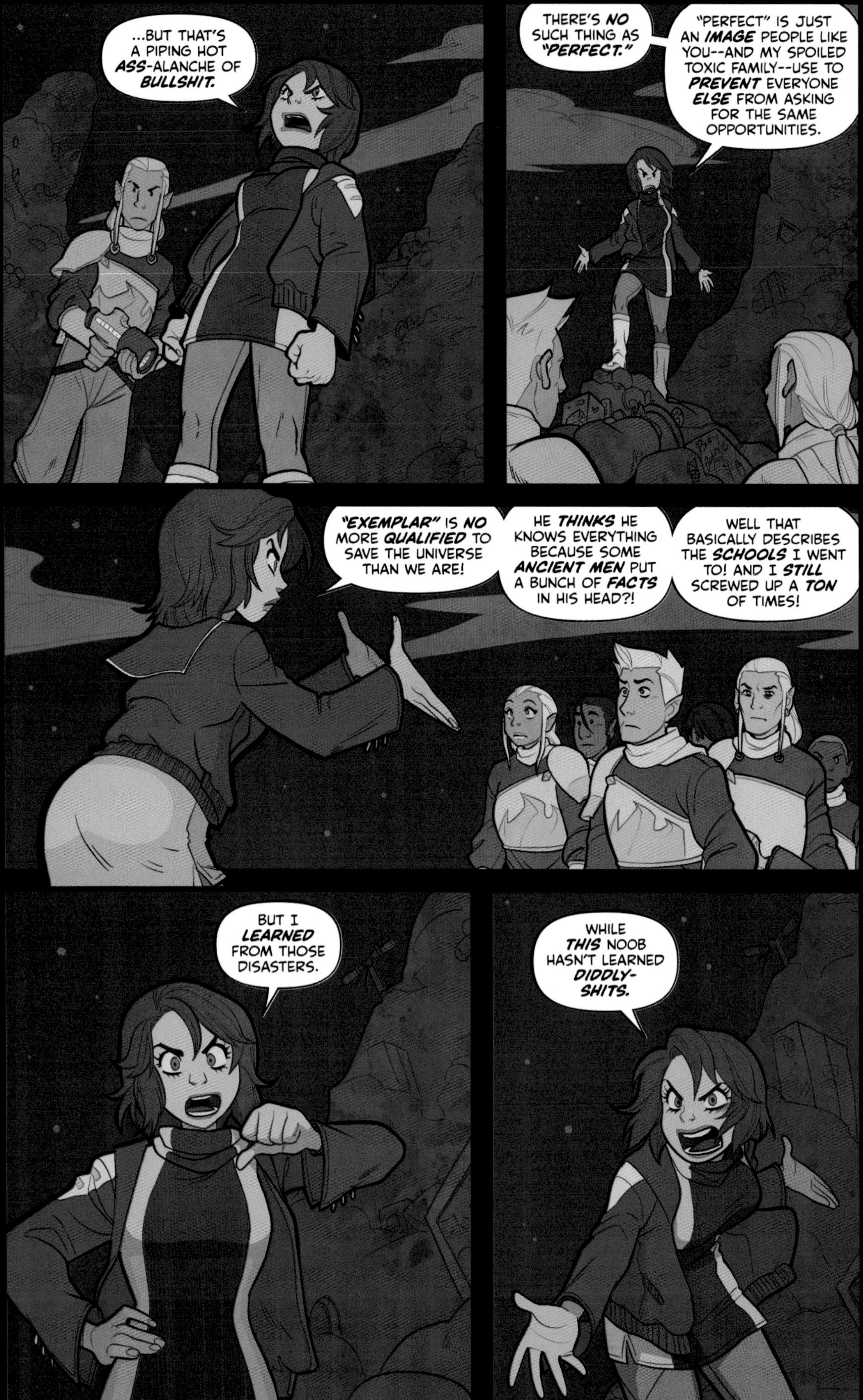
...BUT THAT'S A PIPING HOT ASS-ALANCHE OF BULLSHIT.
THERE'S NO SUCH THING AS "PERFECT."
"PERFECT" IS JUST AN IMAGE PEOPLE LIKE YOU--AND MY SPOILED TOXIC FAMILY--USE TO PREVENT EVERYONE ELSE FROM ASKING FOR THE SAME OPPORTUNITIES.
"EXEMPLAR" IS NO MORE QUALIFIED TO SAVE THE UNIVERSE THAN WE ARE!
HE THINKS HE KNOWS EVERYTHING BECAUSE SOME ANCIENT MEN PUT A BUNCH OF FACTS IN HIS HEAD?!
WELL THAT BASICALLY DESCRIBES THE SCHOOLS I WENT TO! AND I STILL SCREWED UP A TON OF TIMES!
BUT I LEARNED FROM THOSE DISASTERS.
WHILE THIS NOOB HASN'T LEARNED DIDDLY-SHITS.

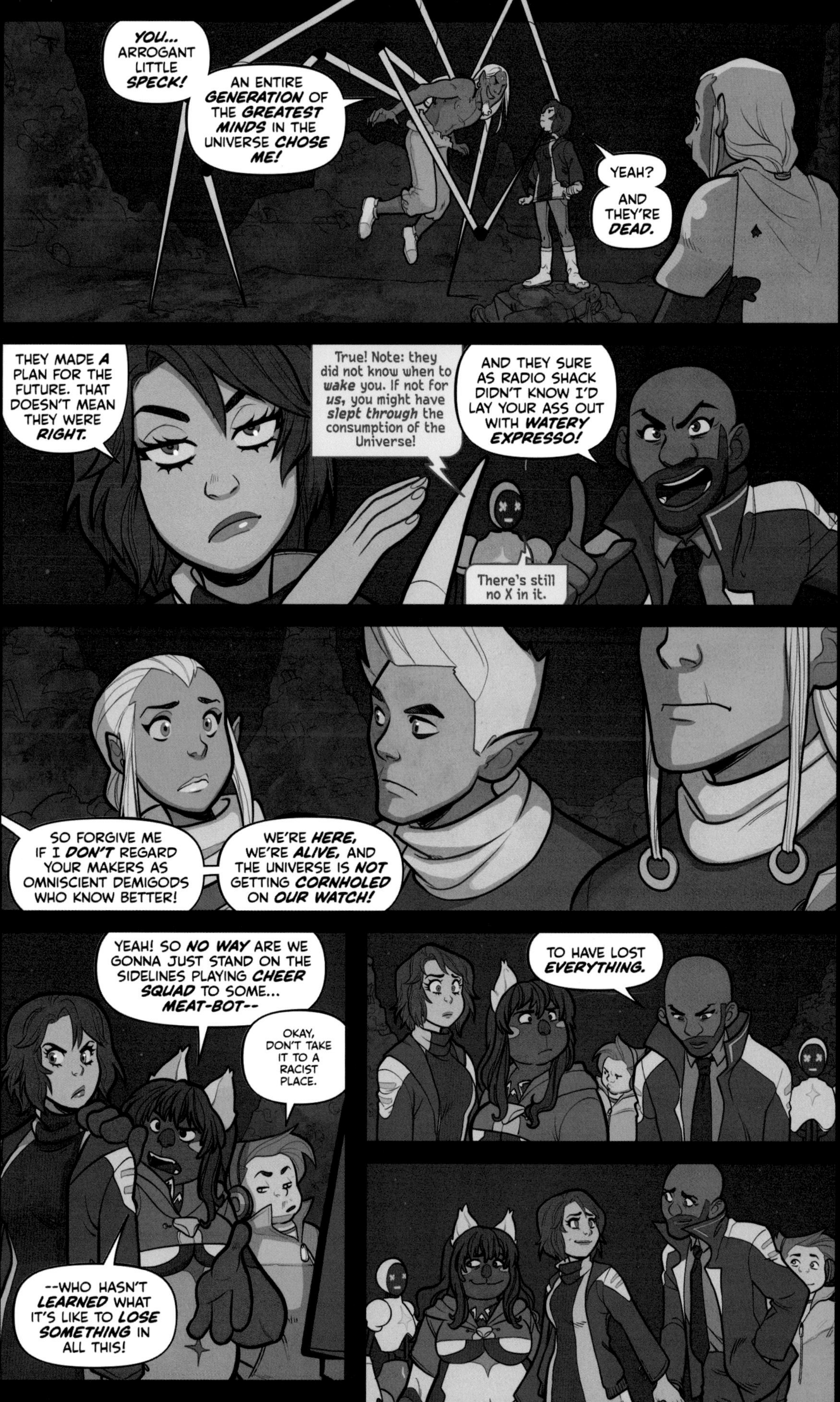
YOU... ARROGANT LITTLE SPECK!
AN ENTIRE GENERATION OF THE GREATEST MINDS IN THE UNIVERSE CHOSE ME!
YEAH? AND THEY'RE DEAD.
THEY MADE A PLAN FOR THE FUTURE. THAT DOESN'T MEAN THEY WERE RIGHT.
True! Note: they did not know when to wake you. If not for us, you might have slept through the consumption of the Universe!
AND THEY SURE AS RADIO SHACK DIDN'T KNOW I'D LAY YOUR ASS OUT WITH WATERY EXPRESSO!
There's still no X in it.
SO FORGIVE ME IF I DON'T REGARD YOUR MAKERS AS OMNISCIENT DEMIGODS WHO KNOW BETTER!
WE'RE HERE, WE'RE ALIVE, AND THE UNIVERSE IS NOT GETTING CORNHOLED ON OUR WATCH!
YEAH! SO NO WAY ARE WE GONNA JUST STAND ON THE SIDELINES PLAYING CHEER SQUAD TO SOME... MEAT-BOT--
OKAY, DON'T TAKE IT TO A RACIST PLACE.
--WHO HASN'T LEARNED WHAT IT'S LIKE TO LOSE SOMETHING IN ALL THIS!
TO HAVE LOST EVERYTHING.

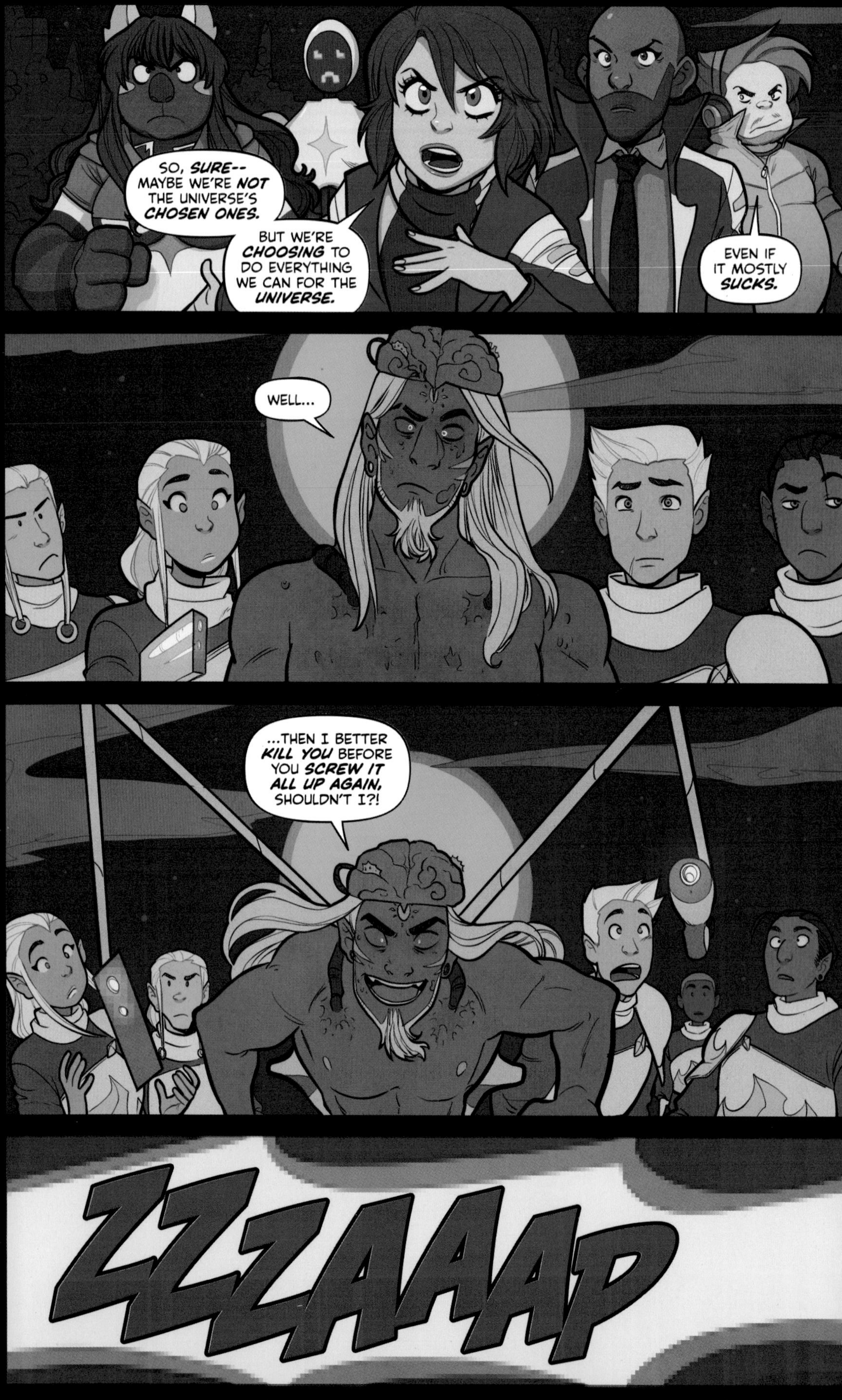
SO, SURE-- MAYBE WE'RE NOT THE UNIVERSE'S CHOSEN ONES.
BUT WE'RE CHOOSING TO DO EVERYTHING WE CAN FOR THE UNIVERSE.
EVEN IF IT MOSTLY SUCKS.
WELL...
...THEN I BETTER KILL YOU BEFORE YOU SCREW IT ALL UP AGAIN, SHOULDN'T I?!
ZZZAAAP

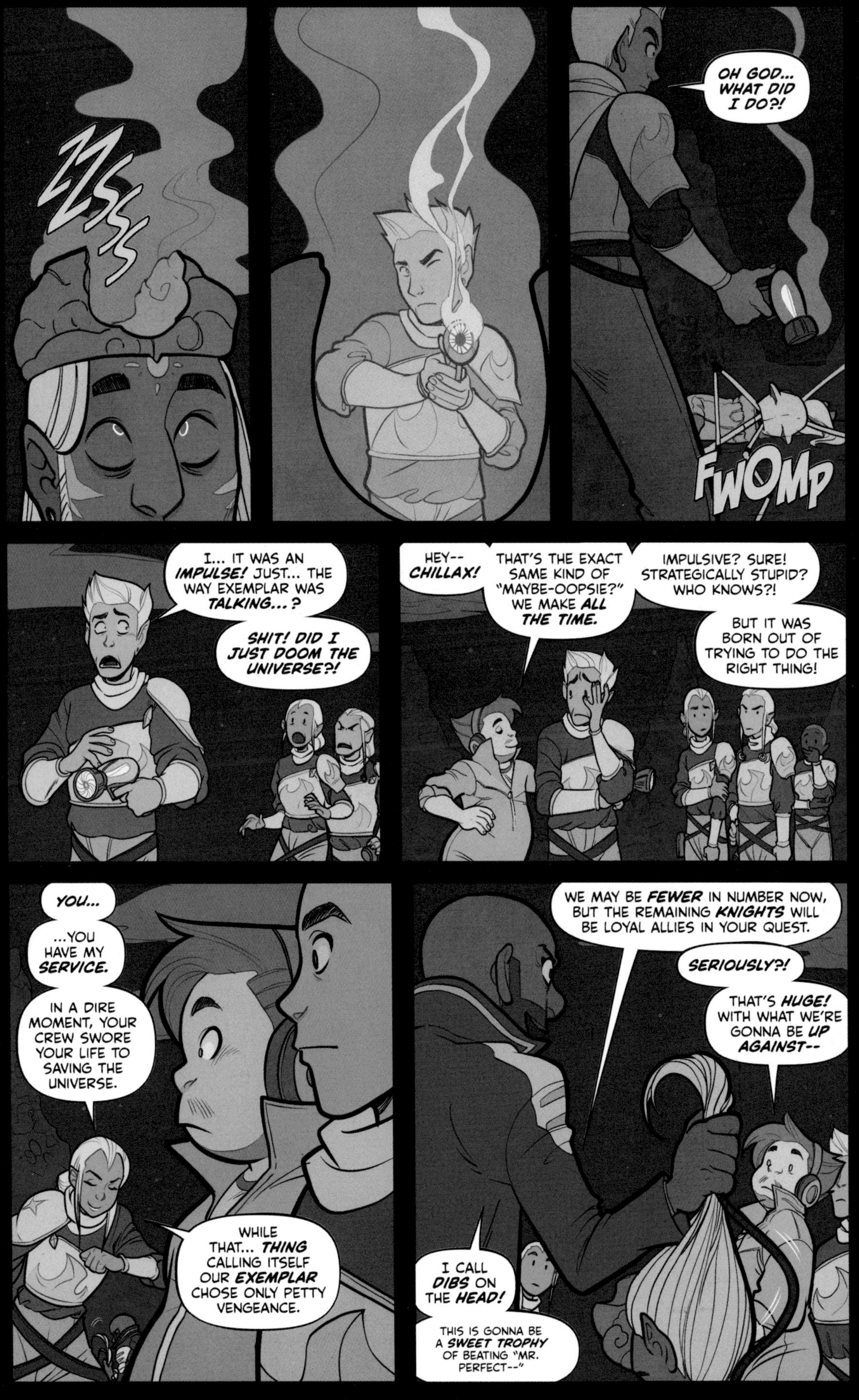

ZZSSS
OH GOD... WHAT DID I DO?!
FWOMP
I... IT WAS AN IMPULSE! JUST... THE WAY EXEMPLAR WAS TALKING...?
SHIT! DID I JUST DOOM THE UNIVERSE?!
HEY-- CHILLAX!
THAT'S THE EXACT SAME KIND OF "MAYBE-OOPSIE?" WE MAKE ALL THE TIME.
IMPULSIVE? SURE! STRATEGICALLY STUPID? WHO KNOWS?!
BUT IT WAS BORN OUT OF TRYING TO DO THE RIGHT THING!
YOU...
...YOU HAVE MY SERVICE.
IN A DIRE MOMENT, YOUR CREW SWORE YOUR LIFE TO SAVING THE UNIVERSE.
WHILE THAT... THING CALLING ITSELF OUR EXEMPLAR CHOSE ONLY PETTY VENGEANCE.
WE MAY BE FEWER IN NUMBER NOW, BUT THE REMAINING KNIGHTS WILL BE LOYAL ALLIES IN YOUR QUEST.
SERIOUSLY?!
THAT'S HUGE! WITH WHAT WE'RE GONNA BE UP AGAINST--
I CALL DIBS ON THE HEAD!
THIS IS GONNA BE A SWEET TROPHY OF BEATING "MR. PERFECT--"

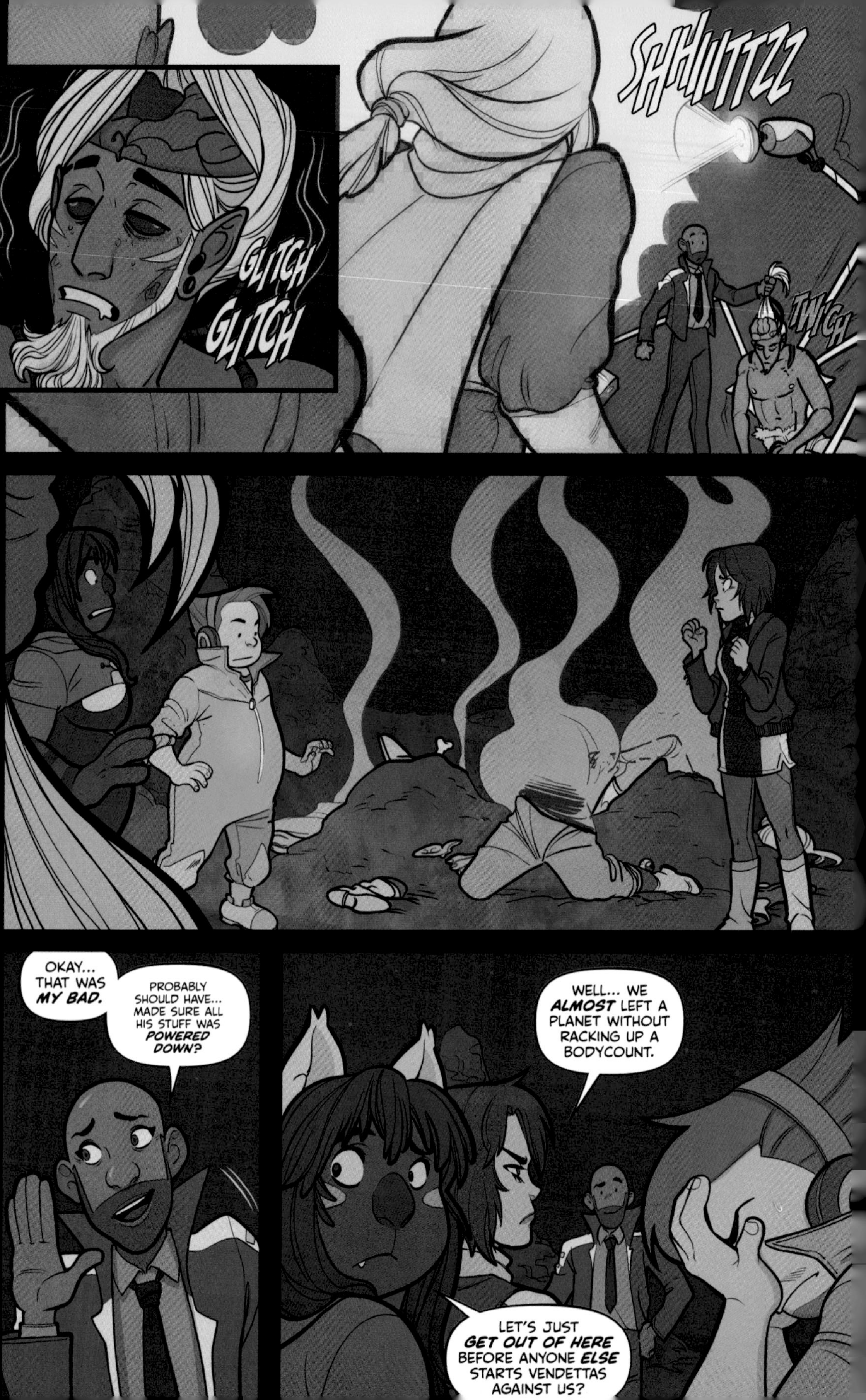
SHHIITTZZ
GLITCH
GLITCH
TWICH
OKAY... THAT WAS MY BAD.
PROBABLY SHOULD HAVE... MADE SURE ALL HIS STUFF WAS POWERED DOWN?
WELL... WE ALMOST LEFT A PLANET WITHOUT RACKING UP A BODYCOUNT.
LET'S JUST GET OUT OF HERE BEFORE ANYONE ELSE STARTS VENDETTAS AGAINST US?

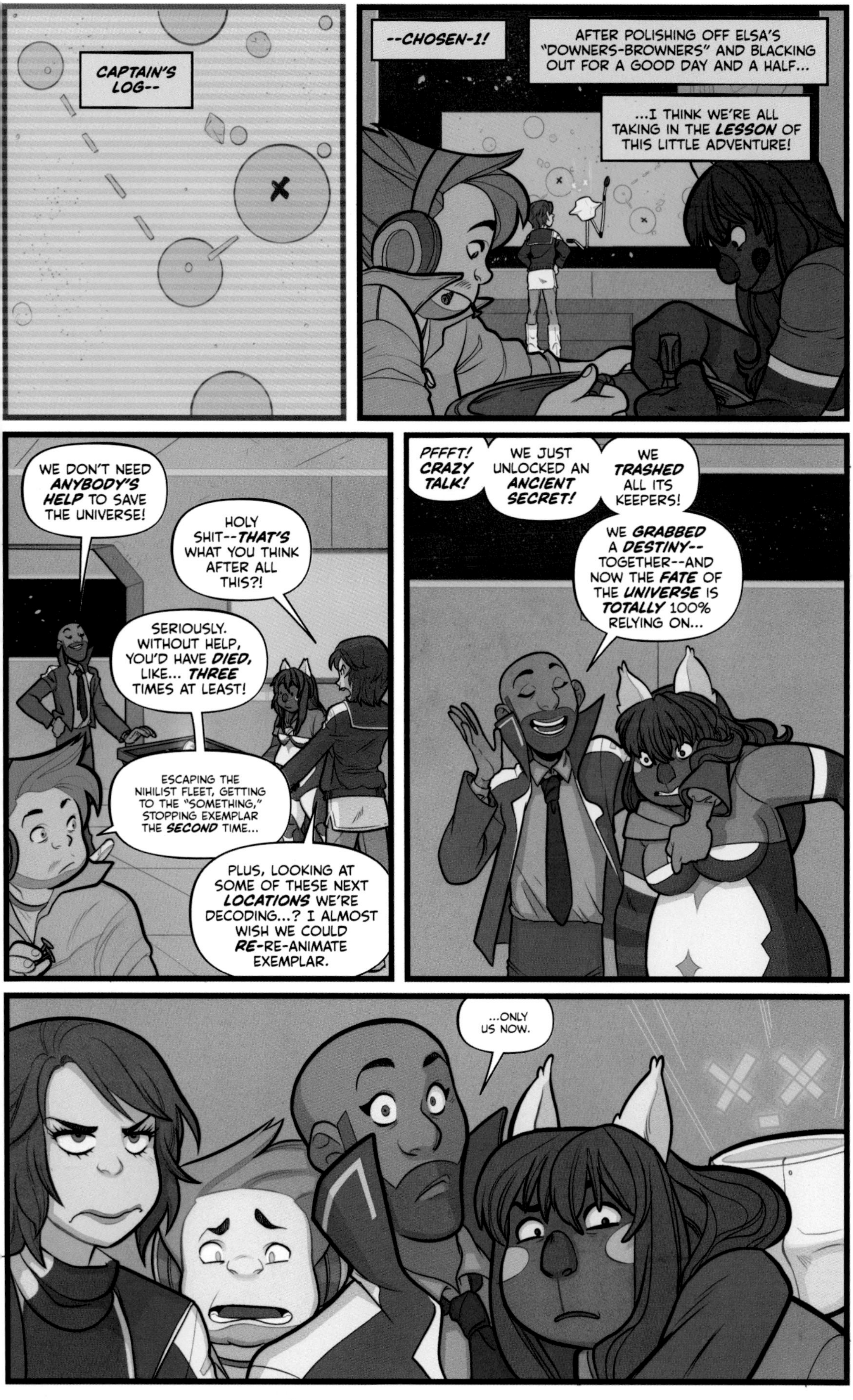
CAPTAIN'S LOG--
--CHOSEN-1!
AFTER POLISHING OFF ELSA'S "DOWNERS-BROWNERS" AND BLACKING OUT FOR A GOOD DAY AND A HALF...
...I THINK WE'RE ALL TAKING IN THE LESSON OF THIS LITTLE ADVENTURE!
WE DON'T NEED ANYBODY'S HELP TO SAVE THE UNIVERSE!
HOLY SHIT--THAT'S WHAT YOU THINK AFTER ALL THIS?!
SERIOUSLY. WITHOUT HELP, YOU'D HAVE DIED, LIKE... THREE TIMES AT LEAST!
ESCAPING THE NIHILIST FLEET, GETTING TO THE "SOMETHING," STOPPING EXEMPLAR THE SECOND TIME...
PLUS, LOOKING AT SOME OF THESE NEXT LOCATIONS WE'RE DECODING...? I ALMOST WISH WE COULD RE-RE-ANIMATE EXEMPLAR.
PFFFT! CRAZY TALK!
WE JUST UNLOCKED AN ANCIENT SECRET!
WE TRASHED ALL ITS KEEPERS!
WE GRABBED A DESTINY--TOGETHER--AND NOW THE FATE OF THE UNIVERSE IS TOTALLY 100% RELYING ON...
...ONLY US NOW.

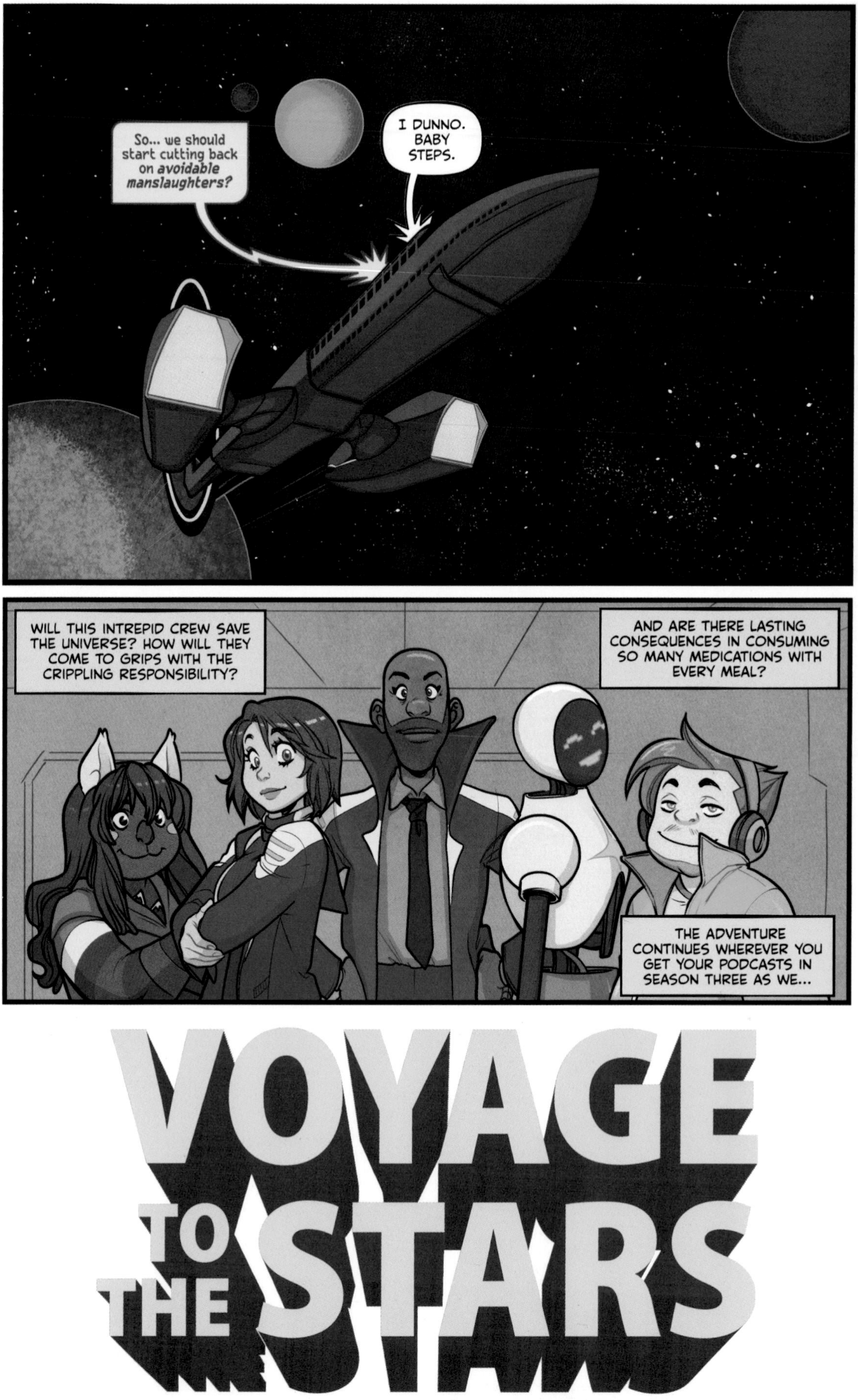
So... we should start cutting back on *avoidable manslaughters?*
I DUNNO. BABY STEPS.
WILL THIS INTREPID CREW SAVE THE UNIVERSE? HOW WILL THEY COME TO GRIPS WITH THE CRIPPLING RESPONSIBILITY?
AND ARE THERE LASTING CONSEQUENCES IN CONSUMING SO MANY MEDICATIONS WITH EVERY MEAL?
THE ADVENTURE CONTINUES WHEREVER YOU GET YOUR PODCASTS IN SEASON THREE AS WE...

VOYAGE TO THE STARS

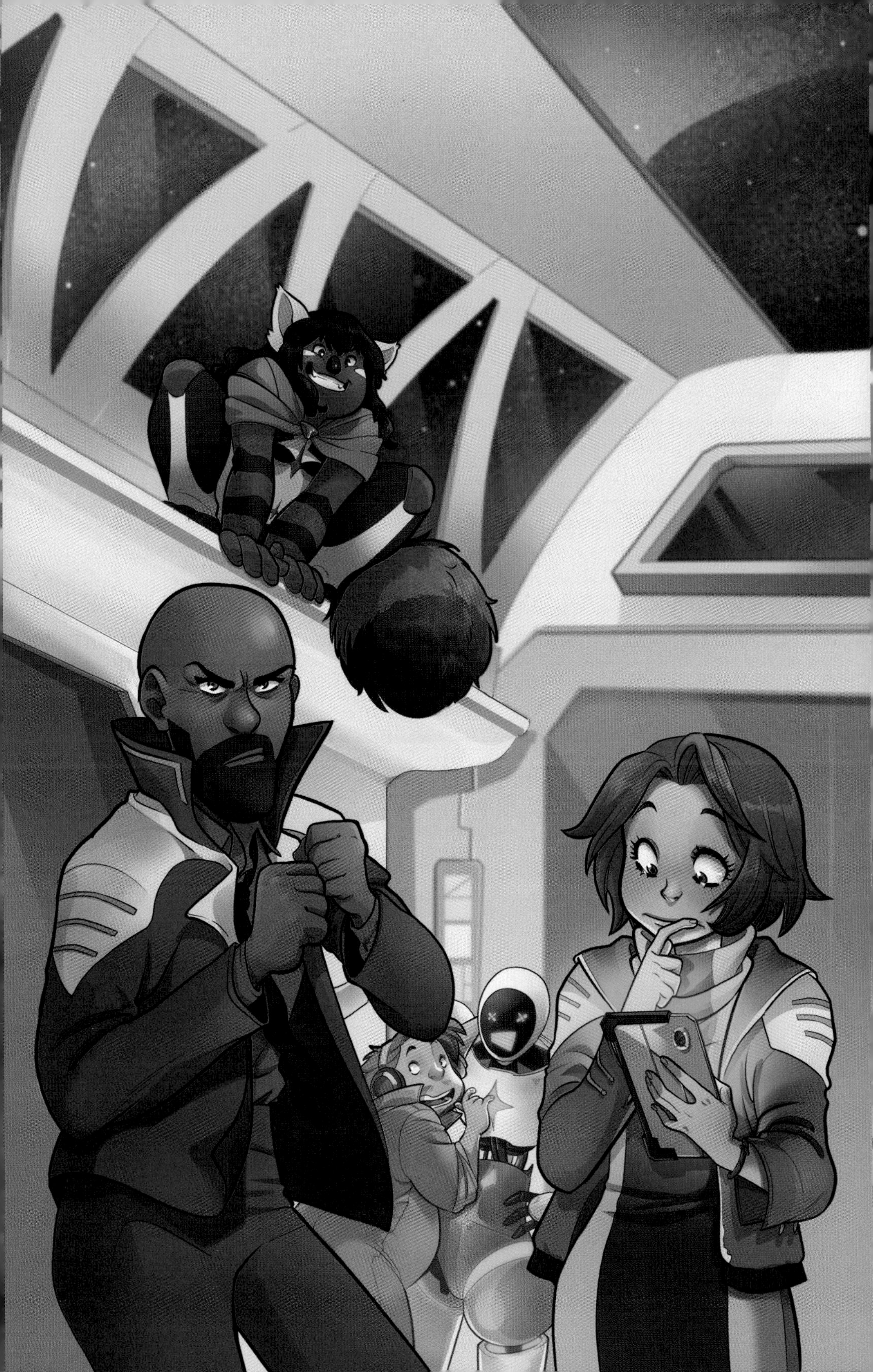

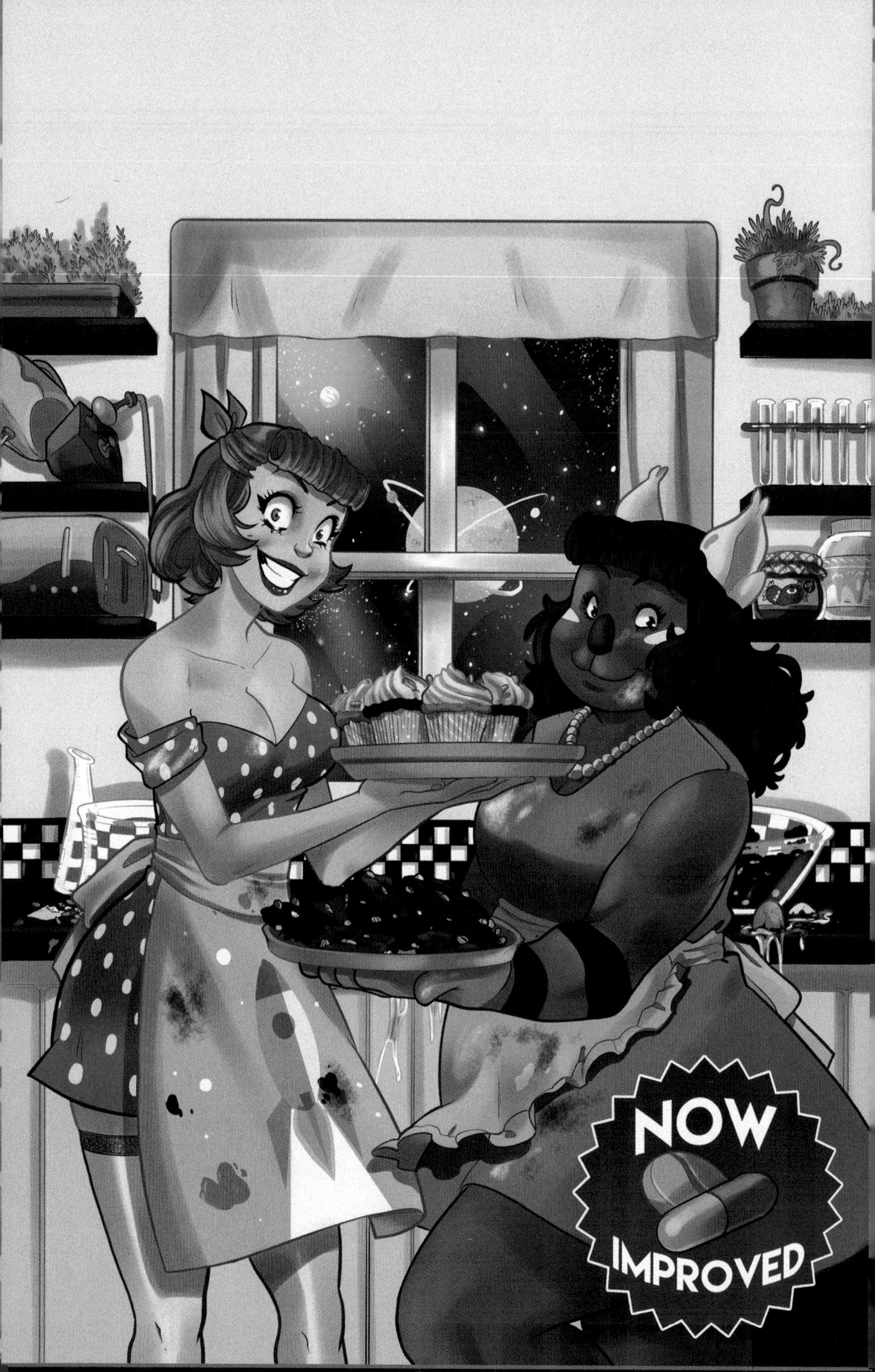
NOW
IMPROVED

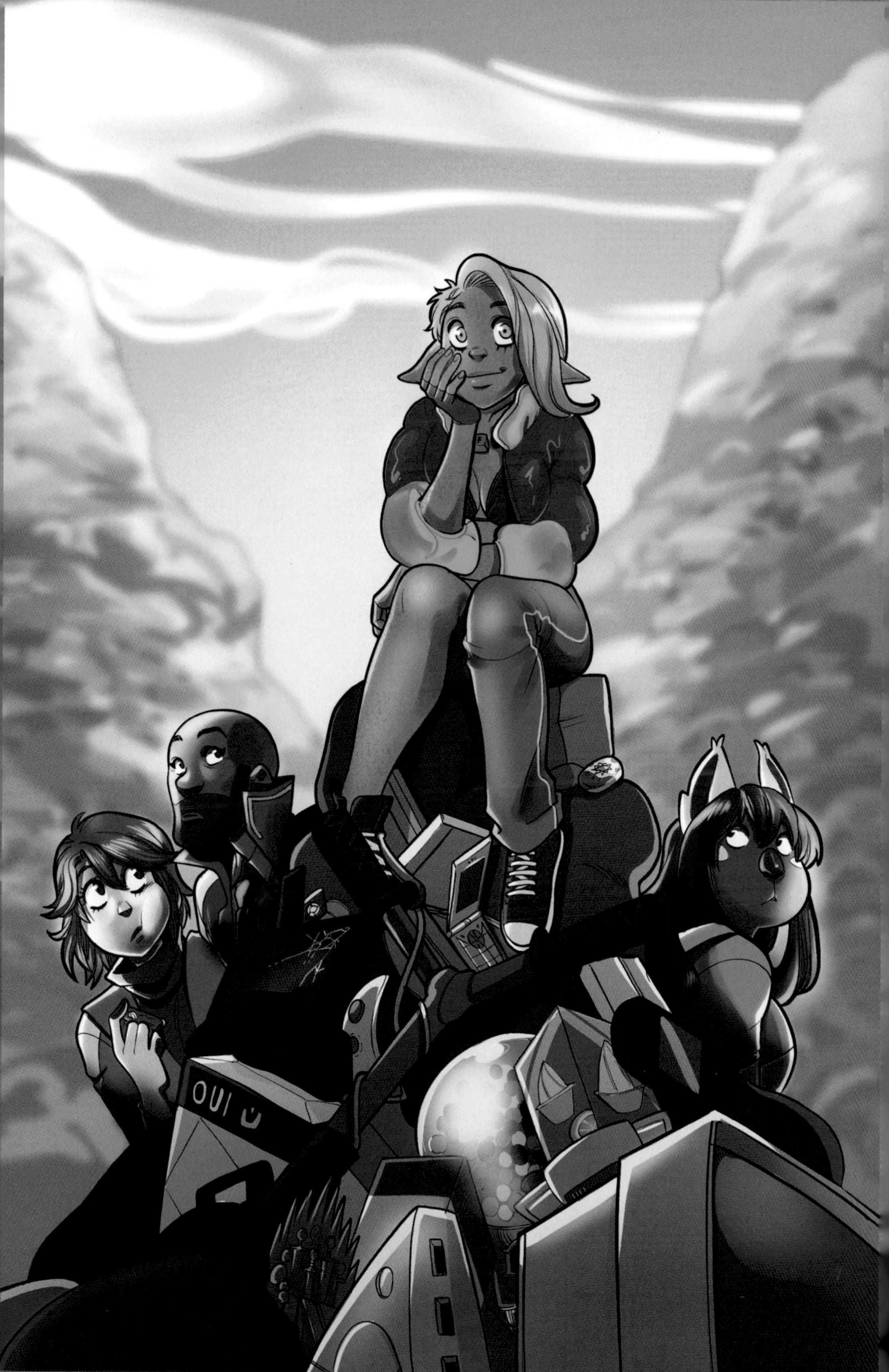
OUI

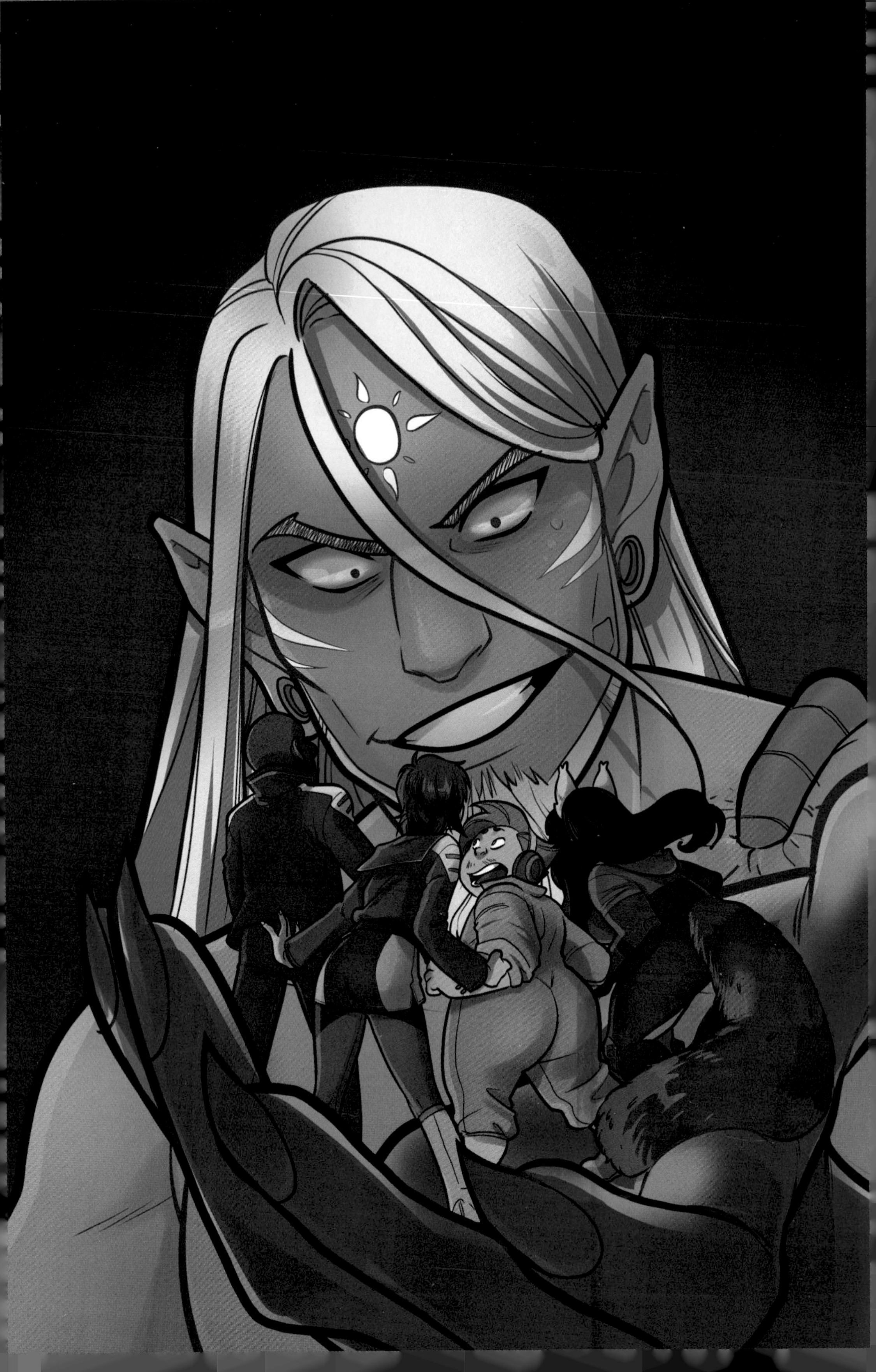